THE
Monarchs
ARE FLYING

THE
Monarchs
ARE FLYING

A Novel by
Marion Foster

Firebrand
Books
Ithaca, New York

Book and cover design by Betsy Bayley
Typesetting by Bets Ltd.

Printed in the United States by McNaughton & Gunn

This publication is made possible, in part, with support from the Literature Panel, New York State Council on the Arts.

Library of Congress Cataloging-in-Publication Data

Foster, Marion
     The monarchs are flying : a novel / by Marion Foster.
          p.   cm.
     ISBN 0-9329379-34-6 : ISBN 0-932379-33-8 (pbk.)
     I. Title.
PR9199.3.F574M6 1987
813'.54—dc19   87-23160
                                                                CIP

For Betty, who makes writing possible and living worthwhile

Chapter One

"**Y**ou got to the motel about three o'clock. You knocked on the door. No one answered. You went off about your business." The stubby fingers with their sprout of fine black hair drummed impatiently. "You'll have to do better than that, Miss Taylor." His emphasis on the word *Miss* turned it into an epithet.

Leslie Taylor stared into the moist black eyes of Inspector Floyd Yarrow and repeated, for the umpteenth time, "I want to see a lawyer."

She had lost track of how long they had been cooped up together in this small, airless room. How long ago was it that she'd opened the door to the warm sunshine of a quiet Sunday morning and found the two plainclothesmen looming on the old-fashioned verandah? Yarrow, heavyset and fleshy; Detective Sergeant Moore, slender and trendy. Trendy, that is, for a hard-rock mining town. A pair of lopsided bookends.

It was not the first time Floyd Yarrow had approached her for information. One of her early projects after returning to her home town of Spruce Falls was a documentary series on battered women. Yarrow, then with the Morality Squad, had been assigned the role of department liaison. Instructed to cooperate fully, he had proved more hindrance than help. When it dawned on her that his sympathy lay more with the men who found it necessary to beat their wives than with the wives who were beaten, she bypassed him and sourced her own leads. The stones she turned over revealed creepy crawlies from both sides of the proverbial tracks. Privy to much information unknown to the police, she occasionally was called upon when background was needed on a suspected batterer.

So it had not seemed too unusual to find two guardians of law and order hovering on her porch, although it was the first time Yarrow had come to her in person for help. In attempting to work with him she had sensed a hint of disapproval under his professional veneer, a resentment of what he probably thought of as a smart-ass intrusion into his territory. He'd made it plain he didn't much care for her. A fair exchange; she hadn't much cared for him, either. Yet seeing him there she had forced a smile, thrown open the door, and invited him in against the protests of Duchess, her one-of-a-kind reject from the Humane Society.

They had not wanted to come in. They preferred to talk to her downtown. And like a fool—thinking perhaps they wanted her to flip through some mug shots, maybe even sit in on a lineup—she'd gone with them willingly. Not until she was in this room, his darting black eyes aglint with triumph, and the seemingly aimless questioning escalating into a full-scale interrogation, had it occurred to her that instead of aiding in an investigation she was the object of one.

"I have a right to make a phone call." Her voice held more conviction than she felt. My God, she thought, I'm beginning to sound like a broken record. It would help if she knew what she was doing here. Oh, it was obvious enough it had something to do with Marcie. Marcie and the motel she had checked into and the message she had left on Leslie's answering machine saying to meet her there as soon as possible. No matter where the questions led, they always came back to the motel. Whatever it was, they had no damned business holding her like this. "I want to see a lawyer, Inspector."

Yarrow set his hands flat on the desk and leaned forward. "Forget the goddamned lawyer. You just get your head on straight and start coming up with some answers. Now what the hell were you doing in that motel room?" He was so close she could see the pores on his nose and the oily globs of sweat on his forehead.

"I've been answering your questions all day. The same things, over and over. If you'd tell me what this is about, maybe I could be more helpful." Her precise Virgo mind functioned on the premise that if you wanted a specific answer, you asked a specific question. That was much too simplistic for the Inspector. His approach was to go round and round in circles with an occasional squiggle off to the side. But the squiggles were short-lived. Always he returned to where she had been, what she had done, who she had seen the day before.

"We know all about you, Taylor." Another of his quick forays into the underbrush, but this time he was not on a fishing expedition. His voice held the flat, metallic ring that distinguishes fact from supposition.

Leslie stiffened. She had known and dreaded that tone from grade school onward. She'd had it from her classmates: Leslie likes girls better than boys. She'd had it at home: if you're not careful, you'll end up being an old maid. She'd had it from women: how come you never go out on dates? She'd had it from men: what are you saving it for, your old age? Questions, comments, sly remarks—freighted with meaning that put a knot of fear in her stomach. And here it was again, coming from a man who looked as though he'd like nothing better than to squash her underfoot. We know all about you, Taylor. We know you're one of those.

"Inspector Yarrow, I'm perfectly willing to cooperate with you." Thank God for all that radio training. There wasn't a flutter in her breathing. "I've been here all day. My dog has been locked up alone. My parents are expecting me for dinner. I have an interview to format for the morning. I simply can't stay here any longer." She stood up and started for the door, telling herself he had no right to hold her, he was contravening his authority. If he laid a finger on her, she would have him up before the Complaints Board so fast his head would swim.

"Sit down." The full-throated command bounced off the walls and reverberated through the fusty air. It was the first time he had raised his voice, the first indication his control was only skin-deep.

The door opened and Douglas Moore appeared as though on cue. A glance at Leslie, then past her to Yarrow. "I thought I'd spell you. You must be ready for a break."

Leslie felt a flush of gratitude. His arrival had to be more than coincidence. He must have had his ear pressed to the door, waiting for Yarrow to dip over the edge. The Inspector was a throwback to the era of naked light bulbs and sand-filled socks that could rupture the innards without leaving a mark. Beer and pretzels, compared to the Douglas Moore image of Perrier and a twist of lime.

Yarrow heaved himself upright and reached for his jacket. His shirt was blotched with sweat, the collar limp and curling at the edges. His hard little eyes fixed on Leslie and he said, "We are speaking here on equal terms, Miss Taylor."

Leslie stared after him as he lumbered from the room. What did he mean—we're speaking on equal terms? A strange thing to say. Stranger still, the manner in which he said it. Low-key. Offhand. Almost pleasant. But her ear, trained to catch nuance and inflection, detected significance beneath the surface.

"Please." Moore smiled and motioned toward the chair. "The Inspector tends to get a little steamed up." He pushed his arms out of his jacket until the cuffs showed. French with gold links. Snow-white against the navy serge of his blazer. "Speaking of getting steamed up, it's stifling in here. Would you like something to drink?''

"I'd rather go home."

"We won't be much longer." A reassuring smile, followed by, "We've got some Cokes downstairs. I'll just be a minute." Unlike Yarrow, he moved gracefully, with a slight, almost provocative sway.

Alone at last, Leslie stared off into space and tried to bring her mind into focus. This couldn't be happening. No one could be whisked off, held incommunicado, subjected to hours of questioning, without being told why.

How many *whys* in a bushel: Why had she come with them so willingly instead of insisting they talk to her at home? Why hadn't she phoned her mother and told her where she'd be? Why hadn't she worn her watch so she'd at least know what time of day it was? Why had Yarrow said, with that near-leer, "We know all about you?"

How much did they know about her? About Marcie? About the relationship they'd kept hidden from their families and friends here in Spruce Falls? It all seemed so far away. So irrelevant to the life she had built since coming back home. Her life had been torn apart by Marcie's marriage four years ago. Slowly she had managed to put it back together—to think of herself as an individual rather than the other half of a pair and the occasional point of a triangle. And now this. An insane set of circumstances with Marcie once again hovering in the background.

A minute ticked by on the stopwatch in her brain. She could clock a thirty or sixty-second commercial to the dot. Too bad her sense of timing didn't include hours as well as minutes. Was it past Duchess's feeding time? It was certainly well past the time when she should be let out.

Another minute went by, followed by another and still another. The relief she had felt at being alone gave way to a new bout of edginess. The walls began to close in. The air was thick with humidity. Moore was not coming back. They had put her in this cubbyhole and gone off about their business and forgotten about her. Panicky, she jumped up and tried the door. It was locked. He had gone out and locked the door. God knows when she'd be discovered. They'd come in the back way, climbed the stairs to the second floor. The offices they'd passed were deserted, probably par for the course on a Sunday. After all, Spruce Falls wasn't exactly a hotbed of crime—a skeleton staff could surely maintain order on the Lord's Day at least.

Pacing the floor she fought off the rising waves of panic by concentrating on thoughts of Marcie. They had met in Spruce Falls when Leslie was just starting out at the radio station and Marcie was a freckle-faced sixteen-year-old. One of the career counselors at the high school had invited Leslie to give a talk on radio as a career option. Marcie had come up to her afterward and said that Leslie was by far the most interesting speaker they'd had. Leslie had forgotten about the girl with the wide, innocent blue eyes and long silvery hair until she showed up at the station a week later on her way home from school. She was just walking past, she said, and decided to stop in and say hello. The visits became more frequent, until finally they were a daily occurrence.

It was inevitable that the staff would notice the tiny blonde with her arms full of schoolbooks and her heart on her sleeve. The receptionist was the first to mention it. "That kid's got a crush on you, Leslie. You'd better watch it." Then one of the announcers, miffed when she turned down yet another date, sneered, "I guess you'd rather rob the cradle than rock it, eh Les?" Having grown out of her own schoolgirl crushes without mishap, Leslie ignored the warnings and spent more and more time with Marcie. Innocent time, until the afternoon Marcie made love to her and the bits and pieces of her life that had never seemed to fit fell into place and made perfect, glorious sense. Marcie was eighteen. She was twenty-two.

A year later, pressured by gossip and the gnawing fear that their parents would find out, they moved to Toronto and began living together. Their relationship—happy at times, stormy at others—had lasted for eight years. It came to an end when Marcie met Charles P. Denton, a bachelor architect who was considered by some to be a super catch. Marcie called within days of returning from the honeymoon and said she had made a mistake and wanted to come back. Having survived months of turmoil and the pain of that decisive parting, Leslie said no.

There had been other phone calls and a few arm's-length meetings over lunch. Once there had been bruise marks on Marcie's arm. And once she had called in the middle of the night saying that Charles had stormed out of the house in a temper and she was afraid of what he might do when he returned. Frightened by the note of hysteria in Marcie's voice, Leslie came close to breaking her self-promise to stay out of the Dentons' affairs. Call the police, she had said. And if you don't want to do that, pack up the kids and go home to your mother.

When her old boss bumped into her at a radio/television conference and offered her a job at double what she was earning, she accepted on the spot. It would be safer, she felt, to put some distance between herself and the Dentons. Besides, Toronto held too many memories, memories that surfaced when least expected. She had called Marcie to say she was leaving, and they had met for a drink. Leslie had been shocked by the change in that once bright, vivacious face. I'm going to leave him, Marcie had said. As soon as Charlie and Emily are old enough, I'm going to take them and go.

Leslie rubbed absent-mindedly at the spot on the scarred wooden table top. When she and Marcie split, she'd vowed to remember only the good times. But this dismal day served as a reminder of the stormier, more troublesome side of their relationship. Scrapes Marcie got into and expected Leslie to get her out of. Harmless flirtations that threatened to explode into violence. Short absences, never explained. Periods of withdrawal when she railed against society, not being able to have children, being forced to live a lie.

She had thought she was finished forever with Marcie and her problems, yet here she was, back on the same old merry-go-round.

Her ear caught the rasp of metal on wood, a creaking hinge. "Sorry it took so long. I got hung up on the phone." Moore stood framed in the doorway, an apologetic smile on his face and a can of Coke in each hand. "Did you think I'd forgotten about you?"

"I was beginning to wonder." She was ridiculously, childishly pleased to see him.

He punctured the flip-top and handed her the can. "Sorry. We don't supply glasses and we're out of straws. I'm afraid we're a bit on the primitive side."

"I noticed," she said drily.

The irony wasn't wasted. "Floyd gave you a bad time, did he? He can be pretty unpleasant when he gets the wind up." He sipped his Coke, careful not to let it dribble. Leslie, who had never learned to drink from a can without spilling, marveled at his finesse.

"What did he mean by that remark?"

"Which remark was that, Leslie?"

"Something about speaking as equals. . . right after you came in, just before he left."

"Oh—that." He shrugged, an eloquent gesture of dismissal.

"I got the feeling he said it for a reason. That it had some kind of special meaning."

"I suppose in a way it has. You've heard of the Miranda rule in the U.S.?"

"Where a suspect must be read his rights or what he says can't be used against him?"

"That's it. That doesn't apply here in Canada. We follow British Law, and in Britain they have what they call the English Judges' Rules. We can ask questions, but we can't force you to answer them. Not you, specifically," he added quickly. "I'm speaking generally. So, legally, we can't force anyone to talk to us although," the boyish smile widened, "they'd be very unwise not to. On the other hand, we are not required to advise a suspect of their right to silence until they are taken into custody or charged."

"What does that have to do with . . . ."

"With speaking on equal terms? There is a British court ruling that if two parties speak on even terms but one remains silent—contradictory perhaps but the meaning is clear—in such instance, silence can be taken as an indication of guilt. He was merely trying to warn you that it would be best in the long run if you made a full statement now."

"I've been answering the same questions over and over all day. Either you take me home, or call me a lawyer and he can take me home."

"Let's just go over it one more time. To keep him off both our backs. Where were you Friday night?"

"The station threw a farewell party for Jim Clark, one of the TV newsmen. We had a banquet room at the Queens Hotel. I left at 3:00 a.m. and went straight home to bed."

"I'm sorry, Leslie. Do you mind if I tape this?"

Sorry on her behalf because he felt it was an imposition? Or on his own, because he hadn't started the damned thing soon enough? "I don't mind if *you* don't. Yarrow used up reels of tape. The same thing, over and over." She glanced at the old reel-to-reel Ampex on a stand in the corner. "That thing must be hot enough to blow a tube. It's silly."

"Floyd does things the hard way." He reached inside his blazer and produced a cassette recorder the size of a cigarette pack. "We may just pick up some little thing that sets us on the right track. You'd be surprised how often a word or two will throw a whole new light on a case."

"A case? What case? How can I help you if I don't even know what you're talking about?"

"We'll get to that, Leslie." He leaned forward and lowered his voice to the intimate level of a candlelight-and-wine dinner conversation. "Actually, I was getting worried about you. Yarrow isn't above getting physical when he doesn't get what he wants. We had a guy a few months ago who walked out of this room without a mark on him. He collapsed in his cell, and two days later he was gone." Noticing the gleam of interest in her eyes, he backtracked. "Don't get any ideas, Leslie. If you're thinking you've got a hot scoop, forget it. Yarrow's been investigated before. Always comes out smelling like a rose. Which is more than you can say for the people who've lodged the complaint: he makes their lives a living hell."

"Maybe he can bully someone he picks up off the street, but I'm not afraid of him."

"You should be. He has things pretty much his own way around here. Anyway, I felt you needed a break. He's been going at you for hours."

"What I need, Sergeant, is to get out of here."

"Call me Doug." The blue eyes smiled into hers, easing the tension cramped between her shoulder blades. Eyes familiar in their frankness and lack of guile. "I'd like us to be friends, Leslie. You spent some time in Toronto, didn't you?"

He shifted the cassette and when he removed his hand, she noticed that the Record button was depressed. Not that it mattered. If he wanted to run off a batch of idle talk, it was nothing to her. "I lived there for eight years."

"It's my home town. I really miss it. Did you work in radio there, too?"

"Yes. I was in the news department at CKAN. The last couple of years I did some free-lance television. News items, mostly. And a couple of documentaries."

"I saw the one you did here. On battered women."

No indication of whether he considered it good, bad, or indifferent—an omission which in itself was an indication. Leslie knew from experience that an acknowledgement without elaboration leaned toward the negative. It hadn't been one of her best efforts. Most of the women had been afraid to talk on camera, and the authorities hadn't gone out of their way to cooperate. "I plan to do a follow-up. Also something on abused children."

"Folks around here aren't much interested in that kind of stuff. You're still thinking big city. It must have been quite a shock to come back here after living in TO."

"Not really. I was getting tired of the rat race. I guess my work is more important to me than where I live."

"As long as you're allowed to live. Spruce Falls is redneck down to its toes." He finished his Coke and tossed the can into the wastebasket. "It's really a pleasure to get to talk to someone like you, Leslie. Most of the locals are strictly hick, about as sophisticated as beans on toast." Then, a switch of subject that caught her off guard, "You and Marcie lived together, didn't you?"

"Before she got married." It was an effort not to glance at the tape machine.

"You were best . . . friends?"

"I suppose so. We've known each other for a long time." The red light flashing in her mind was as bright as the light she knew was pulsing on the recorder. "Lately we haven't seen that much of each other."

"What did she do before she got married?" An offhand retreat from the earlier quick thrust.

"She was a copywriter." Obviously whatever was going on, Marcie was involved. "Is she in some kind of trouble?"

"Why would you think that, Leslie?"

"We keep going in circles, but we always end up at the same place. Saturday. The motel. I'm not exactly stupid, Sergeant."

"Not stupid. And certainly not plain Jane. You must have made quite a pair. Marcie with her blonde hair and you with those dark eyes and great cheekbones. No wonder you moved over to television. No one with your looks should be hidden away in a radio studio." A pause to let the compliment sink in, followed by a nonchalant, "Did you get around much while you were there?"

"When you work in news you don't get much time to yourself. I put in a lot of overtime." She worked. Marcie played. Perhaps if she hadn't spent so much time running around the city with a microphone in her hand they'd still be together.

"Too bad. It's an exciting place to live. Rated in some circles along with New York and Los Angeles." The gold identification bracelet jangled as he straightened the crease in his trousers. "Did you ever get to Crispins'?"

Accompanied by a faint smile and slight arching of the wrist, the question answered more than it asked. He was telling her they were two of a kind. She could speak freely. With him, at least, there was no need to be concerned. But she was concerned. Had been for so long that it was second nature.

"As I said, I didn't get around much." She knew about Crispins', of course. Frequented by gay yuppies, it was an elegant downtown bistro that catered to the affluent and near-affluent. She had avoided it because it was predominantly male. In clear conscience she could say, "No, I have never been to Crispins'."

"Too bad. They have a wonderful Sunday brunch. It's one of the things I really miss. The best you can do here on a Sunday is Chinese smorgasbord." A shudder of mock horror, followed by a supercilious smile. "What about the Cameo Club?"

The Cameo Club. A dance-hall-cum-bar in the basement of an old building on a side street well away from the beaten track. *The* place for lesbians. Where she and Marcie had gone whenever the pressure of masquerading as straight became too much. She was not about to lie about it, but she was not about to admit it, either. "There's a Cameo Motel, as I recall. On the airport strip."

"Not that one. This is a club. For women. In the east end." His voice dropped to a confidential whisper. "I had a friend at CBC who took me there a few times."

"I thought you said it was for women."

"Men are allowed, if they have the right credentials." She half-expected a wink to drive the point home, but the blue eyes remained fixed and friendly. "I miss my friends. I haven't met anyone here that I can sit down and talk to. It can get damn lonely."

Leslie tried to imagine him having this conversation with Floyd

Yarrow—a Falwell clone if ever there was one. "I haven't had time to be lonely."

"You're lucky. And the people you *do* meet! But I suppose it's not the occupational hazard in your business that it is in mine."

It was the type of conversational game playing that demanded a response. "What isn't?"

"Narrow-mindedness. That terrifying small-town inability to look at life from another point of view. Take Crispins'. Or the Cameo Club. If Yarrow ever wandered into either one of them he'd go right off his head. Berserk."

A chill ran along Leslie's spine. "I have a feeling it wouldn't take much of anything to send him berserk. He seems to hang by a pretty thin wire."

"That's right. It's one of the reasons I wanted to run interference. You're my kind of people. I'd a lot sooner you gave your statement to me than to the Inspector. Would you like to do it now and get it over with?" Struck by her baffled expression he added, "If you're ready to make a statement, I'll see about getting you out of here as soon as I can."

"I'll give you a monologue on the topic of your choice if it will help."

"A simple statement will do, Leslie." Some of the cordiality was missing.

"I don't know what you mean by a statement. Ask me questions and I'll answer them."

"You and Marcie Denton were lovers, weren't you?"

Although he'd been edging toward it, the question came so quickly, was so blatant, she felt her breath constrict in her throat. "We were good friends."

"Come on. Yarrow's got the picture. And there's nothing in the world he hates as much as a queer. Don't get excited. That's his word, not mine. He'd rather do in a gay than catch a serial killer."

She had no illusions about Yarrow, but where did that leave Moore? True his wrist hadn't collapsed until the Inspector was out of sight but surely he must suspect something. At any rate, there was no law against being gay. Not if you followed the government guidelines and remained within the prescribed boundaries. And no law at all against lesbianism, thanks to Queen Victoria's refusal to believe that women did such things.

She was about to insist yet again that she be allowed to leave when the door swung open and Yarrow bulldozed into the room. He motioned Moore to follow him outside. A moment later they reappeared, stone-faced and deliberate. "Leslie Taylor, I place you under arrest for the murder of Marcie Denton. I warn you that anything you say can be used in evidence."

Leslie felt as though a deep hole had opened before her and was sucking her in. Images flashed across the screen of her mind. Marcie at breakfast, her pale, silvery hair damp from the shower. The soft, undulating feel of Marcie in her arms. Marcie laughing, serious, happy, frightened and discontent. But always, while they were together, a Marcie brimming with life and vitality. The hole closed over her head, and she felt herself slipping down the never-ending tunnel.

Vaguely, far in the distance, she heard Yarrow say, "Book her. Then let her call her lawyer." And Moore, also far away, his voice echoing from a long way off, murmuring, "I wish you had told us about it first; before he had a chance to charge you. It would have weighed in your favor."

They turned and she walked between them, her back rigid and her legs moving like a wind-up toy. Out of the small airless room. Along the wooden corridor flanked by empty offices, heavy with foul air. Down the stairs to the main floor, then down again to the basement and a vaultlike booking area with cells beyond.

"One call," Moore said. She looked at him blankly, struggling to find meaning in what was nothing more than a jumble of sound. He tried again. "You can call a lawyer now."

What was it they had said? Marcie was dead and she, Leslie Taylor, had killed her. Pain shot upward through her flesh, leaving an imprint of throbbing grief. With the pain the fog started to lift, and her mind began to function.

"I should call my mother and tell her where I am." How could she sound so cool when everything inside was bleeding?

"He said only one call, Leslie." Sensing her distress, he laid a comforting hand on her shoulder and said, "Go ahead. Call her. I'll get your lawyer for you."

"I don't have one. I'll have to look in the phone book."

"I know one who's pretty good. Suppose we see if he's available?"

While she dialed home, he leafed through the cards in his wallet. When her mother answered the phone, she took a deep breath and said, "Mom, would you go over to the house and pick up Duchess? I won't be home for a couple of days." Quickly, before her mother had time to reply, she hung up. She would find out soon enough that her daughter was accused of murdering her best friend. Unless, by some miracle, Moore's friend the lawyer managed to set things right overnight.

Yarrow's face as he rendered the charge rose in her mind. The satisfaction in that jut-jawed countenance had been absolute. He knew she was guilty: if not of Marcie's death, guilty of poisoning part of her life. And the one would weigh as heavily in his scales as the other.

What was it Moore had said? "He'd rather do in a gay than catch a serial killer." The terror of knowing he would never let go mixed with the pain of realizing Marcie was gone forever. Leslie knew in that moment that never again would her life be the same.

Chapter Two

*H*aberdash Poulis was five-foot-five, lean at both ends and pot-bellied in the middle. He wore his suits and shoes into the ground but carried a clean shirt in his briefcase against the possibility of sudden appearance before the bench. This idiosyncrasy led to much good-natured joshing from his colleagues and the eventual substitution of *Haberdashery* for his given name of Simon. What Haberdash lacked in presence was more than made up by a formidable grasp of the law and a threshing machine efficiency in separating the wheat from the chaff. Were it not for a quicksilver interest in whatever happened to catch his fancy, his success as a lawyer would have been assured. The modest reputation he did enjoy was due in part to accepting only those cases that could be resolved quickly, favorably, and with the least amount of effort.

Contacted on Leslie's behalf by Detective Sergeant Douglas

Moore at nine o'clock on the evening of Sunday, July 14, in the Judicial District of Spruce Falls, Attorney Poulis threw a handful of food into the aquarium, changed his shirt, and moments later found himself seated in the small room on the second floor of the police station waiting for his new client to be brought up from the holding cells.

On his way in he had passed the Inspector, who was on his way out. Here to see Taylor, Yarrow had asked, then winked and said, "You've got a live one this time, Hab. Better fasten your seat belt."

Hab did not know Leslie personally, but like everyone else in Spruce Falls he knew who she was. A crossover reporter with the local radio/television station. He also knew, thanks to Moore's telephone briefing, that she stood accused of the fatal bludgeoning of a female younger than herself; she was seen leaving the scene of the crime; she was the last known person to have had contact with the deceased.

Open and shut. If the facts were as stated, there would be little for him to do except go through the mechanics of arranging the best deal possible.

A creak of the door and his new client stepped into the room, followed by Yarrow's elegant young assistant. Appreciative of the growing number of cases being shunted his way by the Detective Sergeant, Hab greeted Moore before turning his attention to Leslie. What he saw was hardly encouraging. In shorts and a T-shirt, haggard and hollow-eyed, Leslie Taylor had the drained appearance of a marathon runner fighting to complete the last mile. The shorts and top told Haberdash that she'd been picked up earlier in the day and had been given no inkling that she would be subjected to anything more than routine questioning. Not, in itself, surprising. The longer a suspect could be kept on ice, the more time investigators had to come up with incriminating evidence. It was on such evidence that bail was granted or denied, that charges were laid or not laid, that a case went to trial or was filed in the wastebasket.

"How long has Miss Taylor been in custody?" The question

was directed to Moore, who was in the process of leaving.

"Since just before I called you. About half an hour."

Leslie's eyes flashed fire. Hab held up his hand to silence her and asked, "When did you pick her up?"

"Earlier today." The slender body shifted uncomfortably.

"This morning," Leslie snapped, her voice crackling with anger. "Right after breakfast. I've been here, God knows why, all day." She dropped into the chair across from Haberdasher, the same chair she had occupied most of the day, and propped her chin in both palms. "They've got it in their heads that I killed someone. It's insane. How soon can you get me out of here?"

"As soon as we can arrange a bail hearing."

"Twenty-four hours." She'd picked that up during the documentary on wife abuse.

"I'm afraid not." Haberdash glanced at Moore. "You did say Murder One?"

Moore nodded as he backed over the threshold, leaving Leslie and Hab alone.

"That twenty-four-hour business doesn't apply in capital cases, Miss Taylor. It could take awhile."

"You mean I have to stay here overnight?"

"I'm afraid so. I'll file application in the morning, but the best we can hope for is one week. Usually it takes more." He pulled a lined pad from his briefcase. "Now, I want you to tell me everything that happened. Everything."

Mind reeling from the discovery that she was not free to leave, might not be free for days and even weeks, she attempted to describe what had happened since she was picked up that morning. Pen poised, Hab said, "Never mind that. Tell me about Marcie Denton. Was there bad blood between you? Why did you go to see her? And why was she in a motel with family in town? Why were you in the motel room with her?"

"I wasn't in her motel room. I don't know what she was doing here. I didn't get to see her." She didn't add that the reason Marcie was in Spruce Falls was that she was probably trying to get away from that crummy husband of hers.

He'd heard it more times than he could count. I'm innocent. I didn't do it. I wasn't anywhere near the scene. They were always the hardest to do anything with, these diehards who refused to own up. And Leslie Taylor had all the earmarks. Guilty as hell. It was in the crossed arms hugging her chest as she came through the door; the dark eyes capable of hiding a glance, but now flat and expressionless; the withdrawn demeanor—understandable under the circumstances, although a manner you sensed was more inherent than immediate.

Neither judge nor juror, it made no difference to Haberdash whether she was guilty as hell or innocent as a newborn. The important thing was that she level with him so that he knew where he stood. "If I'm going to help you, Miss Taylor, you'll have to trust me. I want to hear your side of the story before I get it from Homicide. What exactly was your relationship with Mrs. Denton?"

"We were friends. We'd known each other for a long time." She looked down, avoiding his eyes to hide the tears misting in hers.

Hab made a mental note to tell her to look straight at the jury. Providing, of course, they got that far. Look at the jury. Keep your shoulders back and your head up. And try to show a little emotion. He scowled. If she expected twelve persons, good and true, to believe they were such close friends—that neither bore the other ill will—she had best dredge up a modicum of grief. "Had you quarreled?"

"No. We haven't even seen each other for months." It was easier to think about Marcie in the past tense than to talk about her with such dreadful finality.

"Then you weren't as close as you had been? Why is that?"

"For one thing, she was in Toronto and I was here. We just didn't have that much opportunity. If Marcie's dead, they should be talking to Charlie, not me. Why would I want to kill her? I was in . . . ." Catching herself, she said lamely, "I was very fond of her."

"Why would her husband want to kill her? I take it you mean Charlie Denton, the architect? What reason would he have?"

"What reason would he have to beat her up? She was scared to death of him. Why don't they go get him instead of wasting time with me?"

"They've already talked to him. He flew up as soon as he was notified about the body. He's staying with Mrs. Denton's parents." Obviously Charlie Denton was in the clear. Obviously Leslie Taylor wasn't. You couldn't blame her for trying to divert suspicion, but the sooner she stopped muddying the waters and faced the issue at hand the better off they'd both be. Try again Poulis, and this time keep her on track. "What sort of mood was she in when you saw her? Did she seem upset?"

"I didn't see her."

"Why would she check into a motel when her family is here?"

"I have no idea."

"What were you doing there?"

"She left a message on my answering machine that she wanted to see me. I drove over, she wasn't there, and I left."

For a supposedly intelligent person she was remarkably obtuse. A schoolgirl could come up with a better story than this. Perhaps what she needed was the blunt edge of truth. "Let me lay it out for you, Miss Taylor. You're charged with Murder One. That's twenty-five years. With maximum time off, you're still looking at twenty big ones. Suppose we manage to get it down to second degree. That's ten-to-twenty. The best we can hope for is manslaughter, and even there you're looking at the best part of your life down the drain."

"You make it sound like a fait accompli. They bring me in for questioning and you talk as though it's all over but the hanging."

"Look. A hell of a lot of people are behind bars because they didn't wake up until it was too late. I know Yarrow. He wouldn't have charged you unless he had enough right now to go to the Crown. Tomorrow morning I'll get an application in for bail. He'll do everything he can to show cause why you should be kept locked up until you go to trial. Unless you start giving me some help, your chances are pretty slim."

"Help how? I haven't done anything. Isn't that enough?"

"No. That isn't enough. First I want to get you out. One step at a time. Then we'll decide how we're going to handle this. We'll find a way around it. There are options. We'll get to that later. I want you to get a good night's sleep. If you'll give me someone to contact, I'll try to get a change of clothes to you for the morning. And just in case, I'd better have the name of someone who is willing to assume custody."

"Custody?" Brief horror, quickly shuttered by a masklike impassiveness. "There's no one."

"I thought you were hometown. Isn't your family here?"

"I don't want them involved."

"Involved?" Hab ran his finger around a collar that was growing limper by the second. "They *are* involved. Before this is over, everyone you've ever known will be involved." My God, what did he have to do to get her to comprehend the predicament she was in? "From now on, your life is an open book. Everything you've ever done, everyone you've ever talked to, will be grist for the mill."

The icy control broke without warning. Leslie dropped her face into her hands and her body convulsed. Hab watched, eyes narrowed and speculative. No stranger to delayed reaction, he congratulated himself on his decision to get tough. She hadn't seemed overly perturbed when he hit her with the ten-to-twenty-to-life, but she'd caught it all right. Just as well. If they got down to the wire and had nowhere to go, he'd push for a guilty plea and leniency. Depending on what Yarrow had up his sleeve, he just might try to swing her around off the top. It would be a hell of a lot easier than going through the full rigmarole, to say nothing of sympathy earned through a saving of taxpayers' money.

Reasonably pleased with the result of this first meeting—with having finally gotten through to this client he still wasn't sure he wanted—Hab Poulis packed up his briefcase and strode toward the door. "I'll see you tomorrow, Miss Taylor. And I'll get the application for bail in, first thing. It will take about a week. And remember, don't say a word to anyone. From here on, the only time you talk is when I'm with you."

Moore led the way back downstairs, and Leslie followed like an automaton. Her mind, usually so precise and well-ordered, was functioning like a jack rabbit engine. Fits and starts. Clarity and haze. She asked for a lawyer and got a funny little man in a wrinkled suit who seemed intent on destroying her. She demanded to be let loose, and he said yes, I'll see about it tomorrow, and tomorrow turned out to be a week away—and then only if she was lucky.

Dad and Mother. What about Dad and Mother? They'll have to know, he said. Everyone will know. God. Wasn't it enough that Marcie was dead? Eager, willing, lovely Marcie. Wasn't it enough that she was gone without branding her, branding them both, with the details of that other life they had tried so hard to hide?

Sound rose above their footsteps echoing on concrete, and she was aware, dimly, of a voice speaking. With a politeness born of habit, she said, "I beg your pardon. What did you say?"

They had reached the row of cells and Moore held the door and repeated, "We've decided it's best to keep you here overnight. You'll be moved to the regular facility in the morning."

Best? Best would have been not answering the door when they knocked. Not flipping on the answering machine when she got back from the lake which would have meant not getting Marcie's message which would have meant not going anywhere near the Dalton. Maybe the best of all would have been keeping Marcie at arm's length, pretending shock when Marcie blurted out that she loved her, keeping that other part of herself locked up in a dark little corner and never admitting, even to herself, that it was there.

She walked into the cell, turned, and said, still hoping there was some mistake, "Is it true? Is Marcie really dead?"

"Yes."

"But how? Was it in the motel?"

"I can't discuss it, Leslie." His voice was gentle, sympathetic. "Would you like me to stay awhile? If you feel like talking you'll find I'm a pretty good listener."

"I just don't want to be alone."

"I know. I'd feel the same way. What did you think of Poulis?"

"He seems. . . I don't know. I guess he's not what I expected. He kept asking the same kind of questions Yarrow did. He acted as if I was lying."

"Lawyers are like doctors. They all have a different bedside manner."

"He's not very pleasant."

"It's not a very pleasant occupation. He gets mixed up with some pretty shady characters." He smiled apologetically. "Present company excluded, of course." He disappeared into the outer office and returned with a chair that he propped against the wall opposite her cot. The cell was so narrow that when he rested his feet against the edge of the bed his knees folded into a chin rest. "Now. What would you like to talk about?"

Marcie. More than anything, she wanted to talk about Marcie. "Anything. The weather."

"At the moment, it's raining." Eyes fixed on the ceiling he said, more to himself than to her, "Sometimes I get so fed up with this town I could take off and never come back. It's an anachronism. I swear some of these people are still stuck back in the forties and fifties. So much has happened in the world, yet none of it's sunk in."

"It's no different than most places this size. Spruce Falls isn't exactly a major metropolis."

"It's not one-horse, either. But God, it's backward. Some of us used to get together in Toronto and read poetry. A couple of times a month a bunch of guys sat down and read each other poetry. Can you imagine that happening here? We'd be run out of town on a rail. If Yarrow ever got wind of it, he'd have my tail."

"Is it hard? Working with him?"

"Not if I remember to be careful. But I'm always afraid I'll let something drop. You know what I mean?"

Indeed she knew what he meant. That feeling of caution had been so ingrained during her years with Marcie that she had forgotten what it was to be spontaneous. Every word weighed before it was uttered. Every ad lib scripted in advance. A contradiction in terms, but a necessity for survival. "What made you decide to be a policeman?" Make talk, Leslie. It will keep your mind off what's happening. What *has* happened.

"You're interviewing me, Miss Taylor." He laughed good-naturedly. "Bacon said 'we are all debtor to our professions,' or words to that effect. What we do for a living is what we are."

"I don't know that that's entirely true."

"Nothing is *entirely* true." Moore's gaze was concentrated on the tips of his shoes—was he studying his reflection, she wondered—and giving thought to each word, he said, "I wanted to be a musician. I play a pretty mean piano. But Dad thought that was sissy stuff. He was on the force. One of the old beat patrolmen. I guess I just wanted him to be proud of me."

"Is he?"

"I hope so. He doesn't say much, but I think he feels I've turned out O.K."

"And what about you? Are you happy?" She would have preferred to ask if it was worth it, but didn't out of fear the question would be interpreted on a personal rather than career level. If the Sergeant had skeletons in his closet, better they stay there.

"Do you remember Oscar Levant? I have most of his records. Seventy-eight's. Collector's items." He paused, waiting for a reply, and when Leslie shook her head, baffled by the seeming lack of connection, he continued, "He was big in Hollywood for a while, back in the studio days. Not the greatest pianist on record, but he had a tongue that could cut through metal.

Somebody asked him that question once, and do you know what he said? 'Happiness is not something you experience. It's something you remember.' I think he was right."

The handsome face, minus the smile that Leslie had come to believe he wore even in his sleep, looked old and tired. The features, no longer boyish, were razor-sharp, the skin taut and translucent over bone. She wanted to reach out to him, to tell him that there was such a thing as happiness; and although it was fragile and fleeting and rare in the extreme, it did exist and could be experienced—but one must know when one had it and never, ever, try to hold it beyond its time anymore than you would close your hand on a shimmering, iridescent soap bubble floating free in space.

She wanted to reach out and comfort him but she said nothing. They sat facing each other, each locked in a private world. The light bulb, high in the ceiling, created eerie shadows on the scene below. Overhead there was the faint sound of footsteps. In the cell, no sound but that of breathing. An iron lung, Leslie thought. We're no better off than those polio patients who used to live out their lives in those terrible iron breathing machines.

As the silence wore on, the walls began to close in. In Toronto she had never ridden the subway because it gave her claustrophobia. When she and Marcie rented their first apartment, they picked one with windows for walls and a view of lawns and trees. Always, from the time she was a child, she had needed the sense of freedom that came with open space and clear horizons. To be here, in a restricted enclosure of steel and concrete, was mind-numbing. She began to shake, shivering as much from panic as from the cold and damp. Oh God, oh God, oh God. Her mind spun a silent mantra, the segued repetition of a tape spliced end to end. Arms clasped round her middle, she rocked back and forth, setting the metal cot into a jangle of slats and springs.

"Leslie, I'm sorry." Moore's chair clattered as the front legs hit the floor. "You must be freezing. I'll get you a couple of blankets. And something to eat. Are you hungry?"

Someone else had asked her that earlier. Was it Yarrow? It must have been the Inspector. He had said are you hungry, and she had said yes, and time had gone by and eventually that particular question had been lost in a welter of other questions that had nothing to do with food or drink or personal comfort. And now it no longer mattered. She shook her head, wanting, suddenly, nothing more than to be left alone.

Moore unwound gracefully—strange how even in this environment he managed to portray the model host—and said gently, "I'll be back in a minute."

Leslie heard the door swing shut, a thud that resounded in her head with chilling finality. She did not look at the door, knew that if she saw it closed and locked and with bars in place, something inside her would snap. Moore said he'd be back in a minute. His minutes had a tendency to run off the clock, but however long it took she would sit with eyes closed and mind blank.

Moore found her as he had left her, seated on the edge of the cot, staring at the wall. He paused for a moment, studying her unobserved. Aside from the shivering—even warmly dressed this dank basement was enough to set your teeth chattering—she was remarkably composed. In her position he'd be beating his head against the wall. By now, he'd have spilled his guts. Yet there she sat, as remote and unemotional as a statue. "Leslie." The door swung open with a faint rasp. He dropped the blankets on the end of the bed and held out a cardboard box. "I hope you like chicken."

"You shouldn't have bothered." When she made no move to take the box, he deposited it on the floor.

"I got you some coffee, too. I want you to drink this." He forced the paper cup into her hands, then picked up one of the blankets and draped it around her shoulders. "There's an extra blanket here that you can use as a sheet." The mattress ticking was frayed and discolored. A flicker of distaste crossed the handsome face. He'd sleep on the floor before he'd lie down on that bag of scruff. ''I'll have to leave you now. Try to get some rest.''

As the shaking subsided, Leslie looked up, smiled stiffly and said, ''Doug, thank you.'' Grateful for the food she wasn't about to eat, for the coffee and blankets and company, she held out her hand in a gesture of friendship. Conscious of her use of his first name, he twined his fingers through hers and squeezed an acknowledgment. ''Things will look better in the morning. They always do.''

Turning quickly, he was gone. Leslie listened to his footsteps and, as he neared the end of the corridor, the first few bars of a lilting tune. A happy whistling. Meant as a signal to keep her spirits up? She sipped the coffee and thought how kind he was, how good it was to have someone who cared. If it were up to Yarrow, she'd have been thrown in a dungeon and left to starve.

Wrapped in the blanket, with a corner pulled over her head to block out the light, she closed her eyes and imagined herself in a pleasant garden with Duchess at her heels. Slowly she drifted off into a light, then deeper, more troubled sleep. The garden disappeared, and she was lost in a tangled thicket that caught at her clothes and blotted out the sun. Duchess whined in the distance, and she followed the sound only to have it veer off whenever she came close. At last she broke through the undergrowth into a clearing. There, at the foot of a tree, Duchess lay mangled and bleeding, her leg caught in a trap. Frantic, Leslie tore at the metal, trying desperately to pry the steel jaws apart.

At last, unable to spring the teeth, she sat down and cradled the dog's head in her lap. Weeping, she looked into the soft brown eyes that were pleading for help. I trust you, they said. If you love me, do something. Once lustrous, now glazed with pain, they bore into her soul in mute appeal. In a frenzied attempt to end the suffering of this creature she had raised and loved, she picked up a boulder and brought it crashing down on Duchess's head. The limp body instantly metamorphosed from animal to human. Silvery blonde hair. Blue eyes staring lifelessly into hers. A temple caved and crushed. A trickle of blood tracing the pale skin.

Horrified, Leslie inched free and shook the body. Wake up. Marcie, Marcie, wake up. The trap that had closed on Duchess was now anchored to Marcie, the vicious teeth meshed through flesh that was Marcie's flesh and bone that was Marcie's bone. She knew with the clarity that comes of nightmare that if she could free Marcie from the trap, everything would be as it was. Like running a film backward when you were editing. The temple would round into shape, the boulder would arc into mid-air, Marcie would smile and hold up her arms and say that she loved her.

She reached for the trap. Touched it. It sprang open. Quickly she grasped Marcie's foot to lift it free. With hair-trigger precision, the jaws snapped shut. Both wrists held in a cutting vise, warm flesh pressed against the cold clay of what had once been Marcie, she groped for the boulder that would set them both free.

Duchess ran to the door, tail wagging in anticipation. When she saw it was Adam Taylor and he was alone, the tail drooped and she retreated to the corner of the kitchen that afforded a view of both doors.

Taylor brushed imaginary hairs from his pant leg and called out, "I'm home." Finding his wife alone in the living room he asked, "Where's Leslie? I didn't see her car outside."

"I don't know, dear. She called after you left and asked if we'd look after Duchess." Mrs. Taylor switched off the television set. "I'll get you a cup of coffee." She had spent her entire married life caring for and looking up to her husband. The latter came easily. She was five inches shorter than he.

"Other parents baby-sit their grandchildren. We're stuck with a dog. The next time she asks, tell her we're not running a kennel."

Mrs. Taylor sighed. In spite of her husband's commanding

air of authority, the unpleasantries always seemed to fall to her. "This is only the second time, dear. I'm sure she wouldn't have asked if it wasn't important." She escaped to the kitchen where a trembling Duchess watched as she poured the coffee and set it on a tray with sugar bowl and cream. After years of failing to get it right, she now allowed him to doctor his own brew. "Don't worry," she whispered to Duchess. "He's like you. His bark is worse than his bite."

"Where is she? What excuse did she come up with for missing dinner?" Adding the exact amount of sugar and cream that she would have done, he stirred the coffee into a small tidal wave.

"I don't know where she is, dear. She didn't say."

"Didn't say." The lines around his mouth deepened. "You spend half the day in the kitchen cooking for her, something better comes along, and without so much as a by-your-leave, away she goes. She's changed, Emily. I knew it was a mistake to let her go off to the city on her own. God knows what she got into down there."

"She was over twenty-one, Adam. We couldn't very well stop her."

"Well, you didn't have to encourage her, either. I told you at the time we'd regret it."

Perhaps it had been wrong to let her only child go without an argument, but Leslie would have gone with or without their blessing. Adam didn't seem to realize that the world was a much different one than they had been born into. Not that he was old. Not that either of them was old. But they had both grown up at a time when families were intact and the future predictable.

She thought of the period, early in their marriage, when she decided to get a job to help out. Other women were doing it. Why not she? Because, Adam had said, you are my wife. And my wife does not work for strangers. That had been the end of it, but she recognized in Leslie many of the aspirations she had set aside when she married. She had encouraged her daughter to make her own decisions, to set her own goals and work toward them. It was possible now for women to go into marriage as individuals, to make something of themselves and not have to live forever in some man's shadow. Adam might disapprove, but it was happening. You saw it on TV, read about it in the papers. Even if women's rights were given short shrift in a male-oriented mining town like Spruce Falls, there was a whole wide world out there and Leslie was entitled to it.

"Why doesn't she get married and settle down like other girls? If she waits much longer, she'll be too old."

"Oh, Adam. There's plenty of time to get married. Let her live a little first. You're never too old to fall in love." Her voice was wistful. What had happened to those wonderful years when Adam came courting and her heart pounded whenever she heard his name?

"Children. She'll be too old to have children. She's almost too old now."

"Perhaps she doesn't want any, Adam." Her heart ached as she said it. They had both wanted more children, brothers and sisters to keep Leslie company, to provide a house full of grand-children for what they referred to—jokingly at first but more seriously as the years slipped by—as their golden years.

"Nonsense. A woman is not a woman unless she has chil-dren of her own. Words from your own mouth, Mother." Remembering, the craggy face softened. " 'Now I'm a wom-an.' That was the first thing you said to me when I saw you in the hospital."

His dark eyes brightened, and she saw in them the youthful Adam of the past. Impulsively she walked across to him and brushed his forehead with her lips. He was a good man. The only man she had ever known. There had been times when she had looked at other men and wondered what it would be like. Would they hold her the same way? Would they work so hard toward that one moment and then collapse in almost in-stant sleep? She had wondered, a couple of times had even been tempted, but her infidelities had been imaginary and her virtue remained intact. "I'm sure she's thought it all out, dear. It's not up to us to interfere."

Lately, talking about Leslie seemed to upset him. They had been delighted when they heard she was returning to Spruce Falls. Having her at home again would be wonderful. It was a terrible disappointment to find she had no intention of moving back into her old room. Using up her savings to buy a run-down house at the edge of town was, in her father's eyes, the height of foolishness. A shack, he called it, and after a quick tour of inspection he refused to have anything more to do with it. If Leslie wanted to see him she could come here. To her real home. Not having seen the shack since it was transformed into a neat cottage with a flower garden in front and a spacious run for Duchess out back, he pictured his daughter living in squalor. "It's time for the news." Looking at the world's troubles would take his mind off his own imagined woes.

The screen lit up, and the weekend anchorman came into focus. Not nearly as good as Leslie, Mrs. Taylor thought, but then, he was just a fill-in. The weekend news never amounted to much. You'd think everything stopped for tea between Friday and Monday. It wasn't true, of course, but that was the impression you got watching the newscasts. Leslie said it was because they were on skeleton staff and unless something really earth-shattering occurred, they didn't much bother with what was going on locally.

Car bombs in Beirut. A spy scandal in Germany. An earthquake in California. Another ambush in Ireland by the IRA. The international news was so predictable you could hardly call it news. "And here at home...," the announcer paused for effect, "the body of a woman found early this morning in the Dalton Motel has been identified as that of Mrs. Charles Denton. Mrs. Denton, the daughter of Sven and Anna Bergstrom and a native of Spruce Falls was married to Charles P. Denton, the well-known Toronto architect. A suspect is in custody."

Adam Taylor stared at the screen. "That's Leslie's friend." He turned to his wife. "Marcie Bergstrom. The girl Leslie went to

Toronto with. That's probably where she is now. Over at the Bergstrom's. Funny she didn't say so when she called."

Mrs. Taylor's eyes widened in horror. She had talked to Marcie. Was it only yesterday? Marcie had called saying she was trying to find Leslie. It was important. Yes, she had Leslie's home number. Yes, she had called her there but there was no answer. She'd left a message, but if Mrs. Taylor saw her in the meantime, would she please tell her it was urgent.

And now Marcie Bergstrom was dead and Emily Taylor knew—her mother's instinct told her—that her daughter's terse phone call was connected with the death of her best friend. Shivering, she reached for the sweater draped over the back of her chair. Adam turned off the TV set. Duchess whimpered in the kitchen. Emily Taylor sat unmoving and afraid.

Chapter Three

*H*arriet Fordham Croft paused on the courthouse steps while her eyes adjusted to the bright morning sun. Brilliant aquamarine fringed by thick dark lashes: they were compelling eyes. For that matter, Harriet Croft was a compelling woman. With the poise of a model and the memory of a computer, she had, as her friends said, everything going for her. In point of fact, Harriet Croft—successful attorney-at-law—was fed up with her life and bored to tears.

"I was hoping I'd catch you." Clarence Crossley bounded up the steps. "I called the office and they said you had a court appearance. Are you coming or going?"

"Sometimes I wonder." The firm mouth relaxed into a half-smile. "You're up early." Clare was a night prowler who rarely surfaced before mid-afternoon. It was thanks to him that so many of her cases ended in acquittal. With a network of contacts and the nose of a bloodhound, Clarence Crossley could find out anything, anytime, anywhere. He was Harriet's winning edge, and she prized him accordingly.

"Haven't been to bed yet." Grinning, he pulled a tattered notebook out of his pocket. "I got those names you wanted. The people Reilly said he was with the night the old doll was off'd."

Harriet flinched. Although it was five years since she'd switched from corporate to trial law, street talk still bothered her. Especially from an associate. She suspected Clarence knew this and tossed in the occasional vulgarism to tease her. He was the only person she'd ever come up against who refused to be intimidated by the formidable Croft presence. Yet in many ways she felt closer to him than to most of her friends and acquaintances. "That's wonderful."

Crossley's quick ear caught the lack of enthusiasm. "Feeling down this morning? How about a bun break?"

Harriet manufactured a smile. Crossley, the Danish freak. Sticky buns washed down by a Coke were all he ever seemed to eat. "Sugar is bad for you."

"So is living." He took her arm and propelled her across the street. Shorter by a head, Crossley walked with a slight swagger that made up for his lack of height. He waited until they were seated in the coffee shop on the second floor of the Sheraton, a hangout for lawyers and their clients because of its convenient location across from the courthouse, before getting around to what was uppermost in his mind. "I see your friend Charles P. Denton has made the headlines again." He had met Charles Denton only once, a brief encounter in Harriet's office, and had taken an instant dislike to the man. Forever after he articulated the name with emphasis and dripping scorn.

"Not friend, acquaintance." How many times did she have to tell him?

He ordered two Danish and a Coke for himself, a black coffee for Harriet, and without pausing for breath said, "He had the hots for you."

The waitress looked up from her pad and stared at Harriet, her button eyes alive with interest. Flushed with embarrassment, Harriet waited until the woman was out of earshot and said, "I wish you wouldn't talk like that in public, Clare. Charles Denton was a client. We had a business relationship. I hardly know the man."

"You went out with him."

"For heaven's sake. Once to his association's annual dinner. Once to the theatre. Hardly what you'd call a deep personal involvement."

"Maybe on your part. But I never saw a guy more anxious to get a dame in the sack. It was sticking out all over him, if you know what I mean." Their order arrived, and he leered at her over his Danish.

Harriet set her cup down carefully and pushed back her chair. "You're giddy from lack of sleep. I'll talk to you when you're in a more civilized frame of mind."

"I'm sorry. Don't go." He bit into the Danish and munched happily. "I'll be a *verray parfit gentil knight*. That's Chaucer, Mrs. Croft. *The pine-apple of politeness.* Richard Brinsley Sheridan." A sip of Coke with pinkie extended. "I'm couther than you think." Eyes glinting mischief, he wiped his mouth with the back of his hand. "Do you think he did it?"

"Did what?" She asked the question idly, not really interested in what Charlie Denton might or might not have done. He was one of the clients she had dropped when she gave up her corporate practice. Getting rid of him had caused no loss of sleep.

"Haven't you read the papers?"

"I haven't tuned in on anything all weekend."

"In retreat again?" Having bird-dogged for Harriet for the past five years, Clarence knew that periodically she shut herself off from the world. At times she went on long, aimless drives, stopping overnight when she was tired. Other times she holed up in her apartment with a stack of books and stayed there till Monday morning. Crossley, along with everyone who knew her, respected her need for privacy, but of late it worried him. The withdrawals were becoming more frequent and seemed to be doing less good. "His wife was murdered." He said it bluntly, wanting to see her reaction to the bare bones of it.

"Really?" The green eyes widened with interest. "That sweet wee thing? How awful." The wedding had come close on the heels of her corporate practice wrap up. She had received an invitation and dutifully put in an appearance. Charles had made a point of introducing her to his new bride. Rigidly correct as usual, his manner nevertheless hinted at malice. This could have been you, he seemed to be saying. See what you missed by being so standoffish? She had looked at him, then at the new Mrs. Charles P. Denton, and felt a wave of sympathy for the girl. While she had feared no good would come of the marriage, she certainly had not expected anything like this. "Do they know who did it?"

"They've picked someone up, but they haven't said who. Usually when a woman is battered to death, the husband is number one on the suspect list. I thought you might have an opinion pro or con."

"You can forget about Charles. He's not the type. I don't imagine he's ever acted in a fit of temper in his life. Where did this happen?"

Crossley told her what he knew, which wasn't much. Marcie had gone home to visit her folks except that instead of visiting her folks she checked into a motel room and some time between high noon Saturday and the small hours of Sunday morning she had a visitor who bashed her head in. "I hope," he said pointedly, "that if Denton's the guy on the mat and he hollers for help, you'll have the good sense to say forget it."

The green eyes flashed fire. "I'll overlook that, Clare." Shards of ice tinkled in the expressive Croft voice—a voice renowned for its ability to flay hostile witnesses and sway juries.

Clarence Crossley knew well that no one told Harriet Croft how to run her affairs. You could suggest, advise, offer counsel. But the one thing you could not do was tell her *what* to do. This was one of the rare occasions when he was willing to risk her wrath. "I'd hate to see you mixed up with him. And I know, sure as fate, that if he needs a lawyer, he'll come running straight to you. Do what you like, Harriet. Just be careful. The man's a snake."

They left the hotel in strained silence. Clarence hailed a cab that was cruising out front; Harriet picked up a paper from the corner box and walked the three blocks to her office. Donna, her receptionist/secretary, greeted her with a "Thank God you're here," and handed over a stack of telephone messages.

Harriet fingered the pile and groaned. "It's not as bad as it looks," Donna said quickly. "Most of them are from a Mr. Denton."

"Charles Denton?" Silly question. Of course it would be Charles Denton. No wonder Clarence had gone on about him. Not wanting to be caught as a snoop, he'd led her to believe he'd telephoned the office. Obviously he'd stopped in, seen the messages—he was a magnet when it came to stray bits of information—and decided to get a word in before she made what he considered a Grade A mistake.

The phone rang. "It's him again," Donna whispered. "Are you in or out?"

"In." Harriet took it in her office, door closed. Charles was delighted to hear her voice, how had she been, would it be possible to see her for a few minutes? He was in a pay booth just up the street, could he drop over now?

She cradled the phone and stared at it, perplexed. Not a word about his wife. Her death. The manner of her death. His voice was hurried, but not unduly upset. Whoever was in custody in Spruce Falls, it certainly wasn't Charles. But if he wasn't a suspect, why call a lawyer? And why, in the name of God, was he here in Toronto when he should be with Marcie's parents, tending to the final disposition of the body of the woman he had loved enough to marry?

With time on her hands she took out the envelope Clare had

handed her and sorted through the list of witnesses he'd un-
covered. Scheduled for the Fall Assizes, the case—an armed
holdup of a convenience store—was weighted against her client.
Thanks to Clare, the teeter had tottered in their favor. The witnesses he'd come up with provided an airtight alibi. They were
with him, miles away from the scene, solid citizens all. The case
would be thrown out of court. Her client was off the hook and
the police, not above cutting the pattern to fit the cloth, were
back to square one.

Head bowed, and deep in concentration, she didn't hear him
come in. When she looked up he was framed in the doorway:
the shoulders were just as stiff, the back just as straight, as
she remembered.

"It's good to see you, Harriet." The pale grey eyes were unnerving. She had seen that fixed, unwavering stare demolish
opposition in board meetings and reduce underlings to jelly.
He was dressed in his customary three-piece suit, vest buttoned
and watch-fobbed, trousers creased to a razor's edge.

"I'm sorry to hear about. . . ."

He seemed not to have heard her. "I need some advice. I
didn't know who else to call."

While she waited for him to continue, Clare's warning flashed
through her mind. The man is a snake. Clare was entitled to
his opinion, but he was not about to foist it on her. She would
hear what Charlie Denton had to say and decide for herself.

Speaking slowly, his voice clear and controlled, he began
with, "You may not believe what I am going to tell you, but
I swear it's true." For the next hour he talked without pause.
When he finished, Harriet walked him to the door, went back
for her briefcase and told Donna she was taking the rest of
the day off. If anyone wanted her, she'd be at home.

Leslie woke with a start and scrambled to her feet in panic.
The alarm hadn't gone off. She had an early morning interview at the station and a million things to do at home before
she took off for the office. She looked around the room, at

the bars on the door, at the strange woman sitting in the corridor watching her, and slowly it came back to her. Marcie was dead. She was in jail. They said that it was she, Leslie, who had killed her.

"You sleep sound," the woman said. "I was just thinking I should call you." She disappeared down the corridor and returned a few moments later with a constable in tow. He unlocked the door and motioned her into the hall.

"They shouldn't of kept you here," the woman said accusingly. "Called me down in the middle of the night just to sit with you." She looked at Leslie as though she expected an apology.

The constable produced a pair of handcuffs and clipped one on Leslie's wrist, the other on his. Numbly she allowed herself to be herded up the back stairs and into the parking lot. There was a cruiser at the door, the motor running and a driver behind the wheel. Expecting to be taken to the courthouse which was just across the street, Leslie pulled back, alarmed. "Where are you taking me?"

The matron said good morning to the driver; the constable in the back stared straight ahead. No one bothered to answer her. The car sped up the street and pulled in behind the local jail. "I'm supposed to see my lawyer. He's arranging bail."

The officer got out and pulled her after him. Leslie looked at the squat red building and her knees turned to rubber. If she went through that door, into that place where names became numbers and days became years, she would be lost forever. No one would know where she was. She would never see her family again.

Pain shot through her wrist as the constable started across the tarmac in full stride. Not until they were inside, in a small room off the matrons' office, did the policeman unlock the cuffs and turn her over to the tall, heavyset woman who appeared to be in charge.

While Leslie was strip-searched, her overnight friend stood by as insurance against sudden attack. "My back is killing me," she complained. "They drag me downtown. I sit up all night in that creepy basement watching her ladyship here, who sleeps like a baby, and I get here and your relief's not in and you expect me to do double-shift and my back is killing me and I'm out on my feet and the minute you're all clear I'm out of here. You better call for help now or hack it on your own."

The grumbling continued throughout the search, during the march to the shower room, on the way back to the cell block with its row of cages within the one huge cage that doubled as mess hall, recreation area, and social center. The matron opened the main door, motioned Leslie inside, and slid the bars into place behind her. Dusting her hands, she turned to Miss Aching Back and heaved a sigh of relief. "There. That's over with. I can manage the rest on my own."

Leslie stood in the center of the room and stared around uncertainly. The only furniture was a plank table under the window with a long bench running along either side. The window, set high in the wall, was covered with grime and wire mesh. The individual cells were just long enough to accommodate a cot, wide enough for the single-width bed, basin and toilet.

One of the girls seated at the table stood up lazily and called out, "Hey Les, come on over and meet your new roommates." The shapeless cotton print housedress—standard jailhouse garb, Leslie thought, glancing down at the faded smock issued in place of her own shorts and top—looked out of place on the hefty body. "I'm Josie. That there is Marj. And Elsie. Dinny. And Baby. She cries all the time." She draped a heavy arm around Leslie's shoulders and drew her toward the table.

Leslie sat at the end of the bench and tried not to look frightened. Josie was clearly the person in charge. A huge woman, with thick arms and a fleshy face topped by brown hair pulled back into a ponytail, she looked as though she could clear the bench with one swipe of her forearm.

"It's not the Ritz, but we get by, don't we girls?" Her small blue eyes peered through folds of flesh. Shrewd eyes, but it seemed to Leslie that they held a softness. A hint of compassion.

"We heard about you." A voice from the far end of the table. "We were making bets on what you'd be like."

Josie withered the speaker with a savage look. Then, in answer to Leslie's stunned expression, she explained, "Word gets around. Old lady Klyk was full of it when she came on shift this morning. We don't often get cel-eb-erteries in here."

"I'm hardly. . . ."

Josie talked over her. "The first few days are worst. It's not so bad once you're used to it."

"Did you really hit her with your shoe?" The girl called Baby watched her with wide-eyed fascination.

"My shoe?" This was the first Leslie had heard of a shoe. She looked down at her sneakers, flapping now because the laces had been removed. Inexplicably she began to laugh, a wild, frenzied sound bordering on hysteria. Dimly aware of the women drawing away, huddling against each other for protection—of shouts from Matron Klyk—she rocked back and forth, tears streaming down her cheeks.

Without warning, Josie leaned across the table and slapped her across the face. The blow exploded in her brain, jarring her senses and snapping her back from the edge of a yawning chasm. Quiet now, she hunched into herself and wept inwardly. Josie rounded the table and held her in arms as strong as steel bands. "Don't cry," she whispered. "Never let them bastards see you cry. You gotta act like you got nothing to worry about. Like you're innocent and let them prove otherwise." The warmth of the large body and soothing voice was strangely at odds with the tough veneer.

"I *am* innocent."

"I know." Josie shrugged. That's what they all said. Oh, she'd known a couple of trippers who got a belt out of owning up, but you could tell them a mile off. So what if this kid had bopped her friend. Probably an accident. Got into an argument, lost her temper, hit her with the first thing handy. The next thing she knows the chick is dead and she's in the slammer. Either way, it was no skin off her nose. She'd seen this doll on TV, liked what she saw, would help her over the rough spots if she could.

"Taylor. Visitor." Klyk's voice cut through the air.

"Put a face on," Josie ordered. "Look like you got it all together."

Klyk waited in the corridor, buttressed by a male guard as wide as he was tall. Leslie's first thought was of her mother. "I don't want to see anyone." Her mother would have a stroke if she saw her like this.

"You'll want to see this one. It's your lawyer."

Poulis was waiting for her, open briefcase at his feet, notepad at the ready. "How are you feeling this morning, Leslie?" Fully at ease, he behaved as though this was an ordinary encounter on an ordinary day in an ordinary place.

His business-as-usual attitude deepened her sense of unreality. She glanced at Mrs. Klyk, who had settled in an easy chair near the door. "I prefer to talk in private."

"Don't worry about Matron. She's not interested in what we have to say, are you Mrs. Klyk?" The camaraderie suggested they had been through this before and had come to a mutual understanding.

"I thought what a lawyer discusses with his client is confidential."

"Now, now. You're not in the big city, Leslie. We don't believe in standing on too much ceremony. Nothing you say will go beyond these walls." Another ingratiating smile for Mrs. Klyk. "I've made application for bail."

"How soon will I be out?"

"Impatience. The curse of youth." He shook his head reproachfully. "These things take time. Your 'app' will be heard on Monday. What they call a show cause."

"That's a week away. You mean I have to stay here for a whole week?"

"The time will go fast. The important thing at the moment is to do everything possible to get you released pending trial.

I'll be seeing your parents later today. We'll need their help."

"I told you last night, Mr. Poulis, I don't want them mixed up in this."

"Without them you don't stand a very good chance, Leslie. We're not dealing with a misdemeanor here. This is a capital offense we're up against." He drew out the phrase *capital offense*, lingering over it with relish. "I also have an appointment set up with Inspector Yarrow and the prosecutor. I thought I'd best get that out of the way before Monday, too. I don't want them pulling any surprises on us. They'll try every trick in the book to keep you off the street. They have to show cause why you shouldn't be released. Convince the judge you're a danger to yourself and/or others. And I have to convince him that you aren't. Also that you won't skip bail and disappear."

"I don't believe this. There's a killer out there. Why aren't they looking for him?"

Haberdash didn't bother to explain that the police weren't looking because as far as they were concerned they had their killer. He, Haberdash Poulis, did not know whether or not Leslie Taylor was guilty. But he did know that to Yarrow, it was case closed. From now on, Homicide's attention would be focused on gathering evidence and plugging loopholes all with one end in view—assembling a body of irrefutable data that would place Miss Taylor where they felt she belonged, locked up for the maximum period allowed by law.

The drama would unfold, and Leslie's role would diminish. He and the prosecutor, Jeremy Frost, would become the key players. Witnesses, pro and con, would be the supporting cast. Justice Nystrom or one such would produce and direct. Leslie Taylor would be the trophy awarded for best performance.

He'd been through it so often, yet it never failed to amaze him. Those who abided by the law knew it least. A con would have spilled his guts by now, would be helping to work out a strategy that would beat the system. He tried again. "Is there anything you'd like to tell me before I go?" The shake of her head triggered an urge to shake her. "What about your mother?

Is there anything you'd like me to tell her?"

"Stay away from her." The words crackled with anger.

"I asked her to pick out something you can wear when you go up before the judge. Unless, of course, you prefer to look like a beachcomber." He regretted the sarcastic remark the moment it was out. "There'll be reporters," he said lamely. "I want you to look your best."

He was packing his briefcase, getting ready to leave. "Will I see you before the bail thing?" She said it quickly, aware of Mrs. Klyk bustling toward her.

"I've asked for disclosure this week. That's when the Crown lays its cards on the table. As soon as I see what they've got, I want to sit down with you. Then we'll decide on the approach we're going to take. There's not much we can do until we know where they're coming from."

Padding along the corridor beside her, Mrs. Klyk said, "You've got a good man there. He's looked after a lot of our girls."

And where are they now, Leslie wondered. Two meetings, and still nothing concrete. If he was this ineffectual with someone who was innocent, God help the guilty. She consoled herself with the reminder that Doug Moore had recommended Poulis. He seemed fond of her. They were, she felt certain, a pair of kindred spirits. He wouldn't have suggested Hab Poulis if he hadn't felt the man was competent.

Doug Moore. Would it be out of line to ask to see him? She would like to see him. Not an official visit, just a personal coming together one on one. To talk about Marcie. To air some of the grief bottled inside like nitro waiting to explode. She considered it and decided no, not yet. But one day soon, she'd ask them to get hold of him.

Harriet Croft stepped off the high-speed elevator directly into the living room of her penthouse apartment. The first thing she did was pour a finger of brandy and set the snifter in a patch of sunlight to warm. Next she crossed to the bathroom, sifted a handful of bath salts into the tub, and ran a warm bath.

Tossing her linen suit and silk shirt on the bed, she stepped out of her panties and walked, naked, back into the living room. She did not wear a brassiere. There was no need. Her small breasts were high and firm, in perfect scale with the slender hips and long, beautifully proportioned back. Harriet was one of those rare specimens of either gender who look better with their clothes off than on.

For a moment, brandy snifter in hand, she looked out over the city to the lake beyond. Although she had just returned from a weekend away, she was exhausted. She was beginning to feel as she had during the last months of her marriage. The solution then had been divorce. Too bad you couldn't divorce yourself: wipe out the old to make way for a new you.

She added more brandy to the glass and took it with her into the bathroom. The water, skin temperature, was silky smooth. Closing her eyes she made waves with her toes and sipped the brandy and then, only then, did she allow herself to rethink the conversation with Charlie Denton.

"You know, Harriet, that I have the highest regard for you. It was a grievous disappointment when you decided to withdraw your services. I considered it a personal as well as professional loss."

"It was a business decision, Charles. I wanted to change direction."

"I understood that, Harriet. It did not make it less distressing. The point I am getting to is that there is no one in whom I feel more confidence than you."

"That's very flattering."

"I had hoped that some day the two of us might . . . well, at any rate, shortly after you left our employ I met Marcie and you know the rest of the story."

"I'm terribly sorry about what's happened, Charles. I thought she was most attractive." There. She'd finally managed to offer her sympathy.

"Yes. Well, it really is terribly unfortunate."

At this point Harriet had felt, but not shown, the first nick in her composure. "I don't understand." What did you say to a man whose wife had just been bludgeoned to death?

"Unfortunately, Marcie wasn't what she seemed. You're aware, Harriet, that we are speaking sub rosa. I wouldn't want any of this to be repeated."

"Of course." Whatever it was, she did not want to hear it. The last thing she wanted to share was Charlie Denton's private life.

"The unpleasant truth is that my wife was being pursued . . . by another woman." Light glinted on his spectacles. Naked under glass, his pale eyes were round and owlish. "Amorously pursued," he added, mistaking her lack of expression for naiveté.

"Charles, that's ridiculous." Had the circumstances not been so tragic she'd have burst into laughter.

"It's the truth. She wanted Marcie to go away with her—which she wouldn't, of course—and when Marcie refused, she killed her. She was picked up yesterday and charged last night."

Harriet reached for the newspaper she had tossed aside earlier. Sure enough. There was a photograph of Marcie and next to it a head shot of a dark-haired young woman with high cheekbones and a strong chin. An attractive, intelligent face—unsmiling but not unfriendly. She did not look like someone who went around clubbing people on the skull. The caption underneath gave her name as Leslie Taylor and said that she had been charged in the murder of Mrs. Charles P. Denton.

"Did you know this was going on?"

"Of course not."

"When did you find out?"

"Yesterday. The officer who came to the house to tell me about Marcie suggested we look through her things. We found a letter in the pocket of one of her suitcases. How much she missed Marcie. How wonderful it would be when they were together. She was counting the days. You know the kind of thing."

Never having written or received such a letter from either

sex, Harriet had no idea of "the kind of thing." "It sounds more like a schoolgirl crush than cause for divorce, Charles."

"There was never any mention of divorce." A noticeable tightening in a body already rigid. Another notch and that lean frame would surely snap. "It wasn't Marcie's doing. That Taylor woman met her when she was just a child. Dragged her away from her family. Got her off in the city by herself. When Marcie met me and finally managed to break away, she was determined to get her back. When she saw that Marcie wasn't about to give in, she lost her head and attacked her."

"Why are you telling me this, Charles?"

"Because I want you to do something for me. The bail hearing is scheduled for this coming Monday. I want you to be there, as my representative, and do whatever you have to do to keep her inside. I don't want that bitch to see sunlight until she's eighty. Not even then, if I can prevent it."

The word *bitch*, propelled with such venom from the ever-so-proper mouth of the ever-so-proper C.P. Denton, had shocked her then and it shocked her now, recalling it in the solitary luxury of a scented bath with a generous measure of fine brandy on the side.

There was more. He wanted as much of the sordid detail kept under wraps as possible. The less the children knew about their mother's aberrant behavior, the better. The way to keep publicity to a minimum was to keep the case from going to court. Didn't she agree? And the way to do that was to get Taylor to offer no contest. Plead guilty. It would be best for her, best for her family, best for Marcie—what difference to Marcie, Harriet wondered—best for Marcie's children. "It will be hard enough for them as it is," he pointed out. And then, without a change of tone or blink of eye, "I'd like you to meet them, Harriet. Some evening for dinner. I'd like to marry again as quickly as possible. More for their sake than mine. Children need a woman. If you like them and they like you, I thought perhaps we might pick up where we left off."

Rendered speechless by a welter of emotion—shock, anger,

disgust, incredulity—Harriet had taken him by the arm, steered him into the elevator and left him there without so much as a good-bye.

She had closed her mind to the whole sleazy business, refusing to think about it until she reached the safe ground of her apartment. If the wires and wheels and springs that held her together suddenly went whizzing off into space, she would at least have the protection of privacy.

Thoughts disallowed until she was ready to deal with them now floated to the surface like the bubbles in the bath. What manner of man could write off, without the flicker of an eyelid, the woman who had borne his children? And what manner of woman could write schoolgirl mash notes to a wife and mother and then, in a fit of frustration, attack her with such violence that she brought about her death?

Stretching to reach the hot water faucet with her toes, she raised her right leg out of the water and sighted along it through the balloon glass that was now almost empty. Slender ankle. Elegantly shaped foot. Toenails that could do with a pedicure.

Her mind drifted. The snifter clouded, then, crystal ballish, it cleared and cast up the reflection of the photo from the newspaper. Leslie Taylor. Thirty-five years old. I want her locked up till she's eighty, Charles had said. That wouldn't happen. She'd be out in twenty years maximum. Not long enough to satisfy Charlie, but more than long enough to destroy whatever dreams she had for her life. It was too bad. Too bad she hadn't exercised better judgment. Too bad that if she had to play around with someone of her own sex, she hadn't the sense to stay with her own kind. And of all people to latch onto— the wife of a man as influential as Charles.

And what about Charles? Why so matter of fact about Marcie's death yet so vehement about the woman who caused it? The anger was understandable. The indifference was not. And how dare the man assume that she was a candidate for the position so newly vacated? It was this more than anything that triggered such rage she was afraid to trust her voice in reply.

Add to that the matter of the bail hearing, and you had a very strange scenario.

In a capital offense, bail was automatically denied. What they were looking at was a review, not a hearing. In a major center, the application would come before a justice of the high court who could approve or reject, demand surety or release without bond, sit in open or closed session, impose conditions as he saw fit. It was an arbitrary procedure, solely dependent upon the justice presiding. In smaller centers, however, an application could be brought before a local judge. Either way, it was highly irregular to have a third party represented by counsel. Yet Charles had spoken as though there wasn't the slightest doubt that she would be allowed to appear.

It was not, strictly speaking, playing by the book. Damn. If she hadn't been so quick to show Charles the door she might have found out just what was going on. It was true that victims and their families were finally being allowed to speak up in court. But their input was restricted to the sentencing phase, after the fact rather than before. If a precedent was being set, though, it would be interesting to observe it firsthand. Monday, he'd said. She could fly up and back the same day, treat it as a learning experience.

Wrapped in a bathsheet, she padded into the living room and poured herself another brandy. Then, before she had time to change her mind, she picked up the phone and called Charles at the office. Charles, she was told, was in a meeting. "Tell Mr. Denton Mrs. Croft called. Tell him I will be available on Monday. He'll understand."

It did not really strike her as strange, given his presence in the city rather than at the Bergstroms' side, that Charles P. Denton would be in his office conducting business as usual.

Chapter Four

"*W*hy didn't you tell me you and Mrs. Denton had something going?"

Leslie's stomach tightened into a knot the size of a fist. From the corner of her eye she saw Mrs. Klyk lean forward, face avid with interest. "What do you mean?" A wooden response, forced through equally wooden lips.

"If you expect me to help you, you're going to have to be up front with me. I told you, I don't like surprises."

"Mrs. Denton and I were friends. We'd known each other for a long time."

"Listen, Leslie. I don't care what the two of you were up to." (But he did care. It was reflected in the subtle change of attitude, the shift from professional objectivity to unprofessional familiarity.) "As a matter of fact, this can work for us."

The fist in Leslie's stomach moved into her throat, choking

her. Forcing a deep breath, she said, "I don't know what you're talking about, Mr. Poulis. The last time I saw Mrs. Denton was a year ago. We had lunch together before I moved back here. I haven't seen her since."

"It won't wash." Hab began ticking items off his notepad. "You talked her into leaving home against her parents' wishes. You tried to prevent her marriage. You phoned her repeatedly. You talked her into leaving her family once before. You continued to write to her. Letters you wouldn't want read in open court."

Knuckles pain-white, Leslie clung to the edge of the table for support. "None of that is true."

"I saw one of the letters, Leslie."

"That's impossible."

"I *saw* it. That letter alone is enough to put a noose around your neck. Figuratively speaking, of course. The letter is bad enough. The condition of the body. . . ." His eyes bored into hers. "What went on in that room? Her hair. . . ."

"She had beautiful hair," Leslie interrupted. "She was always so proud of it."

"So you shaved it off. All of it. Not just on her head. Everywhere."

A rustle of fabric as Mrs. Klyk shifted position. The humming of an air conditioner. The ring of a telephone in the adjoining office. The sensation of floating, looking down at three people stopped in time. The face across from her opened and closed, the mouth formed words, a jumble of sound as meaningless to her ear as pig Latin. Gradually the sounds sorted themselves out into a semblance of order. "Do you agree?" Agree to what?

"We plead guilty and avoid a trial. The charge will be reduced from First to Second Degree. There'll be a minimum of publicity. You'll save your family a lot of unnecessary heartache. They've got you pinned down so tight, Leslie, that I don't see any way around it."

The numbness gave way to anger. Would her family really prefer a daughter who killed other women to one who loved them? Was that what he was saying? And did she not, in part, subscribe to a similar view? Why else would she have lived in dread of being found out for the better part of fifteen years?

"Shall I talk to them? See what I can work out?"

Her mind was functioning now. She had waited for this meeting with Haberdash since Monday. Their strategy meeting, he had called it. The time when, having seen what the Crown had in evidence, he would sit down with her and they would work out a plan of action together. First the bail hearing. Then the strategy for his defense. One step at a time. All week she had waited and tried not to think, and now the waiting was over and the best advice he had to offer was worse than no advice at all. "No. I don't want you to talk a deal. I want you to tell them I am not guilty."

Not the answer he wanted, but not entirely unexpected. "In that case, we have one clear-cut defense. And considering the circumstances, we just might pull it off. As I said earlier, your. . .ah. . .your unnatural obsession with the victim can work for us. Not guilty by reason of insanity. We'll opt for a jury. Bring in experts. Maybe we won't even need experts. Any woman who could write a letter like that to another woman is so obviously off base that we needn't even argue the point. You're better not going to trial at all. But if that's what you really want, we'll have to do it on a plea of insanity. It's the only chance we have of winning."

"Winning?" If this was his idea of winning, they were both in trouble. "That's almost the same thing as pleading guilty, isn't it? Except it's worse because this way you go to trial and the other, you don't."

"You don't go to jail, either."

"But they lock you up in an institution. And keep you there until they're good and ready to let you out."

"I'm afraid you're going to have to decide on one or the other. There aren't too many options open to us. Frankly, if I'd known what I know now a few days ago, I wouldn't even have filed application for bail."

A chill slithered along Leslie's spine. "You seemed to feel that was nothing more than a formality." The chill flowed over into her voice. "I'm entitled to ask for bail. The only thing that's kept me from going mad is the thought of getting out of here on Monday. You're a lawyer. Sergeant Moore said you're a good lawyer. I'm counting on you."

Without waiting for a reply she turned to Mrs. Klyk and said, "I'm ready." Haberdash stared after her, nonplussed by the sudden departure. He had intended to ask about the towel bar. To tell her about the fingerprint on the doorknob and the tire tread in the dirt parking lot that forensics had matched to one of her new Michelins. There hadn't even been time to warn her that the Crown had granted permission for some hotshot lady lawyer to appear as an emissary of the victim's husband. He couldn't blame the poor bastard for wanting to get his two cents in. Being cuckolded was bad enough. Being cuckolded by a woman was a real ball breaker. The whole damn case was a ball breaker. He'd near crapped when Yarrow waved that bejesus letter in his face. It was one thing to get your jollies that way. Did she have to put it in writing?

It had been one hell of a session. Frost, who would head the prosecution, pulling one rabbit out of the hat after another. Yarrow grinning like the proverbial Cheshire pussy. That wimp Moore sitting back not saying a word but taking everything in. And through it all, that eerie feeling that there was another hand in the pie. You didn't just ring in someone like this Croft dame. Not without approval from somewhere up there. And the hearing itself. What he told Taylor about the hearing being held on Monday was true. What he hadn't told her was that normally the lower court would reschedule it for hearing by a justice of the Supreme Court rather than a JP. That could take up to a month. But someone had managed to cut through the red tape and arrange to have a full-fledged justice on tap.

Speeding the process was fine by him. Time saved was money earned. It did not, however, bode well for his client. They had her wrapped up and tied with a lavender ribbon. The best he could do was cut her losses. Frost would go for a lesser charge. Anything to avoid the cost of a trial. Yarrow? He'd object, but the decision wasn't his to make. The hang-up, it seemed, would be Leslie herself.

Funny. She had been so malleable. He'd been so sure she'd go along with whatever he thought best. Then—bingo. From meek as a mouse to high and mighty. A passing phase; he'd seen it before. There was no point in trying to talk sense to her until she got down off her high horse, which, unless he was very much mistaken, would occur at some point on Monday. When bail was denied and her situation finally hit home.

Hab picked up his briefcase and started down the long corridor that led to the world outside. A world that Leslie Taylor expected to rejoin, temporarily at least, three days from now. A world that was lost to her forever. Even if by some miracle they set her free, her life would never be the same.

Pausing to admire the flowers edging the walk, Haberdash took a deep breath and thought how good it was to be alive. He had the rest of the day free. Maybe he'd drop by the Legion and try to stir up a hand of poker. He glanced up at the row of windows. One thing you could say about locked doors and steel bars: they really made you appreciate the simple things.

Leslie brushed past Mrs. Klyk and headed straight for her cell. Cage six. End of row. Same address. Why in hell did they have to cart off the mattresses every morning? Was it suicide prevention—swallow the stuffing and choke, strip the cover and form a noose—or one more small way of getting even? Hands behind her head, she lay on the springs and looked up at the ceiling.

"She looks upset." Baby sounded considerably less mournful than usual. One-up for the old adage of misery loving company.

Josie pursed her lips, puffing her cheeks into a comic replica of a fountain cherub about to spout. Weathered by an on-going relationship with the city's constabulary, she knew what the girl was going through. The first few times in the slammer were the hardest. The very first time was a son of a bitch. She walked past the row of cells and into the one at the end. "Hey, Les, do you want to talk about it?" The husky voice was gruffer than usual.

Leslie continued to stare at the ceiling.

"Come on." Hoisting Leslie's legs against the wall, she wriggled her bottom onto the edge of the cot. "They'll have you out of here before you know it."

"I shouldn't even be here."

A good sign. At least the kid was talking. "I'm here on a bum rap myself. I rapped my old man on the ass with a frying pan. Put him out of commission for near a month." The attempt at humor fell flat. "I saw that show you did. On women getting beat up. Too bad you didn't talk to me. I could tell you some stories that would blow your tube."

The bed sagged from Josie's bulk. Leslie's mind slipped into groove. The cell receded, and she was back in the field, doing what she did best. Perhaps, to be fair, she should have included something on husband battering. But then, this was the first case she'd run into. "Was that the first time?"

"The first time I hit him? Yeah. The first time I really walloped him good, the bastard. I got him while he was asleep. Didn't know what hit him till he woke up in the hospital."

"Where is he now?"

"Waiting for me to get out. The day they put me back on the street he'll be right there at the front door. And it'll start all over again." Her large body sagged. "He's never gonna let me alone. Never."

Her coarse voice vibrated with despair. This, Leslie thought, is the real Josie. Not the tough, wisecracking old hand, but a hopeless, frightened woman who can't see any way out of an impossible situation. Still, she was the one who had whacked him. She was hardly a helpless victim.

"Like I said," Josie explained, "I got him when he was asleep. He'd been beating on me all day. Then a friend of his came round and he went out drinking, and when he got home he was meaner than ever. I could see he was set to start in on the kids again, but he was too far gone to do much. I knew what would happen when he got up though."

"Why didn't you just take the children and leave?"

"Leave!" Despair mingled with scorn. How easy it was to come up with solutions. Ready-made answers were a dime a dozen for people who didn't need them. "I been trying to leave him ever since we got together. Every time he finds me and brings me back. And it's worse. It's got so nobody will take me in anymore. My family's too scared of him. Where can I go with five kids?"

"The children—where are they now? Does he have them?"

"He's got them all right. He wouldn't let go of them as long as there's baby bonus coming in. I tried to get them taken away from him, but nobody will listen. It makes me crazy thinking about it. I caught him a couple of times fooling around with the girls. And the boys, he beats on them whenever he feels like it."

"Why haven't you gone to Children's Aid? They'd be better in a foster home."

"*You* say. They think because he's staying with his mother, there's a woman there, everything is O.K. She's as scared of him as the rest of us."

"Then you should talk to the police."

Josie's softness vanished. "They don't care. They laughed like hell when my Legal Aid said I hit him in self-defense. Maybe if he'd been on his feet beating the hell out of us. But he was asleep, so how come self-defense? If I'd hit him when he was awake, he'd have killed us sure. They got him on the stand and he was sweet as honey. With my record, they sure weren't going to go with me."

"I thought you said that was the first time."

"First time for assault. But they've had me on small stuff. Shoplifting. A couple of times for soliciting. Once I rolled a drunk and he caught me with my hand in his pocket." The tough

Josie was back in control. "When kids are hungry you gotta find some way to feed them."

Engrossed in Josie's troubles, Leslie forgot about her own. "Suppose I talk to my lawyer about this? He may be able to help."

"That ambulance chaser? No thanks."

"You know Mr. Poulis?"

"I know *about* him. That's enough. How did you come by him, anyway?"

"He was recommended to me."

"Yeah. It figures. Ten to one, by some guy down at the station."

"That's right. Sergeant Moore."

"Fancy pants. Let me tell you something. When the bastards who are trying to put you away come up with someone who's supposed to keep them from putting you away, you better run in the other direction."

"You don't understand." There was no way she could understand the rapport she and Moore shared, and Leslie wasn't about to enlighten her. That would mean opening a door that somehow she had to keep closed.

"I understand. I understand that he gets more business out of the police than anybody else in town. They finally twigged that he's as much on their side as ours. He's not much for wasting time in court. I know what he's telling you. 'Say you did it. You're a first-timer. Throw yourself on the mercy of the court.' You do that and the only mercy you're gonna get is free room and board in one of them condominiums with barbed wire around them."

Leslie closed her eyes and waited for Josie to leave. She'd struck too close to the bone for comfort. But with the machinery in motion, it was a bit late to pull a switch. Better to wait till the bail hearing was out of the way and then decide. Once she was out of this place, she'd be able to get her head together. Do something about tracking down whoever should be here in her place. To be explicit—Mr. Charles Denton. Who else would want Marcie dead?

Pushing Marcie out of her mind, she concentrated on Josie and the thousands of women like her who had nowhere to turn. When this was over she would do a second, more comprehensive, documentary. Perhaps a series. A format began forming in her mind. Interviews not just with the women but with the men, the children, the families that weren't there when they were needed.

She did not ask herself where this blue ribbon production would run. It was as hard as imagining the charge against her being dismissed, her relationship with Marcie remaining confidential, her life continuing as it always had.

Clarence Crossley wasn't surprised when Harriet called and said she wanted to see him. They hadn't parted on the best of terms, which meant a brief silence followed by a making-up phone call. This time she'd taken longer than usual—four days instead of two. She'd been lucky to catch him this late on a Friday afternoon.

He shouldn't have said anything abut Denton, should have waited until the Monday paper was out and he had the full story. If he'd known about the Taylor woman, he wouldn't have assumed that the suspect in custody was none other than Charlie, and the subject never would have come up. "How did you make out with those witnesses I handed you?"

"They were fine. We got a dismissal." Her slender fingers toyed with her gold ball-point pen, turning it end over end as he had seen her do so often in court. A gesture that usually preceded a particularly telling point in her cross-examination. "Are you free on Sunday?"

"I can be."

"Good. I'd like you to fly up to Spruce Falls for me."

Spruce Falls. Denton. But he wasn't on the hook, so it must be Taylor. Harriet was acquiring quite a reputation in the city, but he hadn't realized it had spread outside. "You got a call from Leslie Taylor. She's smarter than I thought. It will be a tough one, Harriet. It sounds as though they caught her red-handed."

"It's for Charles, Clare. He wants me to do what I can to prevent bail."

Clarence bit back a caustic remark. "That's a bit off the wall, isn't it?"

"Yes. That's why I thought it would be interesting."

"And where do I come in?"

"I thought if you went up a day ahead and nosed around a bit you might come up with something I can use."

"Poor family background. Violent temper. Erratic behavior. That kind of stuff?"

"Anything that will help keep her tied down until the trial."

"You mean Charlie boy is going to pay you hard cash to go up there and do what the prosecutor will do for nothing?"

"I guess he wants to make sure."

"It doesn't make sense. There's something fishy about this."

"Don't start, Clare." The pen spun a little faster. "You can't really blame him. You'd feel the same way if it was your wife."

"I haven't got a wife."

"If you had a wife." Her impatience was beginning to show. "If you're not interested, say so. I'll understand."

"Ah Harriet, of course I'll go. It just seems weird to have Harriet Croft, defender of the downtrodden, crossing the floor. You're not thinking of packing in your practice and going over to the Crown, are you?"

"You're making a mountain out of a molehill, Clarence. Bail. All we're talking about is bail. This won't affect the outcome of the trial. It should be interesting. You can sit in if you like. We both might learn something."

"You mean people can just wander in off the street? I thought most of these things were a private club. No one but principals need apply."

"That's what I mean about it being interesting. I talked to Charles on Monday. He had a pretty good idea then of the agenda. They're not losing any time on this one. A local judge will rule on the application. The court won't be cleared, which means you're perfectly free to come along. It's possible the entire case will be handled locally. Do you realize I've never been in a courtroom outside of Toronto? This will be a new experience."

"For both of us." For Harriet he would go, although some of the pieces were missing, and those that were there didn't fit. Denton wasn't a miser, but he wasn't known for throwing his money around either. If this Taylor woman was dangerous or liable to bolt, she'd be held as a matter of course. If not, what difference did a few weeks of freedom make? And what right had Denton to throw a spoke into the wheels of justice—such as it was?

"Good." Harriet handed him an envelope. "There's enough here to take care of what you'll need. Your reservations are made. You'll be in Unit Three of the Dalton Motel."

The Dalton Motel. That was the motel Marcie Denton had been in when she was killed. That much he knew from the newspaper articles. What he did not know was that Unit Three was the room occupied by Marcie on that final weekend of her life.

Adam Taylor speared the last piece of bacon on his plate and said petulantly, "That dog is beginning to get on my nerves."

Emily Taylor glanced at Duchess, who was shivering on her mat in the corner. "She's no bother, dear."

"She gets on my nerves," he repeated. "All she does is lie there and shake. This afternoon I'm going to take her to the vet and tell him to board her."

"She wouldn't survive, Adam. She's frightened enough as it is."

"That's not our problem. Leslie should have thought of that before...."

"Before what, dear?" She had known he wouldn't be able to say it. All week she had tried to get him to talk about Leslie, without success.

"Before she dumped her on us." He held out his cup for seconds of coffee.

"I'm going to see her this afternoon." This was as good a time as any to tell him.

His hand trembled, sloshing coffee into his saucer. "You're what?"

"I've made up my mind. I'm going to see Leslie. I'd like you to come with me. It would mean a lot to her. We should have gone before this."

"I want you to stay away from that place. I won't have my wife seen in that. . . that jailhouse. Do you know the kind of people they have in there?"

"I know one of them. Your daughter."

"Mr. Poulis will have her out of there on Monday. You can see her then."

"I don't have that much faith in him, Adam. The other day when we went over to Leslie's to pick out some clothes, he talked as if she was guilty."

"That's lawyer talk. He was probably testing you. Wanting to see if you're willing to stand behind her."

"Well, he knows now. I told him right out Leslie didn't hurt that girl. She wouldn't hurt a soul on this earth."

"Then you don't have to worry. If she's innocent, she'll be home before you know it."

Chalk-white, Emily Taylor faced her husband across the table. "What do you mean *if* she's innocent?"

"What I said, Mother. If she didn't do it, there's no cause to worry." Adam picked up the morning paper and turned to the sports page.

"Now you listen to me, Adam Taylor. Leslie is our daughter. There's no one who knows her better than we do. How can you sit there and talk as though maybe she did this terrible thing?"

Adam creased the paper and peered at her over its edge. "You may think you know her, Mother. But she's not the same girl we raised. I told you. From the time she left home, she changed. She used to come to us with everything. It's a long time since she's sat down and really talked to either one of us. You said so yourself."

"You talk as though you don't care what happens to her."

"I care about what happens to us. To you and me. She's made a separate life for herself. You can't just walk away from your family and the minute things don't go right expect to come running back."

"Oh Adam, Leslie's in jail for murder and all it is to you is 'things not going right'? You can't be serious."

"I am serious, Emily. I will do whatever I can. I'll help with the bail money, even though it means taking it out of our savings. She can come back here to stay for as long as she likes. I'll treat her the way I always have. But I will not have either one of us put on public display."

"I don't believe you're saying these things. You're trying to upset me." But Adam, head buried in his newspaper, was no longer listening. Emily cleared the table and stacked the dishes in the dishwasher.

Shocked by her husband's attitude, she decided not to bring up the subject of a jail visit until he was in a more receptive mood. Slipping upstairs, she dressed for the street, then left the house quietly. It was still early. She had time to go out to the mall and do her grocery shopping and see Leslie on the way back. If Adam asked where she had been she could say, in all truth, that she'd been to the supermarket.

Over the years, she'd become accustomed to his moods. Although there were some issues on which he never wavered, there were others where he was up and down like a yo-yo. The visit he forbade today might be encouraged tomorrow.

Adam Taylor might have his faults, but he was basically a decent, fair-minded man. Instead of providing comfort, the thought struck a chill in Emily's flesh. If he, Leslie's father, had doubts—he who was willing to weigh both sides before passing judgment—what of the others? Those who did not know Leslie. Had never met her. Saw and heard only what was presented by media. If even Adam could doubt, who was there to believe?

"I didn't want you to see me here, Mother." How old she looks, Leslie thought. I wonder if I've changed as much in one week as she has.

"You look thin. Are you getting enough to eat?"

"You've been telling me that for years, Mother. The food is fine." She had lost weight. The ring Marcie had given her, moved from her left to right hand, kept slipping off. Twice she had almost lost it, the first time in the washbasin, the second time on the floor in the common area where it was retrieved by Josie. Now she slipped it off her finger and eased it through the mesh. "Keep this for me, will you Mom?"

The male guard jumped to his feet. "No passing things."

Ignoring him, Mrs. Taylor put the ring in her purse. "Is there anything you'd like me to bring you?"

Leslie shook her head. "How's Duchess?"

"She misses you."

"Is she eating?" Leslie had boarded her out once, and she had almost starved herself to death.

"Some." Actually she was down to practically nothing, but there was no point in worrying Leslie. "Dad wanted to come. I thought it would be better if he waited till next time, though." Another lie.

"Is he terribly upset?"

"You know your father." Emily conjured a smile out of the mythical hat. "He said to tell you you're not to worry about money. We'll take care of whatever you need. And we want you to stay with us until this is over, dear."

"We can talk about that later, Mother." There would be a press of reporters wherever she went, lying in wait at all hours of the day and night. There was no way she would subject her family to a media blitz.

"We could go up to the lake. Stay there until . . . ." The sentence trailed off lamely.

"The trial," Leslie supplied, matter-of-factly. Taking a deep breath and praying the tears wouldn't show in her voice, she asked, "Did you go to the funeral?"

Mrs. Taylor hesitated. She had called Anna Bergstrom to offer her sympathy. Frigidly polite, Mrs. Bergstrom had made it clear that she wanted nothing to do with the Taylors. Adam had gone into one of his ups-and-downs when she told him that they were not welcome at either the funeral home or the burial service—furious one moment, lapsing into moody silence the next. "We sent flowers."

"You didn't go? She was buried here, wasn't she?"

"Yes. In the family plot. I would have thought her husband would have arranged for it in Toronto."

"You don't know her husband." Leslie's eyes narrowed, and her voice was grim. She thought of the dog he'd bought for the children. Never mind that they were too young to treat it properly. The moment he realized his mistake, that he should have waited a couple of years, he shipped it off to the pound to be destroyed. Leslie had never forgiven him for that. Nor Marcie, for allowing it to happen. Feeling her grip start to slip she said quickly, "I think you should go now, Mother."

"Perhaps I should. It won't be long, dear. We'll see you on Monday."

Poulis had said they'd be in court, that it would look bad if her parents didn't appear. She had told him flatly that she would take her chances without them.

"I told Mr. Poulis I didn't want you involved, Mother."

"He didn't say that, dear. We'd have gone anyway."

Her mother's face was set with determination. Leslie had seen this granite expression only twice in her life: when she decided to move to the city, and when she returned and announced she was buying a place of her own. In both instances, confounded by a brick-wall stoicism not previously encountered in his mild-mannered wife, her father had wilted. "Then don't let father come. He won't be able to deal with it."

"I'm afraid he'll have to, Leslie."

The chair grated on the floor as she pushed it back. Head

high, trim figure erect, she walked away without a backward glance.

Not until she was back in her cell did Leslie realize that her mother hadn't asked her if she was guilty, and she hadn't volunteered the fact that she wasn't.

Chapter Five

"If you'd told me you were inviting me to a circus, I would have worn my clown outfit."

Harriet raked Clarence Crossley's rumpled suit with a meaningful glance and said, "I thought you had."

They had arrived early, expecting only a handful of spectators. Instead they found a crowd waiting at the door and a full house inside. Harriet had used her credentials to secure a spot for Clarence, or he'd have been one of the also-rans still waiting on the steps.

"They've got enough reporters here to cover World War III. I bumped into a couple from Toronto last night. And this isn't even the preliminary. What the hell is going on?"

"I don't know." Harriet shifted in her seat and looked over her shoulder. "I expected a fair amount of interest, but nothing like this. I suppose, being on TV, Taylor is something of a minor celebrity."

"That doesn't explain the out-of-towners."

Harriet swiveled around to face the front. "Charles just arrived. He's with Mackasey from the *Star*."

"The cop-beat hotshot? I begin to get the picture. He's going to hang this girl out to dry before she even gets to trial."

"She'll get a fair trial. Stop worrying."

"Harriet, I spent all day yesterday talking to people around town. This burg is so right wing, it makes Ronald Reagan look like a progressive. She's up for grabs, even if she's innocent as a lamb."

Harriet's fingers worked her pen through a series of gymnastic loops. "I thought you said her life has been pretty straight-up?"

"Straight-up, yes. Unfortunately, more up than straight. You know she's a lesbian."

"Charles told me. That's not what she's on trial for."

"Oh no? Take a look at this." He pulled a crumpled piece of paper out of his pocket and handed it to her.

The headline read: DO YOU WANT QUEERS TAKING OVER YOUR CITY? That was mild compared to what followed. Harriet skimmed it quickly. "Where did you get this?"

"Would you believe the police station? They had a stack sitting on the counter. The guy at the desk told me to help myself. They had lots of them and they were free." He nodded towards Yarrow who had just come down the aisle followed by Doug Moore. "There's the guy that wrote it. Floyd Yarrow. He's the big wheel in Homicide. When I told him I was scouting the territory for you, he couldn't do enough. I got quite an earful from Mr. Yarrow. It seems he considers you one of the team, Harriet."

"Really?" The query was cool, the face impassive. "And what about Mr. Moore? Did you meet him as well?"

He followed her gaze to the handsome young man tagging behind the Inspector. "That one? No. He wasn't around."

"Too bad. I ran into him a couple of times when he was with

Morality in Toronto. He's an authority on the subject."

Moore was wearing a beautifully cut navy suede jacket over a pale blue shirt. Clarence grinned. "He's a good looking son of a gun. So they run him out of the city and he ends up in the hinterland working for a queerbasher? There ain't no justice."

"They didn't run him out. He's straighter than you are. His specialty is washrooms. More men have been scooped up in his net than Yarrow could come by in his whole career. Dear Doug is society's secret weapon in the washrooms of the nation." Her voice indicated neither approval nor disapproval. "You'd be surprised at how many men have committed suicide because of him—men who couldn't face being exposed to their families. There must be some sort of gay activity in Spruce Falls or he wouldn't be here."

"I'm glad you told me. I'll make sure that if I have to go, I'll do it in private." Forestalling comment he laughed and added, "No, I'm not into that, but it's damn hard to prove it when it's your word against theirs. I have a friend who's straight as a die and ended up pleading guilty because it was cheaper and less trouble. The court appearances were costing him more in salary than the fine."

"He was a fool. If you're innocent, you don't plead guilty. Never. Remember that, Clare."

There was a rustle of movement, and heads turned as Leslie was led in. Flanked by one male, one female officer, she kept her eyes front and composure intact. Thinner, she appeared taller than her actual height. There was a sharpness of bone, a fineness of the skin drawn over that bone that gave her features a luminous sheen. Her head with its cap of dark hair that curled over her collar was the head of a monk: ascetic in profile, brooding and withdrawn full-face.

So this was Leslie Taylor. Harriet stared, transfixed. She had been prepared to feel pity—the pity one feels for an animal, caged and helpless. Instead she felt a stirring of admiration. Either this self-contained young woman was a fool who did not realize what lay ahead, or she was possessed of almost superhuman control. An elbow jabbed her in the ribs, and she was aware of Clarence making words beside her. At the same instant, Leslie Taylor turned and their eyes met. Dark eyes. Almost black. Flat and fathomless. Harriet held her breath, wanting to look away yet unable to move.

A pause. A moment suspended. The dark eyes dropped. Another jab of the elbow, and Clarence's voice, hoarse, whispering, was inquiring, "What's the matter with you, Harriet? You're as white as a sheet."

People around her rose to their feet. Clarence tugged at her arm as a black robe swirled across the dais. "This hearing," said the clerk, "is now in session."

Judge Clement Nystrom rapped for order and smiled benignly at the attorneys seated below him. "I will remind you gentlemen that this is an informal hearing. We will not stand on ceremony. Nor," glaring beyond the lawyers to the rows of spectators, "will I tolerate any outbreak from those of you who have seen fit to join us." Judge Nystrom was prepared to enjoy himself. Most of the cases that came before him didn't amount to more than a couple of lines on a back page. This one had real potential. He'd been told, discreetly of course, that there was a possibility that the actual trial would come under local jurisdiction. "Mr. Poulis, your client stands accused of a most serious crime. We are here at your request in order that you may show cause why her detention in custody is not justified. Are you ready to state your case?"

Clarence nuzzled Harriet's ear. "Hasn't he got it backward? Shouldn't the last word go to Defense?"

"He's running the show," Harriet whispered back. "He can call it any way he wants to."

Haberdash tugged at his jacket, ran his finger around his collar, and said what any attorney in his position would be expected to say. His client came from a solid family background. She had the support of her parents, both of whom were in court today to vouch for her. She had no prior record, had never before been in trouble with the law. She was hard-working, responsible, had a successful career, and had earned her place in the community. With the sole exception of this one unfortunate incident, she was known as an even-tempered young woman who certainly could not be considered a danger to herself or the public.

"As a lawyer he's a great straight man," Clarence breathed. "He's given them enough openings to crucify her."

"Is there anyone you'd like to call, Mr. Poulis?" Judge Ny-strom's attention shifted to Leslie, and a current ran through the room. She was the reason for the large turnout; she was the one the crowd wanted to see and hear.

"Yes there is, Your Honor." Hab allowed a few seconds for the tension to build. Haberdash, like Nystrom, was in his element. "I would like to call Mrs. Adam Taylor."

Leslie was on her feet before her mother had time to leave her seat. "No." Her voice cut through the air like a knife. "I gave Mr. Poulis explicit instructions. He is acting without my consent. Against my wishes."

Nystrom's kindly expression congealed into cold displeasure. "Sit down, Miss Taylor, or I will have you removed." The gavel banged for order. "Mr. Poulis, you may proceed."

Eyes fastened on Leslie's back, Harriet saw the rigidity of the straight shoulders, the defiant tilt of the dark head. She'd learned more from that single outburst than from any of the facts Clarence had dug up. She loved her family and wanted to spare them the indignity of malicious public scrutiny. She knew the trouble she was in and she was determined to face it alone. She was also proud and stubborn and strangely vulnerable for someone of her maturity and obvious ability.

Harriet heard Mrs. Taylor without bothering to listen to what she was saying. What could she say? What would any mother say under the circumstances? She might as well save her breath. Surely Poulis must realize that calling her was an object lesson in futility. At this rate, Charlie could have kept his money and left the hatchet job to counsel for the defense.

Mrs. Taylor stepped down, and Jeremy Frost stood up. The Crown Attorney matched his name. Silver hair. Pale grey eyes. A cold white smile. "Your Honor, I have a number of witnesses I wish to call but first I would like to speak to some of the points brought up by my learned friend. He mentioned the defendant's solid family background. Well, it is Miss Taylor, not her family, that stands accused of murdering Marcie Denton. She has the support of her parents. Would you expect otherwise? She has no prior record. It is not Leslie Taylor's past we're concerned with, but what she was doing on July thirteenth, the day when she knowingly struck down a young woman she claims was her best friend."

Clarence was beginning to vibrate. "He can't talk like that," he gritted.

"He can if nobody stops him." Harriet sounded disinterested.

"With the sole exception of this one unfortunate incident." Frost fixed his attention on the row of reporters. "This *unfortunate incident*, as my friend termed it, was the taking of a human life. A life that can never be replaced. Eight days ago, Marcie became the victim of a senseless act of violence. But she was not the only victim, by any means. I ask you to think of her husband and two small children." He raised his arm in a dramatic gesture, pointing. Bodies swiveled, a gasp went up. Harriet turned and saw Charles standing behind the last row of seats, center-aisle, holding a fair-haired girl in his arms and clutching a small boy by the hand.

"The son of a bitch," Clarence said, not worrying that his voice rose like a foghorn.

Harriet swung round, glancing first at Poulis who seemed surprised but not overly concerned, then at Leslie who remained at rigid attention, eyes front.

Nystrom pounded for order and the clamor gradually died down. He nodded to Jeremy Frost. The prosecutor took a step forward and said, "Would Mrs. Sven Bergstrom please take the stand."

There was another gasp from the spectators as the tall,

heavyset woman moved toward the Bench. With taffy hair wound in a coronet and the translucent complexion and clear blue eyes of her Norwegian ancestry, Anna Bergstrom was an imposing figure. She spoke of Marcie's childhood, the honors she had won at school, how friendly and outgoing she had been until—her gaze swung to Leslie and remained, riveted— until she met that woman. After that she lost interest in her schoolwork, her friends, her family. They were thrilled when she met and married Charles Denton. Twice Mrs. Bergstrom paused to regain control. When she finally stepped down, there was a seething of anger, a muttering from the floor, that prompted the judge to call a brief break in the proceedings.

"What they've got going here is a lynch mob," Clarence groused. "From the Bench on down."

He was interrupted by Frost, who detached himself from Yarrow and Doug Moore and headed for Harriet. "You're next, Mrs. Croft." A sheet of paper dangled from his right hand. "We won't be much longer. You and Inspector Yarrow and we're finished." He rejoined the Inspector and the two bent their heads over the paper, studying it.

"That's the letter." Clarence was breaking into a severe case of fidgets. "They're going to read the letter. I though they had to save that kind of stuff for the prelim."

His voice carried to Leslie, seated on the other side of the railing but directly in front. She turned to Haberdash, said something in a low voice, continued talking while he listened, nodding his head in agreement. When she finished he gathered up his notebook and pencils and stowed them in the brief-case at his feet.

"She's going to withdraw." Harriet sounded only vaguely interested.

"What? What are you talking about?"

"The bail application. She's going to rescind it. I take it that's the love letter Charles mentioned."

"It must be. Yarrow showed it to me yesterday. God, it's mild compared to some of the stuff floating around."

"Maybe to you, but not to her. It's just as well. You didn't come up with anything usable. I'd have had to go into a hearts and flowers, poor bereaved family routine."

Haberdash patted Leslie's shoulder and trotted off to join the huddle at the prosecution table. Together, both men approached the bailiff. Yarrow, thumbs hooked in his belt, radiated smug satisfaction.

"What time are you leaving?"

The very ordinariness of the question made it seem strangely out of place. Harriet was not an emotional person, but Clarence had never known her to be quite so icily aloof. "I haven't even checked out of that rattrap you put me in. If I'd known this was going to take so long, I'd have stashed my bag at the bus station. We're over the check-out time now. For sure they'll charge extra."

"That's fine. Don't worry about it."

"Harriet, are you all right?"

"I'm fine." She smiled, but her green eyes remained opaque. "Why? Do I look sick?"

"You look fine. It's just. . . I don't know. Forget it."

Haberdash and Jeremy Frost returned with the bailiff and moments later the court was called to order. It was ten minutes short of eleven o'clock. Nystrom, pleased that the proceedings wouldn't drag over the lunch hour, wasted neither words nor time. "Counsel for the defense has requested that application for bail be revoked. The accused is remanded in custody pending trial. This court is dismissed."

There was stunned silence in the courtroom. Harriet, who had known what to expect, was on her feet and halfway up the aisle before most of the crowd moved. Clarence stumbled behind her, throwing glances over his shoulder at Leslie who was carrying on a heated conversation with Hab.

Harriet strode out of the building and waved at a passing cab. Out of breath, Clarence scrambled in behind her. "The Dalton Motel."

"Jesus." Clarence collapsed on the seat, huffing. "If you keep this up, I'll be in a basket."

"I'm sorry, Clare. I was afraid Charles would catch us before we could get away."

"And ask for his money back? I don't see why. He got what he wanted. Can you imagine showing up with those two kids? I told you the man was a snake."

Harriet kicked him in the shin as her head tilted toward the cab driver. "We'll talk about it later."

"Sorry." He knew better than to open his mouth in front of a third party. It was one of the many things Harriet couldn't abide. Unless, of course, the third party was a source of information.

"The Dalton. That's where that woman was killed." The cabbie was watching them in his rear-view mirror. "Did they let that Taylor girl out?"

Another ambulance chaser, Clarence thought. He must have been cruising the courthouse all morning in hope of an eye-witness account.

Harriet leaned forward. "Did you ever meet her? Leslie Taylor?"

"Drove her a couple of times. Seemed nice enough. Quiet. You never can tell, can you?"

"No, you can't." Harriet settled back and stared out the window.

The cabbie wasn't finished. "I knew the other one, too. Picked her up at the station one time and drove her to her folks. Had two kids with her. A baby and a little boy. Seemed like they were coming home for good."

"Oh?" Harriet seemed more interested in the houses flashing by than in anything the driver had to say. "I imagine you get to know a lot about people. Driving them around. Listening to them talk. Priests, bartenders and taxi drivers: you're all psychologists."

"That's what I tell my wife. You want to know about people, ask me. Take that Mrs. Denton. She was plumb upset. And the kids. Kids going to see their grandparents, they're happy. Ex-

cited. Not those two. She couldn't get the baby to stop crying, and the boy just sat there. Didn't say a word. Had a heap
of luggage, too."

"How long ago was this?"

"A year. Maybe two. Time runs together when you do the
same thing every day." He wheeled into a gravel drive and
pulled up in front of a door marked OFFICE. "Here you are.
Hope you enjoy your stay."

"Do you have a card? We'll give you a call when we're ready
to leave."

"Just ask for Joe."

Harriet copied his full name from the license suspended from
the back of the front seat.

"We should have hung onto him," Clarence said. The cab was
pulling out of the drive and onto the main street. "It will just
take me a minute to pack up."

"There's plenty of time." She handed him the shoulder bag
that doubled as an overnight case. "Here. Go pour me a drink."

The bed was made and the towels had been changed. He
unwrapped a glass and set it on the chest of drawers next to
the flask from Harriet's grab bag. It was hot outside, hot in
the room. He turned the air conditioner up as high as it could
go and sat down on the bed. Caught in a blast of frigid air,
he knocked the dial back a notch, cursing the insanity of ar-
chitects and builders who could erect skyscrapers but were
unable to cool a limited space without creating an arctic gale.

"That's taken care of." Harriet blew into the room on a wave
of warm air. "I've decided to stay over tonight." She poured
a triple shot of brandy into the water glass, settled in the room's
one easy chair, and propped her feet on the foot of the bed.

"Not here I hope."

"Right here."

"Harriet, it's crummy. I've stayed in some sleazy places, but
this one is the pits. What's the point? There's nothing left to
do. Or are you planning to hide out from Charlie boy forever?"

"Funny you should say that." Flipping back the bed cover

to reveal the sheets, she said, "At least it's clean."

"Sweet Fanny Adams it's clean. Take a look in the corners. And if this rug sees a vacuum cleaner twice in one week it's doing well." Propping himself up on one elbow—the better to see you, my dear—he fired off the question he'd been wanting to ask since he checked in the day before. "You knew this was the room, didn't you?"

"Of course."

Typical Harriet. Neither apology offer nor explanation make. "You should have told me."

"I didn't realize you were so squeamish." She sipped her brandy and looked unconcerned. "Did you find anything?"

"Like what?"

"Like anything. I thought when you realized where you were, you'd at least look around."

"The only thing you're likely to come up with in here, Harriet, is a bad case of pneumonia. That damn vent blows right over the bed. I woke up with sniffles. If you want to stay in Spruce Falls, go somewhere else. The Holiday Inn."

"That thing does throw a draft." She got up and turned the control to low. "It would be cooler if you closed the drapes, Clare." She leaned over to pull them across, paused, then said, "Hello. What's this?"

Clarence slid off the bed and looked at the object she held in her hand. A tiny two-hole button, iridescent in the ray of sunlight. "A cuff button. It could be anyone's."

"It's mother-of-pearl." Harriet slid the button back and forth on her palm, setting off a rainbow of color. "What sort of shirt would a button like this come from, Clare?"

He slid back the sleeve of his jacket and studied the buttons on his own cuff. They were wafer-thin and lusterless. "Not one like mine," he said ruefully. "Probably one of those designer specials. Logo on the pocket and all that jazz."

"Hardly in line with the clientele, wouldn't you say?"

"It does seem a bit out of place. But don't jump to conclusions, Harriet. God knows how many of the local elite drop in for nooners."

She wrapped the button in kleenex and stuffed it in the pocket of her bag. "I'll just hang onto it for a while. You never know."

"I know that if there's the slightest chance that could be used as evidence, you'd better turn it over."

"To that hip-shooting Crown Attorney?"

"No. I wouldn't suggest him."

"Your friend, the Inspector?"

"God, no. I wouldn't trust him with my dirty laundry. I just don't want you to get into trouble."

"How? Once the seal is removed, the scene of a crime is no longer the scene of a crime." She stared at the bed, brows pulled together in a frown. "How much did Yarrow tell you?"

"Plenty. I took him out for dinner. He spilled his guts. The guy's a lush. It cost a packet, but I learned plenty."

Harriet emptied the flask into her glass. "Tell me exactly what they found when they walked in here."

"He showed me a couple of the blow-ups. It was gruesome."

"Where was the body? On the bed or the floor?"

"On the bed. Naked. She'd been shaved, top and bottom. Do you want to know the rest?"

"Everything."

"She'd been raped."

The clear green eyes deepened to a dark emerald. "She was raped? They've got that girl in jail for a murder involving rape? What the hell's the matter with them up here? Are they so damn stupid that they think because a woman is a lesbian she is capable of rape?"

"Your language is going all to hell, Mrs. Croft. It wasn't "just" a rape, but a foreign object special—in this case a towel bar. Shoved it as far as it would go."

Harriet swirled the liquid in her glass and watched it spin into a tiny eddy. Clarence stared at the wall and waited. Still without speaking she set the glass aside, went into the bathroom and closed the door. More time passed. It occurred to him that they hadn't had lunch. She probably hadn't had breakfast, either. Drinking on an empty stomach. Enough to make a truck driver upchuck.

He was about to knock on the door and ask if she was all right when she emerged with the leashed energy of a panther on a chain. "She didn't do it, Clare." The rich contralto held not a shred of doubt. "Leslie Taylor didn't kill Marcie Denton."

"When did you decide this? Before or after you agreed to come up here and do Charlie's dirty work?"

"Don't be churlish, Clarence. When I saw her this morning, I was sure she couldn't have done it. Not with that face."

"With her shoe, not her face."

"Nor is this a time for levity, my friend. Women do not shove things into other women."

"To hell they don't." Sophisticated. Cosmopolitan. And still a babe in the woods.

"Whose side are you on? I got the distinct impression in court that you were leaning in her direction."

"I'm not on anybody's side, for God's sake. If she did it, she deserves what she gets. If she didn't, she needs some help because she's in one hell of a spot."

"Well, she didn't do it, and I can prove it. Come here and I'll show you." She pointed to the towel rack. Made of heavy monel nickel, the bar was securely anchored between two brackets. The fit was so snug that the bar could not be removed while the two end pieces were in place. "Hand me that bar, Clare."

After a bout of pushing, pulling, twirling, he gave up. "The only decent fixture in the place," he grunted. "You'd have to take the whole thing apart."

"Exactly. With a screwdriver. Or, if you didn't come equipped with a tool kit, you'd have to rip it off." She ran her finger over an uneven surface of the wall that appeared to be freshly patched and painted. "Go ahead. Try it." When he hesitated, she reassured, "Don't worry. I'll pay the damages."

Clarence grasped the bar with both hands and tugged. It

remained fast. He spit on his hands, grasped till his knuckles were white, and gave a powerful heave. The brackets held, and the bar stayed in place. "That thing is on there to stay, Harriet."

"Someone got it loose. I think it was torn out of the wall and I know Leslie Taylor couldn't have done it. It would take a lot of strength and a lot of weight and a powerful lot of rage. Did they check that bar for prints?"

"They must have. Even the Keystone loonies would have that much moxie. Yarrow said the whole place was wiped clean."

"So whoever was in here was here for a fair amount of time. After she was either unconscious or dead. No one heard anything, so he must have struck her immediately."

"Who, he?"

"I'm thinking what you were thinking a week ago. It must have been Charles."

"No dice, Harriet. Much as I hate to admit it, he's in the clear. He was in Toronto, with friends. Highly reputable friends, incidentally. The kids were there. The housekeeper was there. One of his business associates dropped in to pick up a set of plans. Whoever it was, it wasn't Charles."

"Maybe someone she picked up in a bar. He followed her back here, she said no, this was his way of getting even. That could account for the kinky rape. But it doesn't explain the shaving bit, does it? Who in his right mind would kill someone, in a motel, with people coming and going, and then take time to depilate the corpse?"

"Who in his right mind would kill someone to begin with?"

"A lot of people. You know that." She brushed past him and sprawled on the bed. "She was lying on her back, right?"

"Yes. With her face to one side. Away from the window."

Harriet turned her head toward the back wall. "I'm Marcie. You're going to shave my head. How do you go about it?"

"I sit down like this and just start shaving, I guess."

"You're not worried about getting blood on your clothes?"

"There's very little blood."

"What about leaving fibers on the sheets? You can be hung

by a thread. Would you think of that?"

"I doubt it. But then I wouldn't think of fingerprints, either. I'd be off like a shot."

"My guess is he touched as little as possible. My guess is he stood up. Leaned over her. Moved around." She swung her legs over the edge of the bed and sat up. "Did you check the carpet?"

"They're not that out of it, Harriet. Forensics does a vacuum job automatically."

"But how thoroughly?" Holding out her hand for him to help her up, she stepped clear of the bed. "Let's move it over."

Smaller than a double but a half-size larger than a single, the frame cleared the floor by only a few inches. High enough for a human foot, too low for a vacuum head or sweeper. Underneath, the shag carpet, matted in the high-traffic areas, was practically brand new—the springy pile marred only around the perimeter by four light sets of toeprints. Two on either side at the top. One halfway down. And one, heavier than the rest, at the foot of the bed.

"God, you were right. We'd better get those jokers back here right away." Clarence had the phone in his hand and the motel operator on the line before Harriet realized what he was doing. "Can you connect me with . . ."

Harriet snatched the phone away from him and said sweetly, "The nearest cab company." Glaring at Clarence, she broke the connection and said, "They have a direct line. There'll be a cab here in a few minutes." Rifling the contents of her cavernous bag, she hauled out her wallet. "Take this. Pick up a bottle of brandy. A camera. Some tracing paper. Onionskin. Can you think of anything else?"

"Yes, the police department. You've got to report this or we'll both be up the creek."

"We will, I promise. But not yet. What else do we need?"

"A ruler. You've gotta be able to measure."

The cab pulled up and Harriet said, "Don't forget the brandy, Clare."

Hand on the doorknob, he said plaintively, "I don't know a damn thing about cameras."

"You point them and go click-click." Then, because he looked so lost, "Tell them you're a new father and you want some shots of the baby. They'll recommend something."

Alone in the room, she tried to imagine what it had been like during those last few moments of Marcie's life. Who had come through the door, walked across this floor, made the indentations around the bed? Had Marcie known the blow was coming? Was she frightened? Was she taken completely by surprise?

Someone walked past the window. Harriet had intended to close the drapes, but had been distracted by the button. As she rounded the bed to do what she meant to do earlier, her eye caught a gleam of silver running through the purplish shag. Carefully, she worked it loose. A strand of hair. Pale as moonlight and almost a foot long. Marcie's hair, shimmering as Marcie must have shimmered in life.

The air moved. Harriet looked over her shoulder, expecting to see someone there—someone watching, waiting. "You're imagining things." She said it in her courtroom voice, the voice that could reach to the last row of a packed chamber. Echoing through the room, the sound added to the chill rather than dispelling it. Feeling the room closing in on her, Harriet placed the hair on the dresser, pulled the drapes shut, and turned off the air conditioner. Clare was right. She could not stay in this room. Not overnight. It was bad enough in the clear light of day.

Pocketing the key, she stepped outside and glanced around. The motel was situated on what had once been a main strip. Set back from the road in a tangle of hedge allowed to run wild, it was as seedy outside as in. A strange place for someone like Marcie Denton to stay. Why here? One more question to add to the list. But what more logical spot to look for the answers to some of those questions? And who more logical to ask than the woman who took in the money and handed out the keys?

The office was deserted, but the creak of the door summoned a body from the rear. "Mrs. Peak, Amanda Peak. My friends call me Mandy. Is everything all right, Mrs. Croft?"

"I'd like to ask a few questions, if you don't mind."

The commercial good humor distilled into caution. "About the room. That poor woman." Everyone who called up asked for Unit Three. Half the units stood vacant, but Three had been occupied from the moment the tapes were removed. With a backlog of reservations, yet. Ghouls. And everyone who checked in wanted to hear all the gory details. "I'm sorry. They told me not to talk about it."

"You're one of the witnesses?" Damn. Her identification was in her wallet, and her wallet was in Clarence's pocket. "I'm Harriet Croft. Mr. Denton's attorney. I came up for this morning's hearing. I spoke with Mr. Frost, the prosecutor, earlier." Misleading, but strictly speaking every word was the truth.

Reassured, Mandy eased onto her stool and said, "I didn't see much. I told that good-looking young fellow from the police everything I know. She came in Friday night. Didn't go out again that I know of. Made some phone calls. Saturday that television girl came. Sunday morning my cleaning woman went in with a key and there she was, poor thing. Nothing like that's ever happened here before."

"How long did Miss Taylor stay?"

"That I don't know. I was watching the baseball on TV. Back there. The phone rang and I came out and saw her drive up and get out of the car and it was a wrong number and I went right back inside. Couldn't say how long she was here."

"What about Mrs. Denton? Did she seem upset? Nervous?"

"Not so I noticed. She didn't say much. Seemed to be in a hurry to get settled. I got her registered and she gave me cash and that was the last I saw of her. It struck me funny. Not many people pay with cash nowadays. Check or credit card, mostly."

"It looks as though you had to do some patching up in the

bathroom."

Amanda's head bobbed confirmation. "Left a hole the size of a fist. Ripped the towel rack right out of the wall."

"It's solid enough now. Whoever repaired it did a good job."

"My husband. When he does something, it's done right." She glanced around apologetically. "Trouble is, he hasn't time for the big jobs. He works shift in the mine. He was on graveyard when it happened. Nobody here but me."

"Too bad he didn't put the first one in. The killer wouldn't have been able to. . . ."

"But he did. Put them all in a couple of years ago. We had some old plastic holders that were glued on. Always falling off. One day he got mad and said he was going to put a stop to it and went out and bought twelve new ones. Got a discount on a dozen. Had two left over. Now we're down to one."

"And no one heard anything?"

"Not a sound. We had two parties in, aside from Mrs. Denton. Nine and Ten down at the end. But they were too far away."

Harriet was about to leave when she remembered the button. "I suppose you go over the rooms pretty thoroughly every time a guest leaves?"

"We do our best."

"Do you have a set cleaning routine?"

"You know what it's like with help. It's hard to get good workers. But I keep an eye on things. If a unit's empty for a couple of days, I give it a good going over."

"Had number Three been occupied before Mrs. Denton moved in?"

"Not before, but it's been going steady since." She shifted her weight uneasily. "Why? Is there something not right?"

"It's fine. I suppose, when you did check it last, you looked for dust." Harriet ran her finger along the counter and held it up for inspection. "Not a speck. That's the first thing I do if I'm away for a couple of days. Give the place a good dusting. Window sills are the worst, aren't they?"

"There's no dust on my window sills," Amanda said. "Ever

since we got those window air conditioners, I've been real careful. Now mind you," she amended, "there's been folks in that room flat out. And I got a new girl. The other one quit. So I can't say what it's like now but I can speak for what it was before."

You may have to, Mrs. Peak. Jubilant, Harriet turned her back on the woman and stopped briefly at the paper box outside to pick up a copy of the morning edition. She stuck her head in the door to say she'd pay later, but Amanda was nowhere in sight.

Anxious to get everything on paper before Clarence returned, she hurried back to the unit and began writing immediately. When the cab pulled up it was all there, a full report, as close to verbatim as she could make it. Which, given Harriet Croft's memory and attention to detail, was very close indeed.

"I'm back." Clarence was hot, cross, and burdened down.

"I see that. Did you get the brandy?"

"Yes, I got the brandy," he mimicked. "Plus some nourishment for yours truly." He set his bundles on the dresser and held out a paper bag. "Have a Danish."

"Be careful, Clare." She rescued the strand of hair and wrapped it in the kleenex that held the button.

"I had a hell of a time. The next time you want a camera, send someone else." Cross-legged on the floor he bit into his bun and washed it down with a huge swallow of Coke. "What's been going on? You look like a cat that swallowed the whole damn aviary."

"How would you like to stick around for a day or two? My treat."

"No way." He looked around and shuddered. "This place gives me the creeps."

"The Holiday Inn. You're big on Holiday Inns, aren't you?" No response. "I'll throw in dinner." Still no response. "Time and a half." A barely perceptible flicker of interest. "Double time. All expenses. A dozen Danish. That's my final offer."

"On one condition. You tell me what the hell you're up to."

"Fair enough. I'm going to take over the defense of one Leslie Taylor and get her out of this mess she's got herself into or my name isn't Harriet Fordham Croft."

Mouth open, Clarence stared at her as though she belonged in a tree. Finally he blurted out, "Your name isn't Harriet Fordham Croft. You're some dizzy bimbo off the street."

"Watch it. You're speaking of the woman I love."

There was a sense of mission, a lively animation long missing in Harriet, that convinced him she was serious. "She's got a lawyer."

"Not worth the powder to give him a head trip."

"Maybe not, but you can't just march in and take over."

"I can't. But you can. There's nothing to stop you from paying her a friendly visit. Tell her. . . I don't care what you tell her. Say you met Marcie in Toronto. Say whatever you have to to get close to her."

" 'Miss Taylor, you don't know me, but I have a lady lawyer who is going to handle your case, so will you tell Mr. Poulis his services are no longer required? Mrs. Croft is now in charge.' You're itching to get yourself disbarred, aren't you?"

"You won't have to mention Poulis. He blew it when he put her mother on the stand. She'll ditch him without any help from you. And when she does, I want her to know there's a better than good alternative."

"Forget it, Harriet. You saw the way she folded when they started waving that letter around. She knows what will happen if she goes into court. They'll pick her clean, and she's not about to let that happen. She doesn't need a lawyer, she needs an undertaker."

"Do you think if we move a couple of these lamps onto the floor we'll have enough light to pick up those impressions?"

It was her way of saying that the discussion was over, her mind was made up. Clarence sighed and reached for the box with the camera. If Harriet wanted him to stay for a few days, he would. If she wanted him to take pictures, get down on his hands and knees and trace footprints, weasel his way into Leslie

Taylor's confidence—so be it.

He would do what he could to help, but as far as he was concerned, they were both wasting their time.

Chapter Six

*H*aberdash drove to the back of the building, turned off the engine, and stared up at the double row of barred windows. It was too nice a day to spend part of it cooped in a cubbyhole. Yesterday, when Leslie had told him she'd changed her mind and wanted to stay put, he'd figured he could knock off for a couple of weeks. The Fall Assizes were four weeks away. Even if they were on top of the list, there was plenty of time to get in some fishing before he had to bone up.

On the other hand . . . it's an ill wind. Maybe, he told himself, she's decided to do the sensible thing and plead herself guilty. That was probably the reason she wanted to see him. He'd felt it coming when she backed down in front of Nystrom and the others. Not surprising. He'd seen people a lot tougher than she wilt under the pressure. What the hell, it was time they got a few money matters straight anyhow. The day wouldn't be a total waste.

He whistled his way past security, down the corridor, through the matron's lounge-cum-office. His good spirits lasted until his client stepped through the door, accompanied by the ubiquitous Mrs. Klyk. Leslie did not look pleased. Neither did she look well. The hollows under her eyes were more pronounced; her skin and hair were dry and lifeless.

"Mr. Poulis." She sat down carefully, grasping the edge of the table as though in need of steadying.

"How are you, Leslie?" Damn, what a stupid thing to say. It was strange how her face said so little, her eyes so much. If looks could kill. . . . "I was pleased you wanted to get together so. . .so soon after. . .after yesterday. There's no sense waiting till the last minute."

"You think I killed Marcie, don't you?"

"If you say you didn't, that's good enough for me. Not that it matters. I'm here to help you, regardless."

"It doesn't make any difference to you one way or the other?"

"No." Here it comes, Hab. She's about to lay it on the line. "I don't judge people, Leslie. My job is to make things as easy as I can."

"Why do you think I killed her?"

"Now, now, I've never said I thought that." Drat the girl. She certainly knew how to be difficult. Better get down to brass tacks before she flew off into another tantrum. "I've been meaning to bring this up, Leslie. My usual fee for a case like this is fifty thousand. That doesn't include expenses. I think it's best to keep the record straight as we go. Suppose we make it ten thousand now, the rest later. That will help defray some of the cost incurred to date."

"I'd like to know, Mr. Poulis. Why do you think I killed her?"

As bad as a dog with a bone, she was. "I told you. I have no opinion on the matter."

"Then why do *they* think I killed her?"

You might as well tell her and get it over with, Haberdash. Prompted by the tiny inner voice that gave counsel when counsel was needed, he ticked the points off on his fingers. The eyewitness who saw her arrive at the motel. The love letter. The shoddy motel. The weapon, a woman's shoe—hardly something a man would use. Her reputation as a man-hater, due in part to her sexual preference for women, in part to the bias she had shown in her special on battered wives. And motive. Marcie had left her for a man, ergo the defacing of her body and the symbolic rape.

"Rape?" Nothing registered in the gaunt face, but the liquid eyes blazed fire. Not even Josie's grapevine had come up with the sexual angle. "What do you mean . . . symbolic rape?"

"The towel rod." Brusquely impatient, he wanted nothing more than to get this over with and be off about his business.

Agitation roiled through Leslie's body, but she managed to remain outwardly calm. *Symbolic rape.* The cool tone held an edge of irony. "Is that different from the other? To me, as a woman, rape is rape."

"That's exactly what I mean." Hab's mouth pulled down at the corners. "*To you as a woman.* You have to stop drawing a distinction between men and women. It creates a bad impression. We're all just people, when you come down to it. I have some blank checks here."

While he thumbed through his wallet, Leslie made some rapid notations on his notepad. Relieved, he congratulated himself on having broached the subject at the right time. Ten thousand had sounded like a fair whack when he said it, but it was peanuts compared to what some of those city lawyers charged. "Here you are." He handed her the slip of paper. "Do you remember your account number?"

She filled in the check and handed it back to him. The smile as he accepted it degenerated into a scowl as he read it. "This is for one thousand dollars. Do you want me to talk to your family about the rest?"

"I don't want you to ever go near my family again." She skewed the notepad around so that it faced him. "I don't know what your rate is. I worked it out at a hundred dollars an hour.

Three hours. Plus the time you spent on the application. Plus your time in court."

"It doesn't work that way, Miss Taylor. You're not hiring a plumber. This is your life we're talking about." What the hell. If she didn't cough up, her father would. You could tell by looking at Adam Taylor that he prided himself on being in no one's debt. He'd sat through yesterday's session like a graven image, but at least he'd been there. Pride—the downfall of the middle class.

"You talked about working something out, not going to trial. How much would that cost?"

Perfect. What he'd hoped for from the beginning. They had her by the short hairs, so going to trial wouldn't accomplish a damn thing. And instead of being tied up for weeks, maybe months, the most he was looking at was a couple of hours. "That would drop it by about half."

"Twenty-five thousand? My luck must be changing. It's not every day I have a chance to save that amount of money, Mr. Poulis."

Hab ripped off the top page of the notepad and crumpled it into a ball. "I'll make the arrangements this afternoon."

"Don't bother. I'll do it myself. If I'm going to end up in jail anyway, I'll be damned if I pay someone to put me there."

"As long as I'm representing you, Miss Taylor. . . ."

"You no longer represent me, Mr. Poulis. I don't want to see you again."

"You're making a mistake." He thought of the clean shirt in his briefcase. If ever he needed a quick change it was now. "There's a lot more to it than you think. You don't just walk in and say you're guilty. You've got to negotiate. Get the charge reduced. Have someone working for you on the outside while you're inside."

He was talking to empty air. Followed by Mrs. Klyk, Leslie was making her way through the adjoining office and toward the corridor beyond. Blast. He shoved the check in his wallet and slapped his briefcase against the leg of the table. Then, because he wanted to get to the Taylor house before Leslie had a chance to phone, he did a scout's pace back to the car.

Fifty thousand would have been nice. Twenty-five, not bad. Ten thousand? Well, it would be better than nothing.

Josie was perched on the end of the table explaining the tricks of her trade. *What you've always wanted to know about shoplifting, but were afraid to ask.*

"You get a shoe box and wrap it up with brown paper and string. You make it look like you just bought it. And then you just go around and fill it up with whatever will fit."

"How do you fill it if it's wrapped up?" Baby asked.

"It's not really wrapped up. It just looks wrapped up." Josie drew an oblong in the air. "This end pulls out. It's on elastic bands, see? You slide it open. It snaps shut. You got it right there under your arm and nobody knows a thing."

Leslie slid onto the end of the bench feeling, for the first time, that this group was her group. She no longer felt separate. Apart. For God knows how long, this place, places like this, would be her home. Home. Her father had been unwilling to set foot in the house she considered home. Would he be equally unwilling to sell it? There was no point in keeping it, no point in keeping anything. They could have a garage sale, sell her books and records, the new furniture. Her parents might as well get what they could for it. Compensation for what they'd spent on her over the years. Her personal belongings weren't worth much, but the house would bring enough to make up for looking after Duchess.

The thought of Duchess brought a lump to her throat and made her eyeballs sting. Marcie was dead, her world was disintegrating, and the thing she worried about most was a dog. Maybe there *was* something wrong with her. Maybe her father was right when he said she'd lost the ability to relate to people.

No, she told herself. It wasn't that she didn't care. She cared too much, and it was terrible to care when nothing you could do would change things. Duchess was totally dependent, scared of her own shadow. The dog would have a hard enough time with her mother, who was the soul of kindness. With strangers she'd die.

"Les." Josie had finished her lesson for the day and moved down to Leslie's end of the table. "Do you want to talk?" She nodded toward the row of cells.

"This is fine." Might as well get used to living in a fishbowl. "I just got rid of Poulis."

"Good."

"How do you get to see the Crown Attorney? Do you have to write him a letter, can you phone him, is there some kind of procedure?"

"You get yourself another lawyer and let him do it."

"I'm not going to waste any more money."

"Maybe you can get Legal Aid." Baby was trying to be helpful.

"That's not for people with money," Josie scoffed. "You have to be broke. Are you?"

"Broke? Almost. But I have a house and a car. I suppose that would disqualify me." She gave her head a shake. "What are we talking about. I don't want a lawyer. I just want to get this over with as fast as possible."

Josie flinched as the light dawned. "I know what you're thinking, and it's dumb. Awful dumb for someone smart."

"You're smarter about these things than I am, Josie. What should I do? Is it the judge you talk to or the prosecutor?"

"Neither, if you ask me. I don't want nothing to do with it."

Josie retreated to the far end of the table, taking the attention of the rest of the girls with her. Leslie thought for a moment, then got up and called for Mrs. Klyk. When the woman appeared, she told her she wanted to see her mother and father. Could she use the telephone? And one more thing. Would Mrs. Klyk please get in touch with Detective Sergeant Moore? Tell him that Leslie Taylor would like to talk to him as soon as possible.

"I'd like to see the man in charge of the Denton homicide."

The duty sergeant took one look at the tall, expensively dressed woman and said, "Yes, Ma'am. Who shall I say wants to see him?"

"Mrs. Croft. Harriet Fordham Croft. I think he'll know who I am."

Inspector Yarrow did know who she was, and he was, he confided, delighted to see her. It was too bad things had wrapped up yesterday before she had a chance to speak. He was looking forward to hearing her. Lady lawyers always took a different tack than the men, didn't she find?

She was in no mood for chitchat. "I stumbled across something I thought you should know about. My associate spent the night at the Dalton Motel, in the room Marcie Denton occupied. We discovered a number of footprints under the bed."

The smile froze on Yarrow's face. "How did your friend come to be in that particular unit, Mrs. Croft?"

"He was in town for the night and needed accommodation. Was there any reason for him not to be there, Inspector?"

"Of course not." The smile slipped off his face as it thawed. "You're working for Mr. Denton, I understand."

"I was, but at the moment, no. I'm here as a concerned citizen. We were careful to leave things exactly as we found them. I know how embarrassing it can be when evidence is overlooked."

"Whatever you found, Mrs. Croft, has nothing to do with Mrs. Denton's murder. My men are very thorough." He selected a file folder from the stack on his desk, flipped it open, and thumbed through the photographs it contained. Black and white glossies of the scene as they had found it. He studied the photographs, closed the file, said with an air of smug superiority, "Not even a midget, Mrs. Croft. That bed practically touches the floor."

"I'm sorry, Inspector, I shouldn't have said *footprints*, should I? I took it for granted you'd know what I meant. Toeprints, of course. They're still there. You can see for yourself." She paused in the doorway, a vibrant figure in ivory linen and beige silk. "Incidentally, they were made by a man. All you have to do is look at them."

Joe was waiting out front. She slid into the cab and said, "The burger stand across from the Dalton."

"That's closed. Been closed for years. If you're hungry, I know lots of good places you can eat."

"Just go, Joe. I'll tell you what to do when we get there."

Like the grounds of the Dalton, the burger lot was fast being overtaken by weeds. Harriet pointed to a hazelnut bush and said, "Pull in over there. You can turn off the engine, but leave the meter running."

He turned off both. "Are you supposed to meet somebody here?"

"No. This shouldn't take long. I just want to see something."

Joe got out of the cab and lit a cigarette. He was getting to like this bossy woman from Toronto, but a lot of what she did seemed downright peculiar.

The cigarette was down to the last few puffs when a car came down the street and turned into the motel parking lot. It was an unmarked car and the men inside weren't in uniform, but he knew it was a police car and the men were plainclothesmen.

His passenger stuck her head out the window and said, "We can go now. My friend will be waiting for you to run him up to the jail."

Clarence, waiting in the lobby, saw them drive up and got in one side of the cab as she got out the other. "Good luck," Harriet said, as the taxi pulled away. "And come straight back. I'll be waiting to hear."

Restless, she wandered around the room while her mind kept pace with Clarence. The cab neared the jail. Clarence was climbing the steps. He was seated, waiting for Leslie to be brought in. Her mind went blank. She played it again, and again she couldn't picture Leslie and Clarence together, couldn't imagine what they might be saying.

Exasperated, she went into the bathroom and ran a bath.

When the phone rang, she was dozing in the tub. "It's me," Clarence said. "I'm on my way."

Before she had time to ask him how he'd made out, the line went dead. She dried herself off, threw on her clothes, and poured herself a brandy. Not until she raised the glass to her lips did she realize her hands were shaking and her heart was pounding at double its normal speed.

The service station was one block away from the Taylors' house. Hab asked for two dollars worth of gas and whipped into the washroom to change his shirt. When he came out he felt better, although he was still a bit damp under the arms.

It was early in the day. Mr. Taylor would probably be at work. He would have preferred going straight to the head of the house, but time was of the essence. If Leslie got to them first, there wasn't a hope in hell of getting his money.

Mrs. Taylor answered the door, invited him in, and told him no, her husband wasn't at home, he usually got in around five. Would he care for a cup of tea or a cold drink?

A glass of water would be fine, he said, and sat on the couch wondering how best to open the subject. Mrs. Taylor solved the problem by leading off with a question. "Have you seen my daughter today?"

"Yes. We had quite a long talk."

"How is she? What happened yesterday? My husband had a check ready. We thought she'd be able to come home with us. Was there something wrong with the papers? Weren't they done right?"

"There was nothing wrong with the application, Mrs. Taylor. Leslie changed her mind."

"Changed her mind? Why? Why would she want to do that?"

"I'm sure she'll tell you when you see her. I think one of her problems is money. A case like this can run pretty high. She owes me ten thousand dollars and the best she could do was one thousand. That's nine thousand short, Mrs. Taylor." He cast an appraising eye over the comfortable living room. "I'm sure you're prepared to make up the difference."

"Yes. Of course we will. We'll get a check to you first thing tomorrow."

"If you phoned your husband at the office, I could drive round and pick it up."

"He hates being disturbed at work, Mr. Poulis. Surely one day isn't going to matter."

"Your daughter is in very serious trouble. She is going to need a great deal of help." If Hab had learned anything through his years before the Bench, it was how to play the mind of a reluctant witness or recalcitrant client. Leslie Taylor was just plain stubborn. Her mother, on the other hand—a puff of smoke would blow her away.

"My daughter didn't lay a finger on Marcie Denton, Mr. Poulis. You're her lawyer. You must know that."

"Be that as it may, she could well spend most of her life behind bars. I'm sure you want to do everything you can to prevent that."

"Perhaps you could come by at five o'clock. I know my husband is prepared to do whatever is necessary. It's just that I don't want to disturb him while he's at the office."

"I have a lot to do this afternoon. I don't see how I can possibly get back here later. You don't happen to have a joint account, do you?"

Mrs. Taylor brightened. She did have a signature at the bank. Never having used it, she never thought about it, however. Adam had told her in case of emergency, if anything ever happens to me, you'll need access. Well, nothing had happened to him, but this was certainly an emergency as far as Leslie was concerned. She found the unused checkbook in her dresser and filled in one of the slips.

Hab watched, elated. There was time to get to the bank if he hurried.

"About the bail money," Mrs. Taylor said. "You'll be seeing them about that again, won't you?"

The woman still didn't understand. It was amazing how little people like the Taylors did understand about the workings of the judicial system. Best he spell it out so there would be no misunderstanding. "She has decided to remain in custody until she comes to trial. Also, Mrs. Taylor, she has made up her mind to plead guilty. She dismissed me and said that she would handle it herself. A terrible mistake. I suggest you talk to her. I am prepared to do whatever I can. She's a stubborn young woman and won't listen to me. You're her mother. Perhaps you can get through to her."

He left her there, standing in the middle of the living room, grappling with information that must have struck her like a fist in the stomach. She'd pressure Leslie to reconsider going it alone, of that he was sure.

Smiling, he fingered the check in his pocket and told himself all was not lost. The real paperwork began after sentence was passed. Affidavits, briefs, depositions. It could go on for years. Being retained by the Taylors rather than Leslie would have its advantages. You could see they were the ones with money.

That original fifty thousand wasn't such a remote possibility after all.

"For God's sake, Clare, stop fiddling around and tell me what she said. How is she?"

"Well, she's sure as hell not going to win any personality contests." He pulled the tab on his Coke and drank straight from the can.

"What did you expect? Sunshine and light? The girl's in jail, Clare. How does she look?"

"Terrible. She looks terrible. She sounds terrible. She is terrible. Are you satisfied?"

"Did she open up at all?"

"About this much." The thumb and forefinger he held up were practically touching. "And then only after I told her I was there because of you."

"Clare, you didn't. Poulis will nail me to the cross."

"Forget Poulis. You were right. She turfed him. I got that much out of her before I mentioned you. You'd have been proud of me. I started off by saying I'd been at the hearing. She was lucky to have someone like Mr. Poulis representing her. I've had some experience in similar cases. Digging for the Defense, etc. Would she have any objection to my getting in touch with Poulis. Offering my services, so to speak."

"You told her she was lucky to have him? What if she'd believed you?"

"Not a chance. She froze the minute I mentioned his name. It was after that I mentioned you. That went over like a lead balloon."

"What did she say?"

He held the Coke at eye level. "That she's had it up to here with lawyers. She doesn't need a lawyer." The empty Coke can looped through the air and landed in the wastebasket. "Incidentally, she remembered you. You are not high on her list of people one should get to know, Harriet. I'd say she ranks you about three rungs below Poulis."

"For someone who didn't say much she seems to have communicated a fair amount," Harriet said drily. "Will she see me or not?"

"She'll see you. At least she didn't say she wouldn't. But there's not much point, Harriet. She's got you mixed up in her head with Frost and Yarrow and the others. The only one she seems to trust is Moore."

"Oh my God, Clare. Moore, of all people."

Clarence stood up and stretched. "I don't know about you, but I'm going to head back. This town is starting to get to me."

"There's a flight at six. I booked you a seat."

"One seat? What about you?"

"I'm going to stay over. I've made a list of a couple of things I'd like you to do."

The sheet of hotel stationery was crammed with instructions, each line flagged with a bullet:

• call Donna and tell her I'm delayed

- get a list of people Leslie and Marcie associated with when they lived together
- find the names of couples Charles and Marcie were friendly with
- who is Marcie's doctor
- where does Charles buy his shirts

The list seemed endless. It was also self-explanatory.

"You're biting off something you'll never get to chew, Harriet."

"Does Chrysler tell GM? I'll handle things here. You look after your end, and I'll take care of mine."

Clarence patted his bottom, leered at Harriet's derriere, and cracked, "You win hands down in that department. I just wish your head was in as good shape as the rest of you."

"My head has never felt better, Clare. I know exactly what I'm doing."

There was no point in arguing. No point in telling her that a town like this could chew her up and spit her out in little pieces. Harriet was a superb lawyer, but she was not a street fighter. Her expertise lay in the intellectual thrust and jab of an orderly, disciplined court. The rough-and-tumble tactics of a Yarrow, the ill-informed posturing of a Nystrom—she would be unable to cope with either.

"I know what you're thinking, Clare. It's going to work out just fine."

Her green eyes locked with his—eyes alive and glinting with tiny points of light. She was bathed in light, her sleek dark-gold hair burnished with tints of copper, her skin lighter than the beige of her shirt, but darker than the ivory of her suit. Energy pulsed from her slim body, a flow of electricity that set the air between them into motion.

"I bought you a present. Something to take on the plane." She nodded toward a paper bag on the end of the credenza. "Two Cokes. Six Danish. That should hold you till you get home."

Touched, Clarence mumbled his thanks. Harriet was generous to a fault, but her largesse came in the form of money rather than the feeding of a habit of which she did not particularly approve.

In his room, packing, getting ready to leave, he asked himself which he would rather: the listless, bored, indifferent Harriet of a week ago, or this brilliantly alive, vital Harriet who was ready to do battle with the world.

He wanted her as she was now. But he wanted her to stay that way, not up one minute and torn to shreds the next. Filled with foreboding, he picked up his suitcase and the bag of Danish and went down to the lobby to wait for Joe.

She didn't know how long she had been driving or where she had been. She didn't know how long she had remained in the house after the man who was supposed to fix things for her daughter got in his car and drove away. What she did know was that Leslie was not coming home. That she was in one of her stubborn fits, determined to do things her way with no help from anyone.

When she realized how late it was—that Adam would arrive home to an empty house, with no dinner ready—she was on a dirt road leading to the park where they had picnicked when Leslie was no bigger than a minute. She'd thrown gravel getting back to the highway and held right on the speed limit through town.

Adam's car was not in the driveway. Breathing a sigh of relief, she rushed to the kitchen and turned on the oven. Adam was a meat-and-potatoes man. If he were like other husbands, she could phone out for a fast-food delivery. Cardboard, he'd snorted the one time she suggested it. And that was the end of that.

Sorting through the vegetable bin for potatoes small enough to bake double-quick, she sensed something was missing. The house felt vacant. Dead. Puzzled, she looked around. Nothing seemed changed. Everything was in order. Her eye fell on the mat in the corner and she saw that it was empty. Then she looked at the clock over the stove. It was late, later than it should have been even if Adam had stayed back as he often did.

Heart pounding, she went from one room to another, looking in closets and under the beds to make sure. There was no sign of Duchess, nothing but the mat to indicate she had ever been in the house. It would kill Leslie if something had happened to her. The one thing she had asked was that they take care of the animal, and she was in such a state when she left that the dog must have got out without her noticing. She could be lost, run over. They might never see her again.

For days she had been fighting to hold back her tears. Now they came with a rush. Adam found her at the kitchen table, head pillowed on her arms, weeping uncontrollably. "Duchess is gone," she sobbed. "I went out and came back and she's not here."

Tensed for the worst, Adam Taylor relaxed and heaved a sigh of relief. "I thought something terrible had happened. Duchess is fine. I took her to the vet. He'll look after her better than we can."

"Adam, you didn't! He'll keep her locked up in a cage."

"What's the difference? She just lay in that corner. Hardly ever moved."

"She'll pine away and die in there. What will you tell Leslie?"

"You can tell Leslie whatever you like. The dog's her responsibility, not ours."

"And Leslie? Whose responsibility is she, Adam? Are you going to wash your hands of her, too?"

"Now, Mother, you know better than that. It's not quite the same thing, is it?" He kissed her forehead. "I brought some work home. Is there time for a cup of coffee before dinner? I'll be in the study."

Always the same. Whenever he was upset he buried himself in his job. This was not the time to tell him about the visit from the lawyer, the nine thousand dollars; not the time to tell him that Leslie, for some crazy reason, had decided to say she was guilty of Marcie's death. The moment he heard that Leslie might not be back, he would have Duchess put down. And that would finish Leslie. She'd had that dog since shortly after she and

Marcie moved to the city. It was Marcie who'd found her and brought her home, but it was Leslie who'd looked after Duchess. She hadn't said take care of the house or the car or anything else she owned. Just Duchess.

She fixed a tray and carried it to the study. Then she went to her room, closed the door, and cried into her pillow.

In the room down the hall, Adam Taylor worked on the contracts he hadn't had time to go over at the office. In the kitchen, the potatoes burned to a crisp.

Chapter Seven

Clarence had told her it wouldn't be easy, but he hadn't warned her it would be next to impossible. In spite of the blank expression, so blank that her face resembled a mask, Leslie Taylor's animosity was palpable. Held by the dark eyes that seemed strangely alive in the lifeless flesh, Harriet felt as she had in the courtroom. A drift of time. Disembodiment. Recognition, half-formed and elusive.

"Thank you for seeing me." It had drawn no response the first time she said it. It worked no better the second time around. "Why did you. . .agree to see me?"

"I was curious." The dark eyes smoldered. "You're a friend of Charles', aren't you?"

"No. I know him. We aren't friends."

"He asked you to come here. To make sure they didn't let me get away."

The drip of acid did nothing to mar the rich throatiness of her voice, a voice that matched the color of her eyes. Wonderful on the witness stand. Harriet leaned closer to the mesh and said softly, "I want to talk to you in private. I know you're innocent."

Without bothering to drop her voice in return, Leslie nodded in the direction of Mrs. Klyk and said, "She comes with the territory. They don't believe in privacy, I'm afraid."

"Tell her I'm your lawyer."

"It wouldn't make any difference."

Privy to only one half of the conversation, Mrs. Klyk inched her chair closer.

"Tell her." Harriet's whisper was as imperious as a roar. "You can fire me the minute I walk out. Just hire me now."

"I just got rid of one lawyer. I don't want another."

"You'll have to speak up there," Mrs. Klyk warned.

The interruption came at precisely the right moment. Leslie's chin came up, and she threw a withering glance at the matron. "I'm talking to my lawyer, Mrs. Klyk."

Harriet was on her feet before the sentence was complete. "I'd like to speak with my client in private."

Mrs. Klyk looked daggers at Harriet before turning to Leslie. "Where's Mr. Poulis?"

"I fired him."

"And hired me. Do you have a room we can use?"

Reluctant, Mrs. Klyk showed her to the lounge off her office and went back for Leslie. She was settling in her usual spot when Harriet said brusquely, "You can leave us now, Matron. I'll let you know when we're finished."

Mrs. Klyk's face flushed beet red. "We don't allow prisoners to be on their own." Glowering, she sat down and planted both feet firmly on the floor.

"I told you." Leslie seemed more amused than upset.

"She's not on her own. She's with me. We have things to discuss, and we want to do it in private."

"That's not how we do it here." Mrs. Klyk's mouth was set

in an ugly line.

"Well, that's how you should do it here. You have no right to listen in on a lawyer and client."

"I have my orders." Her hands locked on the arms of the chair in anticipation of being flung out bodily.

"She doesn't listen in, do you Mrs. Klyk?"

It occurred to Harriet that Leslie was enjoying the situation. A break in the boring routine. A minor divertissement. "I'd like to use your telephone, Matron." Harriet strode into the office, conscious of Mrs. Klyk puffing behind her. "Where is the phone book?"

"There's a pay phone at the end of the hall."

"This one will do," Harriet said pleasantly. She picked it up and dialed the operator. "I'd like the number for the court-house, please." Hand over the mouthpiece, she asked, "Matron, where does Mr. Frost have his office?"

White-faced, Mrs. Klyk snaked her hand across the desk and broke the connection. "You can't be bothering him."

"Then who do you suggest?"

It took thirty minutes, five phone calls, and a forceful dialogue with the superintendent of the jail to effect Mrs. Klyk's removal. Steely-eyed, Harriet faced Leslie. "I hope we don't have to go through this again." Her face softened. "You didn't kill Marcie, did you?"

"No. But it doesn't seem to matter." The response was flat, unemotional.

"It matters to me." Harriet's professionalism surfaced. Putting aside the compassion she felt, she said, "I can get you out of this."

"I don't think so. I had a lawyer. You saw him in court the other day. He said the best thing was to tell them I did it. He said they've got so much against me that it will end up that way anyway. He'd do that for me for twenty-five thousand. What do you charge, Mrs. Croft?"

Reminding herself that the girl was entitled to feel bitter, Harriet said, "Much more than that, Miss Taylor. Much, much more."

She dug in her bag for a notebook. "I want you to tell me everything you did over that weekend."

"You can talk to the police department. Tell them Charlie
sent you."

Harriet's temper flared. "Forget abut Charles. I don't like
Charles Denton any more than you do. You'd better get off
that high horse and get involved. If I were in your position,
I damn well wouldn't sit there and let people walk all over me."

"You're not in my position."

The gold pen spun in circles. Harriet's mind spun with it. What
was the matter with her? The girl was charged with murder
and she, Harriet Fordham Croft, she, who should be laying it
all out coolly and logically, she, of all people, was in a snit.

"I didn't ask you to come here, Mrs. Croft. This was your idea."

Stubborn as a mule, Harriet thought. The only way to help
her is to crack through that shell and lay her wide open. "I
know you and Marcie were lovers." The expressive Croft voice
was crisp as iced lettuce.

A muscle twitched in Leslie's cheek. "That's none of your
business."

"It's everybody's business." Harriet felt like a surgeon oper-
ating without anesthesia. "If you think offering no contest will
keep people from finding out, you're sadly mistaken." She saw
the slender fingers clench together, the dark eyes mist. It was
an effort not to reach out and touch her. Briskly matter-of-fact,
she said, "You're a lesbian. A lot of people know that. You can't
stop them from talking."

The veneer was beginning to crack. "They're guessing."

"What about your family? Do they know?"

"No." The corpselike face had come alive at last. "They don't
know. Neither do you."

"I do know, Leslie, and it doesn't matter. My God, you're not
the only homosexual in the world. Not the only one in Spruce
Falls, either. Ask Doug Moore. He'll tell you."

"He's afraid, too."

"Afraid," Harriet said coldly. "The only thing he's afraid of is not getting enough arrests chalked up." Quickly, not hiding the contempt she felt for the sergeant and his methods, she told Leslie of the arrests he had made and the lives he had ruined.

"I don't believe it. He was nice to me."

"I'm sure he was. Take my advice. Stay away from him. He's worse than that Neanderthal inspector." Pen poised, she said, "I want to hear this from you. Firsthand."

"I'm sorry, Mrs. Croft. I've decided what I'm going to do. I don't need any help." The face, now fully mobile, looked thoughtful. "There is something you can do."

Harriet held her breath, anticipating a change of mind.

"There's a woman here. She's worried about her children. Maybe you could do something for her."

Facing a life term and she was worried about someone else? Exasperated, Harriet explained that her field was not family law and that she was not looking for business. At any rate, she couldn't approach the woman, the woman would have to call her. She was in Spruce Falls only temporarily, only because of you, Leslie Taylor, and there were plenty of lawyers in town who could do the job as well as she.

"She hasn't any money."

Harriet wavered between rage and laughter. "You're impossible." She began to laugh and saw with amazement that Leslie was actually smiling. The transformation was striking. With mask discarded and guard down, she was astonishingly attractive. "Tell her I'm at the Holiday Inn."

"I have some money. I'll take care of it." Sombre, she added, "I won't be needing any for a while."

The good humor was gone, but so was the hostility. Harriet sensed she had just been tested and had passed. Would she be equally successful the next time? And the time after that? There was something in the sober face across from her that intimated the setting of a high standard for those allowed to draw close. "You miss her, don't you?"

"Yes." A terse, emotionless admission. Then, responding to

the empathy Harriet no longer tried to hold back, "I miss knowing she's somewhere. We haven't seen each other much since she got married, but when I thought about her, I could imagine what she was doing. You can't do that when someone is dead. The place where they were is just empty."

"Have you been able to talk to anyone?"

"Almost." A self-deprecating half smile. "Doug Moore."

"You can talk to me, Leslie."

"Some of your best friends?" A question heavy with sarcasm.

"It doesn't make the slightest difference to me, one way or the other. Good Lord, you're not the first gay I've ever met. So you sleep with women instead of men. That's no reason to crawl into a hole and bury yourself. You can walk out of here a free woman, with your head up and the rest of your life to do with as you please. If you don't care what happens to you, think about your parents. Their daughter, the murderer. How will they feel? Don't you care?"

"Of course I care." Her face hardened. "It's because of them I'm not going to be put on exhibition like some freak in a sideshow. It would kill them."

"You don't think much of your family, do you? Or of yourself. If you're so damned ashamed of what you are, why don't you just forget it? Get yourself married and live a normal life."

"What I am *is* normal. For me." A flush of color tinged the pale skin as she realized what she had done. They had skirted the issue, alluded to it, and now, with a slip of the tongue, she had confirmed it. From rumor to fact in one split second.

"You're being unfair. Your mother and father have a right to know the truth. This should be their decision, not yours. If you don't tell them, I will." Harriet watched the color drain from the thin face, saw the dark eyes cloud with fear, anger, helplessness. She had no intention of telling Leslie's parents. That was something only Leslie herself could do. But until it was done, there was no way anyone could help her.

Dropping pad and pen into her bag, she said, "Tell your friend if she wants to get in touch, she'd best hurry. I don't know how much longer I'll be in town." She was on her feet, almost to the door, when Leslie stopped her.

"I'm not ashamed of what I am."

"Tell that to your parents, not to me." Harriet did not turn around, did not want the softening she felt to show. What Leslie Taylor needed most was a hardening of will, not a useless compassion. "Call me if you change your mind. I'll be here until tomorrow night."

Hovering on the other side of the door, Mrs. Klyk almost tumbled into Harriet's arms as she wrenched the door open. "You can return Miss Taylor, Matron. We're finished."

Finished for the moment. She didn't know whether or not Leslie would call. She didn't know whether or not, if worst came to worst, she would tell the Taylors this secret their daughter had tried so hard to keep hidden. Chances were they already knew. And suppose they didn't. Suppose it did come as a shock. If they'd rather see her in jail, they weren't worth worrying about.

A fine line separated principle from necessity, a line Harriet was not in the habit of crossing. But what price principle when the cost was a human life? The question was simple. The answer? That she would decide if and when the time came.

"She had it between her legs. A television set between her legs, and she walked clean out of the store and nobody noticed."

"Josie, can you spare a minute?"

Josie called recess and followed Leslie to her cell. "What's wrong, Les? You've got that Poulis look on your face. I thought you got rid of that guy."

"It wasn't him. But it was somebody I think can help you with the kids."

"What kind of somebody?"

"A lawyer. I have a feeling she's pretty good."

"A lady lawyer? No way."

"What's the matter with you? Have you got something against

women?"

"Come on. I like women as well as you do." She grinned, and Leslie tightened under the understanding in that grin. "They don't like me is what it is. I talked to one once. She went away and didn't come back, and I heard afterward she didn't think I was a fit mother and the kids would be better off without me. Because I said I'd rather have them with strangers than with their natural-born father. She figured if I felt that way, I just didn't care about them."

Her face clouded, as it always did when she mentioned the children. Leslie patted her arm. "This woman won't do that. She said you could call her. It won't hurt to talk to her. Tell her about your husband and see what she says. She might even be able to get him to stop bothering you."

"Man, wouldn't that be something? What's her name?"

"Croft. Mrs. Croft. Harriet, I think. You'll have to call her to-day or tomorrow, Josie. Before she goes back to Toronto."

"Toronto?" Hope faded. "She won't want to be bothered with me. Anyways, I couldn't afford it."

"Call her and see. She's at the Holiday Inn." Leslie thought for a moment, then asked, "Have you ever been in Kingston?" Kingston was the ancient penitentiary that housed both women and men. Even saying the name filled her with dread.

"Hey, I've never been into anything heavy. That's for real operators." Remembering, she said, "Gee, I'm sorry Les. I knew somebody once who got sent up."

"What's it like?"

"Bad. Not as bad as it used to be," she added quickly. "It's more like rooms now, and you can keep stuff. Books and things. This here woman, she had a teddy bear. Would you believe it? Real mean, doing hard time, and she sleeps with a teddy bear. I couldn't get over it."

"Tell me what it's really like, Josie."

Josie shuffled her feet and looked down at the floor and up at the ceiling and finally blurted, "Some of the girls try to kill themselves. Some of them try to kill each other. You gotta keep outa trouble, but you can't because that's all there is in there. Trouble. The girls are trouble and the matrons are trouble and the whole place is trouble, top to bottom. If you go in there, Les, there ain't no way you're coming out again."

Leslie lay on her cot picturing dragons and dungeons and her parents trudging through stone gates to visit. When Josie returned, she was still there, one arm shielding her eyes, the other stiff at her side.

"I left a message. They said they'd give it to her as soon as she came in."

Please God, Leslie prayed, don't let her be there talking to Mother, telling her what I am. Thinking of her recent visitor—beautiful, remote, with her emerald ring and emerald eyes and air of superiority—she felt a slow, burning anger. "If you're so ashamed of yourself," she had said. What did she know, with a husband sitting at home waiting to take care of her? She damned well wasn't ashamed, to begin with. Did not wanting to hurt her parents mean she was ashamed? She had loved Marcie. Marcie had loved her. What they did together, as she had told the arrogant Mrs. Croft, was nobody else's business.

"Are you all right, Les?" Concerned, Josie leaned over and started shaking her.

Leslie opened her eyes and saw the heavy face, younger than hers in fact, but a lifetime older in experience, and heard the voice in her head goading, *say it, if you're truly not ashamed, say it. You're both in here together. What harm can she possibly do you? If you're ever going to do it, do it now.* She sat up, took a deep breath, and before she had time to change her mind said, "I'm a lesbian." The word echoed through the small cell, and if she could have caught it in both hands and stuffed it back in her mouth, she would have. It was the first time—the first time ever—that she had actually said it.

When she dared to look at Josie, expecting to see shock, revulsion, God knows what, she saw only the same round face. "Aren't you going to say anything?"

"What do you want me to say?" The expression was nothing more than mildly attentive.

"Do you know what I'm talking about?" Leslie was nonplused. When you drop a bomb that doesn't go off, what do you do next?

"Of course I know what you're saying. I knew before."

"How?"

"We knew before you got here. Klyk knew. Somebody downtown must have passed the word. I'd have known anyway. Why else would you up and clobber that friend of yours?"

"Fournier, you got company." A venomous summons from Mrs. Klyk.

Fournier. That was Josie. "You'd better go," Leslie said. "It's Mrs. Croft. I can tell by Klyk's mood. They had a run-in, and she lost."

"Jeez. She must of flew." Josie smoothed her hair and straightened the shapeless cotton dress. "Wish me luck, Les. If you want, we'll talk when I get back."

Thoughts whirled through Leslie's mind. Incredulity at having said, so casually, I *am a lesbian*. Astonishment at the reaction—rather, the lack of reaction—on Josie's part. Amazement that everyone had known and no one had said anything. And then a wonderful, incredible, exhilarating sense of freedom. She was thirty-five years old, and she was free! Well, half-free. The parts of her that had been covert—scurrying like mice at the mention of someone being gay, at the words *faggot* and *queer* and *dyke*—those parts had come together, and she felt whole and vividly alive.

Loose-limbed and erect, taking pleasure in the mechanics of movement, the placing of one foot before the other and the easy swinging of her arms, she walked up to the group of women and said, in a loud clear voice, "I did not kill Marcie Denton. Someone did, but it wasn't me."

Heart pounding, Mrs. Taylor sat on the hard chair in the grim little visitor's room and tried to look her daughter in the eye. She had dreaded this meeting, dreaded the inevitable "How is Duchess?" When Leslie called and said she wanted to see her, and her father, too, that it was urgent, Mrs. Taylor's first thought was that somehow word had gotten back that the dog had been shipped off for boarding.

"Where's Dad?"

"You know your father. He's got so much to do we hardly see each other, even when he's home."

"I wanted to talk to both of you, Mom."

"That's all right, dear. I'll tell him when I get home." You'd think, after years of practice, being the family buffer would come easier; instead, it got harder. Rome burns, Nero fiddles, she thought bitterly.

Dismissed yet again by Harriet, who was closeted with Josie, Mrs. Klyk presided over the room with malevolent satisfaction. Here, at least, she could not be evicted. She hitched her chair closer, intent on hearing every word and policing every gesture —no matter the mesh prevented contact and mousy Mrs. Taylor was hardly the type to tote a hacksaw.

Geared to tell her parents she was gay, Leslie looked at her mother and knew this was not the time. Nor the place. Her mother deserved a measure of privacy, freedom from prying eyes, a setting where her feelings would not be laid bare before a stranger. And where, equally important, her husband was at her side. But there would never be such a time and such a place. Not as long as she was in custody.

"You look a little better. Have you been talking to Mr. Poulis?" There was a subtle change, an animation that had not been there on her previous visits. Probably because the lawyer had been paid up. Mrs. Taylor decided that if Leslie asked about Duchess, she would lie, pretend the dog was safe at home. Telling her the truth would set her right back.

"I got rid of Mr. Poulis. Don't you have anything to do with him."

"Oh, Leslie. I gave him nine thousand dollars to look after you."

"Mother, you didn't. Does Dad know?"

"Not yet."

"You'll have to stop payment. Right away."

"I can't do that. What will happen to you? You can't sit here without a lawyer working to get you out."

Almost without thinking, as though it had been in her mind waiting to come out, Leslie said, "I have a lawyer, Mother. Her name is Mrs. Croft. I'm going to ask her to see you tonight. Make sure Dad is at home. She has something to tell you, but both of you have to be there."

"Who is she? Where did she come from?"

"She'll explain. Just go and cancel that check." Leslie smiled at her mother, smiled at Mrs. Klyk as she said, "Would you tell Mrs. Croft I'd like to see her before she leaves?"

Humming, she followed the matron back to the cell block. Josie wasn't there. That meant Mrs. Croft was still in the building.

Leslie looked at the women bunched at the table. She looked at the grimy window set high in the wall above and wondered that sunshine could flood through such murky space. Strange that she hadn't noticed it until now.

Mrs. Taylor set the tray on the coffee table in front of Harriet and retired to a chair opposite. Lawyers certainly came in a wide assortment. This one was as different from Mr. Poulis as night and day. Sure of herself, she was. That was good. Leslie needed someone who wasn't afraid to stand up for what was right. But she looked like a lot more than nine thousand dollars worth.

"Leslie told me about the check you gave Mr. Poulis."

Startled by what seemed a tuning in on her thoughts, Mrs. Taylor said, "I phoned the bank. It was already cashed."

"Don't worry about it. I talked to him, and he agreed there was some misunderstanding. He promised to return the money tomorrow." Harriet neglected to say that the "misunderstanding" was resolved only when she threatened to file a grievance with the Bar Association. Mrs. Klyk. Hab Poulis. She might be influencing people, but she certainly wasn't winning any friends.

There was no sign of Mr. Taylor. On this point, Leslie had been explicit. "I want you to tell them, but they have to be together." She had also mentioned a dog. Duchess. The animal was obviously important to her. "Leslie asked me to say hello to Duchess."

"She's not here at the moment."

Reasonable. Were it not for the agitated flutter of Mrs. Taylor's hands, she would have assumed the dog was outside. In a run. She was obviously being walked by Mr. Taylor, which explained both absences. "That's fine. I'll see her before I leave. Your daughter seems more worried about her than about herself."

"She's very timid. That's why Leslie worries so much." On the verge of tears, pinned by a glance so green and piercing that she was unable to look away, she said, "My husband asked the vet to look after her."

"Leslie thinks she's here with you." In spite of the anger lumped in her chest, she spoke softly. Clearly this was none of Mrs. Taylor's doing. "She'll be all right with my mother," Leslie had said. "She's the only person Duchess is not afraid of." Too bad she'd left her father out of the equation.

"Mr. Taylor felt it would be better for her." She added lamely, "I'm going to bring her back. We haven't talked about it yet."

"Where is your husband, Mrs. Taylor?"

"He's here. Working. He's very busy, Mrs. Croft. He said we could talk without him."

"I'm afraid that's impossible. I won't take much of his time."

"It wouldn't do to interrupt him. Especially when he said not to."

"This once he's going to have to be interrupted. Does he realize this discussion concerns his daughter? Doesn't he care what happens to her?"

"He cares too much. It upsets him to think about it."

The anger threatened to spill over. Harriet sipped her coffee and waited for the rage to subside. When the cup was empty, she set it down carefully and, smiling gently, said rather than asked, "You're sure he's not going to join us?"

"Yes." It was such a nice smile that Mrs. Taylor thought, what a pity she didn't use it more often.

"In that case, we'll have to join him."

Flustered, Mrs. Taylor blocked Harriet's entry to the hall. "I'll talk to him. Perhaps he'll change his mind."

There was the sound of voices—one soft and insistent, the other sharp and querulous. Footsteps. A tall, slightly stooped figure with leonine head and craggy, lined features entered the room. "You wanted to see me?" Leslie's father had a peevish, how-dare-you-disturb-me manner that was curiously at odds with the strong chin and determined mouth.

"I wanted to see both of you." She waited until they were seated. "You know your daughter decided not to go to trial?"

"That's the first I've heard of it." Frowning, Adam said, "Did you know about this, Mother?"

"Mr. Poulis mentioned it when he was here."

"You didn't tell me he was here."

"I've hardly seen you, dear. He came after Leslie fired him. Mrs. Croft is handling things now."

The frown deepened. "Of course there will be a trial. Everybody has a trial."

"Not if they plead guilty." Watchful, Harriet waited for the reaction as the words struck home.

"She can't do that." Mrs. Taylor was close to tears.

"My daughter never hurt that girl." Adam Taylor's deep voice lacked conviction.

"I know that." A pause, "She loves you both very much."

"We love her." They said it in unison.

"It's because she loves you that she didn't want to go to court."

Adam put his arm around his wife who was weeping uncontrollably. "What kind of mixed up thinking is that? I'll talk to the girl. Get some sense into her."

"Your daughter is a homosexual, Mr. Taylor. She and Marcie were lovers. She was afraid of what it would do to you if it came out in court."

Tears streaming down her face, Mrs. Taylor turned to the man who sat, frozen, beside her. "Adam, it's my fault. I knew. I've known for a long time. If I'd talked to her this never would have happened."

Adam got up and left the room without a word, without a backward glance. "I think you should be with him," Harriet said to his wife.

She had done what Leslie asked, and now was at a loss what to do next. Perhaps she should have led up to it more slowly, paved the way a little more. Instead of the rational discussion she had planned, Leslie's father was in retreat and her mother was in tears.

"He wants to be alone." Drying her tears, Mrs. Taylor looked Harriet straight in the eye. A proud look. "I want you to tell Leslie not to worry about us. Tell her it doesn't matter." A thought flashed through her mind, and her eyes darted to Harriet's left hand. "Are you one too?"

It was a question Harriet had never been asked, a question one didn't expect to be asked. "No. . .You make excellent coffee, Mrs. Taylor. Could I trouble you for another cup?" She followed her hostess into the kitchen, sat at the table, and said, "My name is Harriet. Would it matter?"

"I'm Emily. No, it wouldn't matter. Not to me. Except it might make things easier for Leslie. Easier to talk, I mean."

"How long have you known about her?"

"I didn't really *know*. But I've had a feeling, since back in grade school. She was always with girls, never cared about boys at all. Only as friends. Then, when she went off with Marcie, in the back of my mind I knew. A couple of times I nearly asked her. I guess I was afraid, afraid she'd say it was true."

"Afraid of what?"

"Lots of things. Her living that kind of life. Getting sick. Losing her job. Not having a decent place to live. The people she'd be with."

"The people aren't any different. They're just like the rest of us. Some good, some bad. And a lot that are happier and more successful than most people you meet."

"It's not just that. You have children, and you expect they will have children and it will go on like that. When you know that's not going to happen, it's hard. Worse even for my husband than it is for me."

"It took a lot of courage for Leslie to ask me to come here tonight. What I'd like is for both of you to visit her tomorrow. She'll be a bundle of nerves until she sees you. Until you tell her that you love her and you're behind her and under no circumstances is she to take the blame for Marcie."

"Everybody seems so sure she's guilty. Maybe even her own father. Does she have much of a chance?"

"Every chance. Providing she doesn't change her mind again about going to trial. That part is up to you. Now what are we going to do about the dog?"

From strangers, to acquaintances, to friends and allies in less than an hour. Emily set another pot of coffee to brew and said, "I've just had a wonderful idea. Are you any good with animals?"

"Hopeless. I've never even owned a goldfish. If she belongs anywhere, it's here."

"She belongs in Leslie's house. It's no good for her here. My husband isn't mean, but she knows he doesn't like having her around. She shakes the whole time he's in the house. Now here's what I was thinking."

She spelled it out and added logic to argument; in the end, it made perfect sense. "Tomorrow," she said, handing Harriet the key to Leslie's bungalow, "I'll pick Duchess up and deliver her myself. It'll be a lot more comfortable than staying in that hotel."

A house. A dog. A woman with no money who was afraid of her husband and worried about her kids. A gay client. A police department that handed out inflammatory flyers about faggots and queers. Not quite her normal routine.

It was time to call Donna and tell her she needed some

clothes. To check up on Clarence and find out how he was doing. And to have both of them make arrangements to join her
here in Spruce Falls. If today was any indication, there would
be busy days and a rough ride ahead.

Chapter Eight

Only three weeks in Leslie's house, yet Harriet felt completely at home. Little more than a garden cottage, the bungalow was bright and sunny and furnished with an eclectic abandon that should have been frenetic but was, instead, homey and in harmony.

It was Sunday morning, and she had promised herself the entire day of doing exactly as she pleased. Emily had invited her for dinner, an invitation she politely declined. Clarence and Donna, who had reluctantly agreed to temporary relocation—dislocation, they called it—had escaped to Toronto for the weekend. Josie's children were being cared for by Children's Aid, and her husband had been slapped with a writ ordering him to stay away from his family, wife included. Leslie and her parents were on speaking terms although, where her father was concerned, that amounted to little more than hello and good-bye.

Breakfasting on the deck Leslie had attached to the rear of the house, Harriet noticed Duchess at the foot of the yard gnawing on a bone. The change in the dog was remarkable. The first few days, she had retreated behind the sofa and refused to come out. Now she was gaining weight, wagging her tail, making tentative efforts toward play. Never having taken the slightest interest in creatures with four legs, Harriet was amazed by the pleasure she derived from watching Duchess emerge from her cocoon.

A shimmer of orange caught her eye directly above Duchess in a low-hanging tree that a few moments before had been green. Now, in place of leaves, the boughs were covered with masses of butterflies, their wings glowing in the sun. Monarchs. No wonder she had used the word *cocoon*. Once, long ago, a friend had pointed them out to her. So beautiful, Harriet had said. So beautiful and delicate and heartbreakingly fragile. What a pity they live only a day. Not monarchs, her friend had told her, and explained that like geese and ducks and robins, the monarchs migrated—riding the wind, despite their fragility, to a warmer and more inviting climate.

Fascinated, Harriet watched the play of color—rising, falling, appearing, disappearing. There was no movement away from the tree, yet the color ebbed and flowed.

Slice of toast in one hand, cup of coffee in the other, she walked toward the tree to investigate. Duchess dropped her bone and bounded up to meet her. Harriet shared the toast, then fixed her attention on the tree. The butterflies were clustered, their folded wings a tarnished beige rather than the vivid burnt orange revealed in flight. Intrigued, Harriet stretched up her hand, and the ornamented tree blazed with flame as the wings opened and hundreds of jeweled bodies readied to rise.

Duchess at her side, Harriet returned to the deck. The monarch was beautiful, but only when it spread its wings and prepared to fly. Wings closed—perhaps a protection against enemies—it was drab and undistinguished.

People were the same, she thought. As Duchess nuzzled her hand, she realized she was not thinking of people. She was thinking of Leslie Taylor. The instant those dark eyes met hers that abortive morning of the abortive bail review, she had known there was a second Leslie Taylor buried inside. Someone locked away. Someone who, if once released, would soar above those around her.

Even now, after only one step forward, there was a change: a new closeness with her mother; a growing lack of restraint with her father; an ease in conversation that was at times unnerving. Like the day she'd talked about heterosexuality, *compulsory heterosexuality*, she'd called it. "A trap. Women are forced into roles someone else believes they should play. They get married without thinking about it. That's what you probably did." Unsettling. Because, Harriet had admitted to herself later, that was exactly what she had done. She had entered into the perfect union: because that's what her family expected her to do.

"Now, if only she could bring herself to stand up in front of the world," Harriet said aloud to Duchess, who wriggled her rump in agreement. Harriet's intelligent eyes narrowed, and her thin face set in concentration. Tomorrow she was slated to sit down with the Crown, to have the case as it stood revealed to her, the evidence in hand. She had intended, at the same time, to inform Frost of her intention to request a change of venue. "Anywhere but here," Leslie had instructed. And she, Harriet, thinking of the bumbling Nystrom, of the small-town mentality reflected in most of the people she had met in Spruce Falls—she had granted the wisdom of moving to a larger, more sophisticated jurisdiction. Never, in an important case, had she delayed so long in asking for discovery. The closer to the wire it got, the less chance the Crown would have of shoring the weak spots in their strategy and anticipating hers from the witnesses she planned to call. Had the delay, Harriet wondered, reasonable on the surface, been prompted by a gut feeling that there was more at stake than holding her cards close to her chest? Acquittal in Toronto would set Leslie physically free. Acquittal in Spruce Falls would liberate her fully and forever. It would depend, of course, on Leslie.

It was not yet noon, a bit early for a jailhouse visit. There was enough time to walk Duchess to the end of the street and turn her loose in the scrub along the creek. One thing about living with a dog: you never had time on your hands. Never felt lonely, either. She rustled through Leslie's closet and pulled out a pair of worn cargo pants. The last time she'd walked the dog she'd ended up covered with mud.

"Your mistress doesn't believe in throwing things away, does she, Duchess?" They were the same pants Leslie was wearing in the photograph on her dresser. A determinedly proper photograph taken under a large tree with a brick building showing in the background. Standing beside Marcie, both staring straight at the camera, untouching, Leslie wore a T-shirt and the pants Harriet was putting on. A pile of leaves at their feet, the snap was obviously taken late in the year. Marcie was smiling. Leslie, bushel basket in her right hand, rake held upright in her left, wore the same dour expression as the pitchfork-holding farmer in Grant Wood's famous American Gothic painting. There was a ring on her engagement finger, too small to see clearly, and a slogan on the T-shirt that read, Popeye eats spinach. Had she kept that, too? What else did she have in her wardrobe?

Curious, Harriet slid the hangers along, gaining from the garments a sense of the persona presented by her client to the work-a-day world. Pants and tops, skirts. A few dresses. A number of suits—some light, some winterweight. Expensive, but unexciting. The blacks and browns and dark greys would work against her coloring, and that wouldn't help in court. Better a cherry red, or perhaps a dramatic orange a shade or two up from umber. Something to add tone to the pale skin and bring out the richness of her dark eyes and hair. Leaning over Duchess, Harriet clipped the leash to the dog's collar. *The woods are lovely. Dark and deep. And I have promises to keep.* She opened the door and stepped onto the porch, the porch on which Moore and Yarrow had stood on a morning so similar and now so long ago.

Straining at the leash, Duchess set off up the street. "This is going to be a short one," Harriet warned, and then intoned, *For I have promises to keep. And miles and miles and miles to go before I sleep.* "That," she added, thinking of Clare and his periodic lapses into pedantry, "is by Frost. Robert Frost. A famous American poet."

Duchess wagged her tail and bounded ahead, and Harriet quickened her step to keep pace.

"My word. So this is the way you look on your day off?"

Leslie cocked an eyebrow and grinned, and Harriet, who never thought about her clothes once they were on, felt shy and self-conscious. "Is this something new? A dress code?" Harriet asked. She'd seen everything from jeans to banker's stripes parading the corridor.

"Snappish, too."

"If you must know, I've been walking your dog." A curt, angry remark. And mean, given the circumstances. Leslie should be out walking the dog herself, not some stranger.

"Not like that, I hope. You look more jet set than Spruce Falls." With a rueful glance down at the faded cotton billowing about her knees, Leslie said, "I'm sorry, Harriet. I didn't mean to tease you. It's just that you look so. . .so terrific. I've always wanted to own a pair of those Garbo trousers."

Harriet's ill-temper vanished. She had debated with herself over the propriety of making a professional call in other than her usual professional dress. In the end, she had opted for the tailored slacks. With one of her custom-made silk shirts, ivory as were the pants, and a scarlet cashmere cardigan, she did present a more informal appearance. But it was more by design than by chance. Aside from it being Sunday—when surely everyone had a right to relax, in dress if not commitment—

she wanted to establish a more casual footing. It would take all her power of persuasion to convince Leslie of the merit of standing trial on her home ground. A lawyer/client relationship was restrictive. Today she was here as much as a friend as a legal advisor. "How are things going with your parents?"

"Better. My father pretends nothing has changed. Mother. . . Mom is wonderful. You don't know what it's like not to have to talk in riddles. Thank you for telling them. And thank you for helping Josie. She used to spend all her time telling shoplifting stories. Now all she talks about is you. You made quite an impression."

"All it took was a couple of phone calls."

"It couldn't have been that easy. She's been trying to get somebody to help for years. You didn't really walk Duchess?"

The sudden shift in conversation was typical. Now that Leslie was more accepting of her, she was more talkative, her conversation leap-frogging from one topic to another. "Why? Shouldn't I have?"

"I'm just surprised she'd go with you. She crawls around on her stomach with people she doesn't know. She's seen my father often enough and she's even scared of him."

Like you, Harriet thought. Hadn't she read somewhere that animals picked up their owner's vibes, reflected their fears and prejudices? "Well, she's not afraid of him now," Harriet said dryly. "We were there yesterday, and she was fine." She could tell from the look on Leslie's face that she didn't believe her. Probably felt she was gilding the lily to set her mind at rest. So be it. She was here to discuss Leslie, not her dog. "You agreed when I took this case, Leslie, that you would do what I considered best."

The smile evaporated. "I don't remember saying that."

"Perhaps I didn't actually say it, but it's implicit. When you hire a lawyer what you're really hiring is that lawyer's expertise."

Shades of Haberdashery Poulis. Leslie's lips turned down. "I didn't hire you. You hired yourself," she said rudely.

"Don't start up. I'm in no mood for one of your sulky fits.

I thought you were past that."

Leslie stopped scowling, a marginal improvement at best. "What is it now? The last time you wanted me to tell my parents they had a queer for a daughter."

"And was that wrong?"

"No." It was a reluctant concession, followed by a lessening of tension. "No, Harriet, you were right. I should have done it back when I first met Marcie, when she started showing up at the house, tagging after me. They must have wondered then what was going on. She was so persistent. I couldn't get rid of her."

Excitement surged through Harriet. This was new ground. The one thing Leslie had refused to discuss was her early relationship with Marcie, how they had come together. She had assumed that Leslie, being older, had pursued Marcie. If it was the other way around, the events leading up to the murder shifted subtly in their favor. "Marcie initiated the relationship?"

"Yes. I wasn't the first, by the way."

"But she was still in school?"

"She was still in school and had been involved with girls since she was thirteen. I didn't know that until later. We moved to Toronto because people were talking, and I was worried as much about her as I was about me. Her family was very strict. Lutherans. They wanted her to be a deaconess, would you believe? I felt guilty about taking her away and I finally talked her into coming back home. She kept writing and visiting on weekends, and I missed her when she wasn't there." Leslie glanced at the square-cut emerald that Harriet had bought for herself from her first major earnings. "She sent me a ring for my birthday. Not as expensive as yours. They took it when I came in here."

"The ring you were wearing in that picture? The one in the bedroom—you and Marcie raking leaves?"

Leslie nodded. "That was taken after she came back to stay. It's my fault she's dead. It never would have happened if she'd stayed here. If she hadn't met Charles and gotten married."

"You think he did it, don't you?"

"I know he did it." Her body vibrated with hot, helpless rage. "Why didn't they arrest him?"

"He was in Toronto, Leslie. He can account for every minute. He married her, you lost her. You had more reason to kill her than he did."

"That's not true, Harriet." Leslie's gaze was direct, steady. "She was trying to leave him. I think the only reason he married her was because he knew she was a lesbian and it was a challenge. That old male ego thing. It was after she started phoning me that he started beating her. That was another mistake: she wanted to come back, and I wouldn't let her."

"You weren't chasing after her?"

"I never chased after her, Harriet. Not in the beginning. Certainly not after she got married. We saw each other a couple of times, but that was all. I was afraid of what Charles would do to her. To me, too. Maybe he didn't kill her himself, but he had someone do it."

An improbable suggestion. Charles shopping around for a hit-man? Even if he knew how to go about finding a contract killer, he would no more lay himself open to blackmail than he would to charges of bribery and corruption. All that was certain was that Marcie was dead, someone had killed her, and whoever it was, it was not Leslie Taylor. "They'll find out who did it. Once they get it through their heads it wasn't you, they'll have to start looking again." Harriet hoped Leslie would accept the assurance at face value. If it were up to Yarrow, the loonies would be running loose and everyone else would be under lock and key. Setting the conversation back on track, she said, "I have a meeting with the Crown tomorrow."

"That's when they convince you I'm guilty." Wasn't that what had happened with Poulis?

"That's when I tell them we want the earliest date we can get. I'm not going to ask for a change of venue, Leslie. And I don't want to wait for an upper court judge."

Taken aback, Leslie said sharply, "Don't you think this is something we should discuss?"

"We're discussing it now."

"Being told what to do isn't my idea of a discussion."

"All right. Let's talk about it."

"We won't have a chance here. They hate queers in this town."

"Don't use that word again. We're talking about homosexuals. You're a lesbian, not a queer. Murder is against the law. Homosexuality isn't."

"Tell that to Inspector Yarrow."

"I will if it's necessary. You're not going to get away from him, Leslie. He'll be there. He'd be there if we went to Timbuktu."

"It can't be here, Harriet. I'm going to have to live here after it's over. If it ever is over."

She was shivering. Harriet took off her sweater. "Here. Put this on." It was useless to tell her that she was bigger than Spruce Falls, that life held more for her than a town like this could offer. Equally useless to point out that she could no more escape what she was, could no more escape people knowing what she was, than she could go on mourning over if's and but's and lost turns in the road.

"My parents...."

"You worried about them before. They're stronger than you think."

"This isn't the same as just telling them. Their friends would know. The neighbors. The people Dad works with. It would be awful for them."

"Suppose they didn't object. Would that make a difference?"

"Maybe. I'd have to think about it."

"Would you like me to feel them out?"

Leslie responded with an explosive "No. I'll do it myself," followed by a contrite, "I'm sorry. I know you're thinking of what's best for me. But you demand a lot, Harriet." She rubbed her cheek against the soft cashmere. "I get so cold. I'll talk to them if that's what you want. When do you have to know?"

"Tomorrow. Before eleven. I guess you'll have to do it by phone." Harriet retrieved the sweater, slipped into it while it still held the warmth of Leslie's body. The imprint remained long after she left the building.

The phone was ringing as she came up the walk. It rang while she hunted for her keys. It was still ringing when she snatched it up and panted into the mouthpiece.

"Harriet, where have you been, it's Clarence, I've been phoning and phoning, I was about to write you off, what's going on, I'm glad I caught you."

"Clare, slow down. What's the matter?"

"Nothing. I hope nothing. I bumped into your friend last night. He knows where you are. He knows what you're doing. He's mad as a hatter. Said he's going to go to the Law Society and have you thrown off the case, that you're working for him and have no business getting mixed up with Taylor."

"Is that all?" Charles was the least of her worries.

"He's jumping ten feet. I've never seen anyone so mad."

"Well, he'll just have to get over it. I returned his check. There isn't a thing he can do."

"I want to stay over a couple of days. I'm onto something that could be important."

"That's fine. There's not much you can do here at the moment."

"I don't want to leave you alone. I'm telling you, Harriet, that bastard is really on the warpath. I wouldn't put anything past him."

"Oh Clare, you're turning into a neurotic worrywart. It's all that sugar. At any rate, I won't be alone. Donna's coming back tonight, isn't she?"

"Donna." Derision yielded to concern. "The mood Charlie's in, what good is Donna? The two of you are a pair of sitting ducks."

"You're forgetting Duchess. What's better protection than a watchdog?"

"Watchdog?" The lighthearted attempt at humor misfired. "Oh God. I'd better come back."

"Clare," Harriet's voice was sharp enough to cut the telephone wire, "we don't need you here."

A pause. "Are you sure?" Another pause. "I've got a line on Marcie I should stay with. It seems Leslie wasn't the only woman in her life."

Harriet gripped the phone and held her breath. When she was able to speak she said quietly, ominously, "If that's true, I want to meet her. As soon as possible. And Clare, let her get away and I'll skin you alive."

Another woman. Perhaps more than one other woman. Harriet opened the cupboard over the sink and took down the bottle of brandy. It had been there for three weeks and was still over half full.

What she wanted for Leslie was more than acquittal. She wanted to prove to this whole narrow-minded town that Leslie Taylor was innocent. And the way to prove innocence was to prove guilt. Someone else's guilt.

She sipped her brandy and thought again that this was not a crime one woman would commit against another, but who could say? People did terrible things to each other. To each other and even—glancing toward the monarch nesting tree— yes, even to themselves.

Everyone was smiling. Frost. Yarrow. Moore. Harriet. The meeting was launched on a wave of social grace.

Frost had skirted the issue of venue. It wasn't often they were honored by the presence of a big city lawyer. He'd been surprised when he heard that she'd agreed to represent Taylor. Spruce Falls was a far cry from Toronto. She'd be mighty homesick before she got back. Mind you, he didn't expect the trial itself to take that long.

The smiles had appeared when she responded to the non-question by saying that she felt quite at home here, that she wasn't the least homesick. If they wanted to know whether or not she intended to ask for a change of jurisdiction, the answer was no. Miss Taylor felt she could get as fair a hearing here as anywhere else. Frost had looked at Yarrow, Yarrow had looked at Moore, and it was at that point that they all began to smile.

"I understand your field is corporate law. Takeovers. Litigation."

"Did Mr. Denton tell you that?"

"Ah . . .yes, as a matter of fact, he did. Have you handled criminal cases at all, Mrs. Croft?"

"I've had some trial experience, yes."

"That's good. You're up against a tough one, I'm afraid. The Inspector has done a thorough job. Hasn't overlooked a thing, have you Inspector?"

Yarrow expanded noticeably. "We may seem like small potatoes up here, but we do the job, don't we Sergeant Moore?"

"That's reassuring, Inspector. Did you manage to get casts of the prints around the bed?"

Frost shot a startled glance at the two detectives. "What prints? What bed?"

"At the Dalton," Harriet said. "The killer left impressions in the shag carpet. I reported it to the Inspector weeks ago."

"We checked it. Mrs. Croft was imagining things. There was nothing there. Nothing aside from normal signs of wear. A lot of people have been through that room since our lab men went over it."

"You found this after our men cleared the room?" Frost settled back into the deep leather club chair. "That explains it. If there'd been footprints there at the time, we'd know about it." Light glittered on his spectacles. "The weight of evidence against Miss Taylor is overwhelming. Nothing will be accomplished by going to trial. The Crown is quite prepared to discuss a guilty plea. Prepared to make allowances in consideration of the saving to the taxpayer."

"You'd reduce the charge?"

"We'd think about it, Mrs. Croft."

"By how much? Manslaughter?"

"Now, now, you know better than that." Jovial, he said, "What would you consider fair, Inspector?"

"Second Degree with a recommendation for parole."

They had discussed this ahead of time. The ball was tossed too quickly, caught too readily. All three had expected her to turn up, hat in hand, begging a deal. They were in for a royal surprise. "Suppose you show me what you have first?"

Tagged and identified, the physical evidence was laid out on a table in an adjoining room. The shoe that struck the lethal blow—a high-heeled sling-back pump. The towel rod—exactly the same as the one now installed in its place. A plastic bag of platinum hair and a smaller bag of pubic hair. A wrist watch with smashed face. A cassette tape—the one from Leslie's answering machine containing the message from Marcie. And—the letter.

She picked up the sheet of paper, skimmed it quickly, and held it out to Frost for inspection. "There is no date on this."

The smile he threw at Yarrow was a near-leer. "It's not *when* it was written, Mrs. Croft. The fact that it *was* written speaks for itself."

"I see." She read it again, this time committing it to memory. "It's just a copy. May I see the original?"

"There was no original. This is all there is."

"This is the letter Mr. Denton found in his wife's suitcase?"

"That's right."

"Doesn't it seem peculiar that she would keep a photostat instead of the original?"

"There could be any number of explanations. It could be anywhere. This just happens to be the only copy that's turned up. Don't worry, it's genuine. We've had it checked by a handwriting expert."

"This letter is the only piece of evidence you have that relates directly to my client. And it really can't be considered evidentiary because it has nothing whatsoever to do with the crime."

"It goes to the state of mind, Mrs. Croft."

"Of course." With an enigmatic smile, she looked once more

at the letter, then replaced it on the table next to a scrap of paper—a receipt from a jewlery store. "There isn't enough here to warrant a charge, much less a trial."

The three men were watching her. Confident. Secure. Predatory. "Harriet—you don't mind if I call you Harriet?—I wanted you to see what we have so you'd know what you're up against. We can tie every one of those items to your client. Witness A will place her at the scene." Harriet made a mental note: Mrs. Peak. "Witness B will speak to the letter. And the hair." Who else but Charles? "Witness C is an authority on . . . I believe the term is alternate lifestyles?"

A psychologist. A handwriting expert. The pathologist. Forensic technicians. Listed alphabetically, but identifiable by category if not name. "You've done your homework, Inspector." To Frost, she said, "What you have is entirely circumstantial."

They both knew that circumstantial evidence could be as binding as direct. In some cases, more so. Direct evidence, if accepted as true, proved a fact in issue. Circumstantial evidence inferred the existence of a fact in issue. Jurors seldom separated the two.

"We might consider Second Degree, Harriet."

In which case she'd be eligible for parole after ten years. But if the judge decided otherwise, they could still be looking at twenty-five years. Not that it made the slightest difference. She had no intention of plea bargaining the better part of Leslie's life into oblivion. "I'll speak to my client, Jeremy."

She would tell Leslie about the offer. It was incumbent upon her to do so. She would mention it. They might discuss it, but consider it? Not likely.

The lights in the club were concentrated on the dance floor. The tables, set back against the wall, were in deep shadow. Even so, Harriet felt conspicuous.

"Feel like a fish out of water?" Clarence teased. She was wearing designer jeans—the first time he had ever seen her in jeans—and a fisherman-knit pullover. On the whole, she blended rather well.

"I do. Because of you. You stick out like a sore thumb."

"I'm not the only man in here, if that's what you mean."

"You're the only one in a suit and shirt and tie." The two men dancing together were wearing jeans and polo shirts; the only other male, seated with a group of women, wore a canvas anorak over a boatneck knit top.

"The next time we do the town, I'll raid your closet. Where did you get those jeans? They look as though you were poured into them. I'll be lucky to get you out of here in one piece. There's a doll over yonder who's had her eye on you ever since we came in."

"Stop gawking, Clare. Why don't you make yourself useful and go get us a drink?"

The bar was located in a separate room at the rear—a large room with pool table, slot machines, extra tables for the overflow, and a line-up of jostling patrons waiting to be served. "No way. This is one time you do the honors, Mrs. Croft. I wouldn't get into that queue for nothin.'"

He feels outnumbered, Harriet thought. She had often seen men on their own in a crowd of women—a male lecturer addressing a women's club, a minister at a church tea, a politician campaigning for the female vote. Far from feeling intimidated, they usually thrived on being the star attraction. Here, men were without special status. It dawned on Harriet that throughout her life, wherever she had been and whatever she had done, there was a tacit understanding among both sexes that the male of the species was somehow special. Why else would married feminists make a point of saying their husbands helped with the housework? Why else would successful career women, women who had reached the top through brains, guts, ability and hours of overtime, why would such deserving women feel privileged to be accepted into the upper echelon? Surrounded by women who saw themselves as entities rather than appendages, it was understandable that Clarence should feel strange.

The bartender was a tall brunette with shoulder-length hair and a flashing smile. Briskly efficient, she suggested Scotch in place of brandy and Pepsi because she'd run out of Coke.

"Do you know Leslie Taylor?" Harriet asked, conscious of the bodies pressing forward behind her.

"Sorry," the girl said, looking beyond her to the next in line. "Maybe some of the others do. Ask around."

Harriet returned to the table and a Clarence grown edgy. "I asked the bartender about Leslie. No luck."

"Your secret admirer just asked about you." He indicated a retreating figure, in starched chinos and a man's vest. "I didn't think she was your type, so I told her you were taken."

"You're supposed to be watching for Elsie whatever-her-name-is, not cavorting with the clientele. Are you sure she'll be here?"

"That's what she said. Every Saturday night. The Cameo Club. Haven't missed since they opened. Her very words."

"There are a lot of people in here. What does she look like?"

"Not too tall. Sandy hair. Hazel eyes."

"That could be anyone."

"Sort of boyish-looking. She walks around with her hands in her pockets. Her last name is Mak. Elsie Mak."

Harriet tapped the shoulder of a woman at the next table. "You haven't seen Elsie Mak around, have you?"

Startled, the woman swung round. "Who wants to know?" As Harriet came into focus the hostility disappeared, replaced by a surging interest. "Haven't seen her. Ask at the door. They'll know. You're new here."

"Yes."

"I'll go ask if you like. They know me here. Been coming for years."

Clarence waited until she was out of earshot. "I don't like the way she looked at you. Don't expect any help from me if you get yourself into a fix."

"She's not here yet, but I told them to tell her you're here. Would you like to dance?"

"She can't dance," Clarence said. With inspiration born of

desperation, he added, "She has bad feet."

"Bad feet?" The woman looked perplexed.

"Malformation of the metatarsus. It's very painful."

"It's not bothering me at all at the moment," Harriet said coolly. "I'd love to dance."

From the dance floor, through a crush of gyrating bodies, she glimpsed the young man in the anorak approach Clarence, bend over in an exchange of conversation, straighten—miffed—and walk away. A couple moving in a sinuous frontal lock-step blocked her view. When next she caught sight of their table, Clarence was standing, beckoning to a sandy-haired girl with thumbs hooked in her pockets. Elsie Mak had arrived. Harriet excused herself and hurried to join her.

Yes, she said. She had known Marcie Denton. Knew her before she was married and after, too. Leslie Taylor? No. Oh, she'd seen her a few times. In the club. Always with Marcie. Kept pretty much to themselves. They'd come in, have a few drinks, a couple of dances, and go home. It was when Marcie came in by herself that she got to talking to her. Got to know her.

"Did she do that often? Come alone?"

"It wasn't a regular thing, if you know what I mean. Now and then. Mostly it would be on a Friday night. Her roomie—that's what she called Taylor, her roomie—she'd be working, and Marcie would get bored."

"Was she. . . ."

"Playing around? Not that I know. She was really hung up on Taylor. All she wanted was some company. It was after. . .after she got married. She'd go home with anybody. Seemed like she was lost."

"Were you involved with her?"

"I slept with her a couple of times. Nothing serious. She was a good kid. I'm sorry about what happened to her. I'd like to see whoever did it get nailed."

"Did she ever talk about leaving her husband?"

"All the time. At first she wanted to take the kids. Twice she did that, and he caught her and brought her back. Then he got a housekeeper who spied on everything she did. Watched the kids like a hawk. That's why they weren't with her."

The music blared. The room pulsed with the pounding beat and shuffle of dancing feet. Harriet's heart raced with its own wild rhythm. "She was running away?"

"Yes. He must have found out. She tried to get me to go with her. Guess she thought it would be safer to be with somebody instead of alone. Maybe it would have been. What she wanted to do was just take off and get lost."

"Then why would she go to Spruce Falls? That was the first place he'd look."

"Nobody was supposed to know she was there. She figured she'd try one last time to get back with Taylor." Pensive, she mused, "I miss seeing her around. She would have given you the shirt off her back. She gave me this . . . for being a friend, she said."

Elsie held out her hand, displaying a birthstone ring. A single pearl, candescent as a tear shed in anger. Expressionless, Harriet stared at the ring. "You've been very helpful, Elsie. Clarence, I'm sure Elsie has better things to do than sit around with us. Are you ready?"

The phrase rang in her ears as they made their way back to the car. *For being a friend.* How good a friend? Good enough to speak for Marcie now that she was gone? To tell this story in court so that the real killer could be found? That would be up to Clarence. He would either have to persuade her or order her to appear.

Out of breath, Clarence scrambled into the car and grumbled, "Why the rush? I thought you were enjoying yourself in there."

"We've got what we came for, Clare." Her face was blank, her voice flat. Her hands on the wheel were steady. There was no outward sign of the adrenaline pouring through her veins, the rush coursing like an electrical charge. "I know who killed Marcie. I don't know how, but I know who. Now all we have to do is prove it."

Chapter Nine

*D*onna typed a final set of instructions for Clarence. Clarence sifted through the masses of information compiled for Harriet. Harriet paced back and forth, sparking the room with energy.

Donna thought: before this is over I'll be cuckoo, a dingdong loony-toon. Clarence thought: she's like a racehorse waiting at the gate. Even the dog knows to stay out of the way. Harriet thought: this is what it must be like on opening night. Either you pull it off, or the roof comes down around your ears.

She felt cold. Clammy. The red cardigan lay over the back of the sofa. She put it on and the chill eased. Tomorrow Nystrom would mount the Bench, strike his gavel, and the case of the Queen versus Taylor would creak into motion. A ponderous affair, this deciding of guilt or innocence. Jury selection could run into a week. Prior to that selection, Nystrom would speak to the pool of jurors. When the panel of twelve was chosen, he would deliver his instructions. Then it would be Frost's turn. It would be days before the first witness was called and the actual proceedings got underway, days that Leslie would sit exposed—an object of curiosity, whispers, innuendo.

Had Harriet done the right thing? Perhaps she'd been wrong to insist they remain in Spruce Falls. To allow Nystrom to preside. Perhaps she should have concentrated on deemphasizing the homosexual angle rather than placing it front and center. Perhaps she should have taken Leslie, Clarence, Donna, into her confidence, shared her suspicions with them instead of keeping them in the dark. Perhaps her whole strategy was wrong.

As of late this afternoon, Leslie was in better shape for the trial than she was. They had spent most of the day together. Under the jaundiced eye of Mrs. Klyk—who said a hairdresser was not a lawyer and she would not, by all the saints, be put out of her rightful place by the likes of such—Leslie had her hair shampooed, trimmed, and set. Afterward, she had tried on the new outfits purchased by Harriet, but paid for out of Leslie's account. The woolen sheath, supple as silk and brilliant as flame, wrought a miraculous change in mood as well as appearance.

"I've never worn anything like this," she had said. "It's gorgeous."

"So are you." It had slipped out so naturally that by the time Harriet realized what she was going to say, it was already said. Hurriedly, she had turned over the other boxes. A soft heather tweed suit with a slender skirt and cardigan-style jacket, and a classic shirtdress in a rich, buttery shade of caramel. "And there's something else I want you to wear," Harriet had said, handing her the envelope pried loose from the Superintendent's clutches.

Leslie's ring. The ring given her by Marcie and worn until it was removed. She had held it in the palm of her hand, studying it in silence, sadly, and then quickly, as though it caused her pain, had placed it back in the envelope and held it toward Harriet. "I've gotten used to being without it," she had said. And Harriet had replied, "I want you to wear it. Later you can do as you wish. But until I say otherwise, I want you to wear it."

Leslie had been in good spirits, as eager as Harriet for the trial to begin. Was she going through the same last-minute jitters? With Josie back on the street, released two weeks ago, she had no one to confide in. Alone. Confined. It would be harder for her to stay up.

"Clare." The bottled nervous energy spilled over. "You're sure Elsie Mak will show?" Yes. She was under subpoena. She'd be here. "The people who stayed at the Dalton?" Yes, Harriet. There had been four days between the removal of the seal on Unit Three and the Sunday when he checked in. The previous occupants were all local. All available and willing to tell what little they knew.

One by one, they went through the list of witnesses, lay and expert. Clarence had done a thorough job, had talked to scores of people, even those only remotely connected. From schoolgirl friends of Marcie's, to Fiona Black, Charlie's secretary who had known and liked her employer's wife, he had collected stray bits of information with the diligence of a squirrel storing nuts. Some of that information would be useless; some would be helpful; some, he feared, downright dangerous. The homosexual stuff, for instance. He'd gone to the Coalition for Gay Rights as Harriet instructed. He'd talked to a Christine Donald, who delivered unto him literature and leads and the assurance that being gay was quite o.k. and did not lead to pathological disorder. Which may all be well and good for someone buttressed by an active gay community, but mere whistling in the dark when it came to places like Spruce Falls.

He had tried before, without success. Now, when it was almost too late for a revised strategy, he tried one last time. "This is a murder trial, Harriet. You don't need all these people talking about homosexuality. That's not at issue. You've got your priorities all mixed up."

"You think I can't see the forest for the trees, don't you?" Ordinarily she would have blown up. Instead, she flashed an enigmatic smile.

"I think . . . . ," a pause before the plunge, "you're too emotionally involved in this one." He knew her so well, knew Charlie so well—the type, not the person. Whether she won or lost, Charles Denton would be intent on destroying her. In oblique warning, he recited, "My candle burns at both ends. It will not last the night."

"You forgot the rest, Clare." The smile now was as close to mischievous as a Croft smile could be. "*But oh my foes and ah, my friends, it gives a w-o-n-d-r-o-u-s light.*" Penned for an earlier generation by the morose Edna St. Vincent Millay, the bit of verse took on a new dimension for Harriet. Not a few throwaway lines strung together because they happened to rhyme, but a proud, defiant challenge. A challenge and a blueprint for the future.

Balance restored, she made out a check and handed it to Clare. "We can manage without you for a couple of days. I want you to fly to Toronto in the morning, rent a car, and drive back here." His eyes widened in protest as she explained what she wanted him to do. "And one other thing," a quick diversion to forestall argument, "See if you can have this preserved. Under glass would probably be best."

Picked lifeless from the base of the nesting tree, the object cupped in her hand was as light as air and fragile as a cobweb. Two broad wings. Two smaller wings. A needle-thin body. A specimen as near perfect in death as it had been in life. "Tell them," she said, "that it is a *Danaus plexippus*. That it's a gift for someone special."

A butterfly, Clarence thought, an ordinary butterfly. If you asked him, Harriet Fordham Croft, attorney-at-law, was on the verge of sliding off the wall.

Coiled for battle, Harriet waited for Leslie to be brought in.

No handcuffs, she had warned, and Yarrow had said smugly, "While she is in our custody, she is our responsibility." Harriet had guessed his intention from the offhand reply and knew that he did, indeed, plan to bring Leslie in with cuffs and heavy escort. What better way to create the impression that this slender young woman had a propensity for violence, that she was a felon now held securely by the hands of the law. Harriet had addressed him with a calmness she did not feel. "If I see anything that is prejudicial to my client, anything that hints at bias on the part of this court or the officers of this court, I will claim grounds for a mistrial." The inspector had said nothing, indicated nothing. She would not know to whom the victory in this opening skirmish was due until Leslie actually appeared—with or without restraint.

Already the courtroom was packed, as it had been for the earlier session when Leslie abruptly decided to forego bail. There were an equal number of bodies, although some of the faces were different. Charles was not there. Clarence had learned from Fiona that he would skip the first two days because he was finalizing the design for a major land development scheme. The Taylors, too, were absent. Harriet had suggested they spare themselves the tedious process of selecting a jury. But the Bergstroms were present, a solid reminder of what this trial was about. And Josie, unfamiliar in her civvies. And Haberdash Poulis, who had made a point of strolling over to the defense table and wishing her luck. The resentment in his darting black eyes made it plain that she would need a lot more than luck for this one.

Frost, seated at the table to her right with Yarrow and Moore, was busily arranging papers in neat stacks. He picked up one of the sheets, glanced at it, and ambled toward Harriet. "Our witnesses, Harriet."

She ran through the names, conscious of him standing there—expectant. "Thank you, Jeremy." He continued to wait. "Thank you," she said again, wanting to get rid of him.

"What about yours? You do intend to call witnesses?" He

had heard she excelled at cross-examination. Was it possible she meant to rely on nothing more than her expertise and the old wives' notion of innocence till guilt was proved without a shadow of a doubt? Ah, how the mighty tended to do themselves in.

"We have a number of witnesses."

"May I have the list?"

"No."

What a pain she was. Hand outstretched, affability frozen, he said stiffly, "It's customary for the defense to make this information available, Mrs. Croft."

"Customary, Mr. Frost. Not obligatory."

Before he had time to reply, a current ran through the room, the charged hush preceding the arrival of each principal. Frost retreated. Harriet, transfixed, watched the door through which Leslie would enter.

The knob turned. The crack widened. Leslie stepped into the room. A gasp went up from the spectators. Harriet felt a sharp triumph mixed with relief. She was not in handcuffs; she was not under heavy guard.

With a male officer on one side, and Mrs. Klyk on the other, the slender figure paused in the doorway, eyes searching for Harriet. In the red dress, hair glistening and pallor eased by a blush of make-up, she was vibrantly alive and radiantly beautiful. Her eyes met Harriet's, she smiled, and Harriet, smiling back, thought, I must remember to tell her not to smile, not to appear to treat this matter lightly.

"You didn't tell me," Donna said, and Harriet, who had forgotten that she was at her side, custodian of the data unearthed by Clarence, still looking at Leslie, said, "What? Didn't tell you what, Donna?"

"That she's so. . .so attractive. She could have anyone she wanted. I don't believe she's a lesbian at all."

Harriet glanced at Donna and thought, wherever have you been all these years? and said matter-of-factly, "Ah, but she is. That's one thing we're going to make absolutely clear."

Leslie, standing behind that narrow door, had steeled herself to step through it into the spotlight, on display like those poor unfortunates huckstered in side shows. But the door opened and she stepped through and Harriet was there, her smile a dazzling shield that blocked out the curious stares and muttered whisperings.

She saw Donna speak, saw Harriet turn to her with a look of bemusement, saw the smile fade and the fine features set in steely determination. And she knew that whatever lay ahead, she would not face it alone.

The jury was finally in place. Thanks to the profile of the ideal jurist submitted by the psychologist Christine Donald recommended, Harriet had managed to weed out most of what might be termed undesirable.

Allowed four challenges, Frost had used only two—striking a male hairdresser and an elderly female librarian who said she had never married because she had never met anyone fit to marry. The accompanying sniff had sealed her fate. Harriet, with twelve challenges to the Crown's four, had used her full quota. Blue-collar laborers were out, although there were a couple she might have passed were the stakes not so high. Also eliminated were a middle-aged married woman who, when asked what she thought of marital rape, said there wasn't any such thing; a married man who had seen Leslie's documentary on wife battering and pronounced it "yellow journalism at its worst"; and a young man so determinedly heterosexual that he would hang Leslie by the noose of his own impulses.

Go for professionals, the psychologist had said. The more education, the better. Stay away from the traditional family types, the macho men and apple-pie-and-cookies women who have their needles stuck in the past. And so, with criteria in hand, she had passed on people she would ordinarily have accepted, and accepted people she would have exempted. A nurse. An accountant. A high school teacher. Of all things, a minister. Sensing that Frost and Yarrow were first astonished and then enthralled by her lunacy, she had crossed her fingers and hoped this Donald person wasn't a ninny and the psychologist knew whereof he spoke and she, Harriet Croft, wasn't blowing the most important trial of her life right off the top.

Nystrom, wrapped securely in his robe of authority, closed his opening instructions to the jury with the hours he planned to sit. Ten in the morning to four-thirty in the afternoon. A midmorning recess at about eleven-thirty. Lunch at one. From two-thirty to four-thirty without recess. "I now call on Crown Counsel to address you."

It was a few minutes after eleven o'clock. Would Frost begin only to break off as he was beginning to hit his stride? No, Harriet decided. He'll ask that we recess now. Within seconds the prosecutor was on his feet requesting that today's intermission be put forward. Predictable. As predictable as Nystrom's amiable assent.

From the corner of her eye, Harriet saw Mrs. Klyk bearing down on them. "Did you manage to get a decent night's sleep?" A hurried question, answered by Leslie with a nod as she was led out.

"Those things he said to the jury," Donna said, referring to Nystrom, "he was reading them."

"He didn't read far enough." Harriet's voice held the rustle of dried leaves. "He omitted to tell them about not being swayed by indignation or prejudice. Make a note to remind me."

Having secured a seat, the spectators remained resolutely in place. Not so the reporters who, assured of their space, rushed up the aisle to mingle and smoke and pick brains in the corridor. They swarmed around Harriet as she emerged, firing a fusillade of questions and comment. Do you intend to plead insanity? Is it true Mrs. Denton and Miss Taylor were more than friends? Will your client take the stand? And, from a woman with microphone and shoulder-slung tape recorder, a sly, "Are you hoping that this new feminine image will put down the rumors about your client, Mrs. Croft?"

"I have no statement," Harriet said pleasantly, making a mental note that the woman with the mike would bear watching. She remembered seeing her at the bail hearing. And the woman obviously remembered the stubborn, sullen, defiant Leslie of those few months before. Given the contrast between then and now, the comment was understandable.

She returned to the courtroom, the order was given to rise, Nystrom swept on stage, and Frost rose to his feet with a clutch of poster-size sheets under his arm. On the wall next to the jury box, working rapidly against Harriet's expected objection, he pinned the blowups of Marcie's body in full view of the court.

Leslie looked at the picture of Marcie on the bed and began to cry. The reporters strained forward. The spectators recoiled in horror. Sven Bergstrom uttered a loud curse, and Anna Bergstrom wept openly. Harriet neither objected nor turned away.

In a voice cracking with emotion, Frost told of Marcie's childhood, what she meant to her family, what she and they had planned for her future. "Until," he thundered, "she met the accused. From that point on, her life was doomed." Leslie Taylor, he said, lured the younger girl away from family and friends, introduced her to an alien and aberrant lifestyle. When Marcie at last made her escape through her marriage to a successful and highly respected member of the architectural profession, Leslie Taylor, in a fit of jealous, impotent rage, struck her, killed her, desecrated her body in an act of revenge—a final unspeakable indignity aimed at Charles Denton through this woman he had loved.

He named the witnesses he would present, the evidence on exhibit, said that the pivotal piece of evidence in support of motive was a letter which would be read to the court. The key elements in a case of this nature, he explained, are motive and opportunity. Here we have both.

The hands on the clock showed 1:00 p.m. He had spoken without interruption for one-and-a-half hours. Ninety eloquent minutes, during which he had moved many of the women to tears and most of the men to anger. A superb performance timed to the second.

Harriet, conscious of Leslie at her side, earlier poise shattered and emotions frayed, said crisply, "I want you to have lunch. And a rest. And try to put this out of your mind."

Leslie stared at her blankly. Lunch. Open your mouth. Fill it with food, chew, swallow. Something you did when your world was right side up. How could anyone think of food in the presence of those obscene posters, those graphic visuals that the eye absorbed but the mind could not.

Barely conscious of Mrs. Klyk's hand on her arm, she felt a deep, engulfing shame mix with the pain. She had looked on this trial as an exposé, an uncovering of a secret part of herself that she had wrapped in batting and kept hidden for years. She had seen herself as the principal figure in a sordid drama. Well, the drama was sordid, but it was not her drama. And the love, if love were the cause, was twisted and unnatural. But it was not her love. And she was not the principal figure. That tragic role belonged to Marcie.

Harriet stood up, her manner unusually brusque. She could imagine the impact of those blowups, the effect they must have had—would continue to have—on her client. "We'd better have something to eat, too. It's going to be a rocky afternoon."

"Couldn't you have stopped him from showing those pictures?" Donna asked, as they crossed the street to the nearest restaurant. "They were horrible."

"I could have. They were highly inflammatory."

Inflammatory? That was an understatement. Donna looked at Harriet accusingly. "Then why didn't you?"

"Because I wanted everyone to see them."

"Leslie Taylor, too?"

"No," Harriet admitted. "But it couldn't be helped."

"It wiped her out. She's not going to be able to take it."

"She can take it," Harriet said. "She'll have to. This is only the beginning."

Dr. Frederick Spellman was as gaunt and cadaverous as the

bodies on the slabs in his morgue. As Spruce Fall's medical examiner, he had taken part in more trials than most lawyers. An experienced witness, Spellman was crusty, didactic, and unaccustomed to having his opinions treated as opinions—which they were—rather than fact—which they frequently weren't. Marcie Denton, he said, suffered a stellate fracture above the right ear, a break in the bone with a surround of star-shaped extensions. The resultant brain damage and swelling had caused her death.

There had also, he said, been severe trauma around the vagina and a degree of internal pelvic hemorrhage. Asked by Frost to explain this in more detail, he told of the penetration by a blunt object, trauma to the rectum and anus, the torn colon and resulting bruising and bleeding of tissues in the middle area of the body. There was extensive tearing of the vaginal wall, lacerations of the rectal wall, and substantial distortion of the buttocks and anal area.

It was a learned and scholarly dissertation, an academic exercise delivered in a voice as dry as dust. A female juror asked to be excused and was led from the courtroom, retching. Mrs. Bergstrom fainted. Judge Nystrom pounded for order and called a brief recess. Dr. Spellman looked puzzled by the fuss and bother. Harriet poured a glass of water and handed it to Leslie with a white tablet. "It's phenobarbital," she said. "Take it. It will help."

Leslie drank the water but refused the sedative. "I'll be all right." She didn't look all right. Her skin was pasty, and it took both hands to hold the water glass.

"Try to think of something else. Try not to listen. This is the worst part. Once it's over it won't be so bad."

Donna was almost as disturbed as Leslie. Harriet had allowed the showing of the photographs, magnified and in full color. She had allowed the minute description of the violation of Marcie's body. How much more would she allow before being moved to act? How much longer would this ghoul be on the stand?

Five minutes ticked by. Ten minutes. Harriet watched the clock impatiently, pen flipping through her fingers. She wanted to complete her cross-examination of Spellman and be done with him. One day of this was about all Leslie could take. The session finally resumed with the witness moving from cause of death to time of death. This, he estimated, occurred shortly after 3:00 p.m. on Saturday, July 12. The statement struck Leslie with the force of a hammer blow. Fingers gripping the edge of the table, she looked helplessly at Harriet. It was at three o'clock that she had knocked at Marcie's door and waited for the answer that didn't come.

"Rigor mortis was showing the first signs of fading." Spellman's monologue was not quite over. "Also," a brief pause to impress upon his listeners that although not scientific, this closing remark was nevertheless pertinent, "Mrs. Denton's watch had not run down. It was still keeping time. Accurate time."

Frost turned him over to Harriet, and she rose and said lightly, "Are we to assume, Doctor, that in addition to your other accomplishments you are also an authority on watchmaking?"

"No, Mrs. Croft, but it hardly requires expertise to determine whether or not a timepiece is keeping time." There was a slight arching of the eyebrows and a smile at the jury, who dutifully smiled back.

Harriet granted him the point and stood there as though trying to get her mind on track. Tall, slender, striking, slightly befuddled. "What exactly is rigor mortis, Dr. Spellman?"

The woman really was a simpleton. Looking down from the twin heights of physical elevation and superior knowledge, he spelled it out, spacing each word so that she would be sure to understand. "It is the stiffening of the body after death."

"But what is it exactly? Why does it occur?"

"The muscle protein coagulates." What difference did it make? Wasn't it enough that it happened? Next she'd be asking him to explain what protein was.

She wanted an explanation, yes. But not of protein. "Can you tell us, briefly, what an autopsy consists of? The steps you go through?"

"Well . . . .," he would have to put it in lay terms, keep it as simple as possible, "you open the body." His finger ran down his torso. "You remove the organs. Weigh them. Measure them. Take tissue samples. Test the blood for alcohol or barbiturates."

"Unembalmed?"

"Naturally."

"The organs that are removed—in a case of homicide, they would be saved for further study? The liver and kidney? The stomach and small intestine?"

"In most cases, yes."

"You've earned quite a reputation in your field. I imagine you work with the most up-to-date equipment. Forensics has come a long way in the last few years, hasn't it?"

Tell that to the city. Maybe it would help get that budget increase he wanted. Still, he did a creditable job with what he had. "We have made strides."

"For blood tests—what equipment do you use for that?" Bless Clarence for telling her everything she'd never wanted to know about this gruesome business.

Spellman hesitated. It was becoming more difficult to keep this simple. "A spectrometer. That's standard, Mrs. Croft."

"Not a chromatograph?"

Damn the woman. She had the greenest, most hypnotic eyes he had ever seen. The spectrometer, which used ultraviolet rays and filter paper to analyze liquid blood, depended for accuracy on the skill of the technician. The gas chromatograph measured gas emitted from heated blood and recorded this information directly onto a graph. It was said to be one hundred percent accurate. "No," he admitted, "we do not have a GC machine." What difference did it make? The cause of death was a blow to the head, not something in the blood stream.

"Do you have a transmission electron microscope? Are you equipped with electromagnetic lenses—or are you still using the old glass lenses?"

"Our microscopes are capable of magnifying up to twenty-five hundred times. That is sufficient for. . . ."

"It hardly compares with computerized magnification, does it Doctor? The scanning electron microscope, for instance. Is it not true that it not only has a capability of projecting in three dimensions, it also magnifies up to fifty thousand times the specimen size? From twenty-five hundred to fifty thousand is a substantial leap. You do have an SEM?"

"Not at present. That is a very sophisticated piece of. . . ."

"Much too sophisticated for widespread use. We understand, Dr. Spellman. Histopathology, serology, odontology. Even anthropology. Not only is it possible to tell race, sex and age from nothing but a skeleton, it is also possible to recreate facial features on a skull."

"Objection," Frost hissed. "This line of questioning is irrelevant."

"It *is* irrelevant," Leslie whispered to Donna. "I don't know what she's talking about."

"She isn't talking about anything." Donna had watched Harriet in action often enough to follow her train of thought. "She's trying to destroy his credibility."

"Sustained," Nystrom ruled. "Please stick to the facts, Counselor. This is a courtroom, not a lecture hall."

"Getting back to rigor mortis. Over what period of time does this take place?"

Spellman relaxed. Back to comfortable ground at last. "It's progressive. The first stage will commence within three to six hours. At this time of year, full rigor will be reached after twelve hours. Fading begins in eighteen to twenty hours, after which, there is a return of mobility."

"And what is taking place during this process is—to use your words—a coagulation of muscle protein?"

"That is correct."

"Would it be fair to say that the amount of body muscle and fat could affect the time required for that coagulation?"

"I suppose it's possible, but. . . ."

"You also used the phrase *at this time of year*. This would indicate that environmental conditions must also be considered?"

"There are a number of variables which must be considered, Mrs. Croft. That is where experience and training come in." His smile was pure condescension.

"Is it not also true that the most accurate test of time of death is the digestive process? That digestion ceases abruptly at the moment of death? You removed the internal organs. Did you make a determination based on the contents of the stomach?"

"Not knowing when Mrs. Denton had last eaten, or what she had eaten, there was no way of telling. . ."

"Are you aware that rigor mortis, depending on temperature, humidity, etcetera, has been know to last up to forty-eight hours?"

"In the month of July, Mrs. Croft, that is highly unlikely."

"Ah yes. Unlikely in July. Possible in early spring or late fall. And of course, Doctor, all of these theories go out the window if a body happens to be frozen."

"This body was not frozen, Mrs. Croft."

"Objection."

"Sustained."

"I was merely trying to demonstrate how many factors are involved here, Your Lordship." Harriet beamed at Nystrom. At Spellman. "Thank you, Doctor. You've been very helpful."

Dismissed, Spellman stepped down with a curt nod to Frost and a lofty disregard of Harriet.

The first day of testimony was over. It had been a bad day for Leslie, even worse than Harriet had anticipated. The impact of the photographs, the grizzly autopsy report—alone in her cell, the phrases and images would resurface. "Would you like a couple of these to take back with you? To help you sleep?" She extended the bottle of phenobarb.

"I wouldn't get them past the showers." Making a stab at humor, she added, "I can see you've never been strip-searched. Mrs. Klyk is an expert." Harriet blushed and Leslie, hearing the innocent remark as it must have sounded to Harriet, blushed in return. Changing the subject, she said, "He hurt us, didn't he? When he said it . . . it happened . . . at three o'clock?"

"He didn't say that, Leslie."

"Harriet, don't you remember? He said the time of death was approximately three o'clock. Donna, you heard him."

The green eyes were as cool and clear as a mountain lake. "You and Donna may think that's what he said. He may think that's what he said. But that's not what I heard him say." And then Mrs. Klyk materialized, Leslie was being led away, the door was closing, and Harriet was left staring at the space she had occupied and thinking of the hours that lay ahead on that cot, in that cell block, in that grim building.

Joe had pulled up in front and was waiting to drive them back to the house. "The money this is costing, you could buy yourself a car."

"She has a car," Donna said. "She does ninety in school zones. We're safer with you."

"I've never had a ticket," Harriet objected.

"That's because they're afraid to give you one." Donna's voice was a mixture of affection and admiration. "Too bad you weren't with us today, Joe. She did a number on your medical examiner that had his hair standing on end."

"On Spellman? I'd like to have seen that. He's a tough nut. Doesn't get much flak from anyone around here." He wheeled the cab into Leslie's drive and jumped out to hold the door. "Looks like you've got company."

The front door was open and Duchess was leashed to the porch. "Thank goodness. I was beginning to think he got lost." She was referring to Clarence who had been gone considerably longer than expected.

It was indeed Clarence. And Emily Taylor. And Adam. The kitchen smelled of fresh bread and roast beef and warm apple pie. The dining room table was set for five. Clarence was arranging cut flowers in a crystal vase; Adam Taylor was supervising. "We thought you might need a little cheering up." Emily tried to smile, but her eyes were searching, anxious.

"You shouldn't have bothered." The Taylors had enough worries of their own without bothering about their daughter's lawyer.

"That's what I said." Clarence jammed the remaining flowers into the vase. "You look as though you've been through a wringer."

"She looks wonderful." Emily relieved Harriet of her bag and briefcase. "She always looks wonderful."

"That's just on the outside." Clarence winked at Harriet then busied himself pouring her a drink. "Here. I'll talk to you while you change."

Adam and Emily looked startled. "It's all right," Donna said. "They do this all the time." The Taylors looked alarmed. "He sits in the corner facing the wall, closes his eyes, and holds his hands over them," said Harriet.

"I'm really a sheep in wolf's clothing," Clarence confided. "I think my hormones are out of whack."

Uncertain, the Taylors looked at Harriet and Donna and Clarence and then at each other, and then Emily laughed and the rest joined in. "I suppose we seem awfully old-fashioned." Coming from Adam, the remark was surprising.

In the bedroom, with the door closed, she said, "Whatever possessed you to make that crack about hormones? You said that deliberately."

"I did. I figure a bit of gentle indoctrination now will keep them from flipping their lids later. I still think it's a mistake to drag in the gay issue."

"Sit in the corner, face the wall, close your eyes, pull your sweater over your head," Harriet sing-songed. "Do you realize they probably think we've turned their daughter's house into a sin bin?"

I should be so lucky, Clarence thought. He closed his eyes and listened to the rustle of fabric. "I'm sorry it took so long."

"That's okay. Did you get it?"

He felt the mattress dip from her weight as she sat beside him, opened his eyes, handed her an envelope. "Where did you get those pants? They look as though they're out of a rag bag."

"They're Leslie's," she said absent-mindedly, skimming the envelope with her thumbnail. "Duchess likes me to wear them." God. Talk about going to the dogs. Bright, brilliant, beautiful, sophisticated. And getting nuttier than a fruitcake. "There's something I've been meaning to say to. . . ."

Harriet was reading, not listening. Suddenly, without warning, she threw her arms around him, shouted eureka at the top of her lungs, and rolled both of them off the end of the bed and into a heap on the floor. The door flew open. Duchess bounded into the room. Behind her, Donna. Behind Donna, framed in the opening, Emily with her mouth open. Behind Emily, Adam rooted in disbelief.

Twined in Harriet's arms and pinned by her body, Clarence, dazed by behavior so completely out of character, said feebly, "We were just discussing the case."

"I see," Adam said. "Perhaps you'd rather be alone for a while," Emily said, backing into her husband.

"No, don't go." Harriet rolled off Clarence and sat beside him, hugging Duchess who had romped forward ready to play. "We're going to celebrate." She pulled Clarence to his feet and brushed him off. "Somebody get this man a Coke. He has this day done us all an extraordinary service."

It was, they would say later, a memorable evening. The kind of evening that can happen, but can never be planned. Yet each would remember it differently. It was, in Adam's mind, the night before his first venture into the courtroom where his daughter stood trial for her life. For Emily, it was an oasis in a landscape grown bleak and frightening. Donna would think of it as the night Harriet let her hair down, after which she was never quite the same. Clarence would feel again the pressure of Harriet's body—see her in Leslie's reading chair, head thrown back in laughter, after-dinner brandy in hand, Duchess at her feet. And for Harriet it was the night when the puzzle was narrowed to the last piece save one.

The Taylors had arrived early. They were seated behind the defense table on the side of the room opposite to the Bergstroms. Harriet noticed them immediately. She did not notice Charles until Clarence whispered, "Charlie Boy is here. And up to no good."

Standing against the wall with Moore and Yarrow, back to the room and deep in conversation, Charles was unaware of their arrival until Yarrow put his hand on his arm and nodded in their direction. He came forward then, body erect, shoulders rigid. "You're looking well, Harriet." He managed to make the compliment sound like a death threat.

"So are you, Charles." Not elegant in the way Moore was elegant, Charles nonetheless was an imposing figure. Faultlessly tailored, linen crisp and tie subdued but expensive, he would pass for a fashion layout of the man at the top.

"There is no need to tell you how disappointed I am to see you here?" The lines around his mouth deepened, and his nostrils pinched with displeasure.

"I'm sorry you feel that way. You build buildings. I defend innocent people. It's as simple as that."

"Innocent people." His voice seethed with menace. The air around him vibrated with sinister energy. "You'll regret this, Harriet. If you're wise, you'll withdraw from this case. Mr. Poulis was smart enough to see it. I'm surprised you aren't."

The clerk called his order to rise as Clarence was preparing to thrust himself in front of Harriet as protection. A round-faced young man with horn-rimmed glasses and long sideburns was first up. His name was Buddy Jim, the forensic technician who had examined the room at the Dalton. He assured the court that the contents of the room were not disturbed. There was no trace evidence to speak of. Very little blood, and what there was belonged to the victim. No telltale fibers. No fingerprints. No hair.

"Actually," Harriet said as she began her cross, "there was quite a bit of hair, wasn't there?"

There was, he admitted, but it, too, belonged to the victim.

He had vacuumed it from the body, the bed, the floor around the bed. It was then bagged and tagged. No, of course he had not examined each hair. You could see at a glance that it was identical. It was so pale, so fine, that a foreign strand would be visible to the naked eye.

Fingerprints? Of course he didn't mean there were no prints in the room. There were none that had not been eliminated. None that related to the crime. What method did he use? The standard method. Dusting. Fingerprints are oily. Fine, dry powder clings. Voila, a readable print.

Rapid-fire, Harriet asked if he had checked the body for prints, the drapes, the bedding. Was it not true that dusting was effective on hard surfaces only, that only ten percent of prints fluoresce naturally which means they are invisible to the eye which means you might easily overlook the one place you should be dusting? Did he not fume with gas to raise and fix these elusive leave-behinds? Was he not aware that there were techniques using lasers, magna brushes, luminol that could lift prints from soft surfaces—from skin, fabric, even vegetables and the insides of rubber gloves?

"Objection. Counsel is badgering the witness."

"Sustained."

"You vacuumed for trace evidence. How thorough were you, Buddy Jim?"

"Very thorough."

"Did you move the bed? Vacuum underneath it?"

"Well . . . I . . . ."

"Objection." Frost was on his feet. Yarrow was half out of his seat. Nystrom looked undecided.

"Did you, Buddy Jim?"

"Objection. Your Honor, the witness has said that he checked the scene thoroughly."

"Sustained."

Harriet walked back to the defense table, smiled at Leslie, took the kraft envelope from Clarence. "Your Lordship, I have here tracings of impressions found under the bed which I contend were made by the person responsible for this crime. . . ."

"Objection."

"Photographs of these prints, with a copy of the *Spruce Falls News* dated Monday, July 22, on which date this room was occupied by my assistant, Clarence Crossley."

"Objection. A week later. This is not relevant."

"I wish to enter this material in evidence."

Frost was apoplectic. "Counsel is engaging in speculation. Creating a smokescreen. This is unheard of. Dozens of people had time to go through that room. Your Honor, I object."

Nystrom's gavel was in midair, about to crack down in Frost's favor. Quickly, knowing she had only a split second before being ruled out of order, Harriet held up the long, silvery hair that had once grown on Marcie's head. Twisting, shimmering under the light, it drew a gasp from the spectators and a nervous wriggle from Buddy Jim. With the prosecution's Exhibit A in one hand, and the single strand in the other, she held the two up for inspection. As Buddy Jim had said, you did not have to be an expert to see that this hair came from the same source as those in the clear plastic bag. "It was found," Harriet said quietly, "on the rug near the toe marks. Clearly both had been overlooked in the initial search."

The gavel descended. "Objection overruled." The items were approved and placed in evidence. Recess was called, with Inspector Yarrow first up after the break.

The Taylors took advantage of the lull to join Leslie. It was the first time since she'd been arrested that they were able to get within touching distance. Emily hugged her, and Adam, gruffly uncomfortable, asked her how she was and said that she looked nice and they were looking forward to having her home.

The fact that he was here, that he had summoned the courage to walk to the front of the room, in full view, was an improvement, Harriet thought. She was pleased by the gesture, the statement it made to those watching. Even more pleased when he leaned over and kissed Leslie's cheek before the couple returned to their seats.

"He hates me," Leslie said.

"Your father? That's ridiculous. He loves you."

"Not Dad. Inspector Yarrow. Look at him, Harriet. He can't wait to get at me."

"That's fine. I can't wait to get at him, either."

Yarrow crossed to the stand with the slow moving force of a bulldozer. Seated, he stared down at the Defense with a cold, implacable hatred. Conscious of Leslie trembling, Harriet whispered, "Imagine him up there with nothing on. Naked." The image of frontal nudity worked. Leslie's trembling stopped, her clenched hands relaxed.

Frost led his star witness through a description of the room as he found it. The body as he found it. The precision and skill of the men under him. The cases successfully solved, the reputation thus earned.

Harriet smiled at the extemporaneous fence mending. Her handling of Spellman and Buddy Jim must have been more damaging than she thought. Yarrow was moving now to the arrest of Leslie. Her attitude. The demand to see a lawyer. Not accused, not charged. Yet she wanted a lawyer. Her behavior was indicative of guilt. No mention of the letter. But then, Harriet reminded herself, it was picked up in Toronto, not in Spruce Falls, so it would come later.

Frost stepped aside and Harriet rose, leisurely, walked towards Yarrow, leisurely, imagined him sitting there with bare rump glued to the chair, bare chest covered with hair, muscles and middle bulging. "You once worked with Miss Taylor."

Yarrow was momentarily taken aback. In place of the cold hostility he had expected, he saw an amused smile. The woman actually seemed to be laughing at him. Well, he'd give her something to laugh about, and damn soon. "Not *with* her, no. I merely provided her with information."

"For a documentary on wife beating. You didn't approve of that documentary, did you?"

"I don't approve of making mountains out of molehills."

"You don't approve of beaten women, either. I don't mean the beating of women, Inspector. I mean the women who are beaten."

Yarrow turned to Nystrom for help. The judge obliged. "Counsel is confusing the witness. Will you reword the question."

"I'm sorry, Your Honor. It wasn't really a question. The fact is, Inspector, that you don't much care for women, do you?"

"I don't like women who kill other women. No, I don't."

Harriet considered having the remark stricken from the record, changed her mind, said instead, "Following Miss Taylor's arrest, you made a point of saying to her that you were speaking on *even* terms."

"I believe the phrase was *equal* terms."

"What did you mean by that?"

"It's a figure of speech."

"Taken, I believe, from the rules drawn up by British judges in 1918. What are those rules, Inspector?"

Again, he turned to Nystrom. "I'm not a lawyer, Your Honor." A faint smile for the jury. "Merely an officer of the law who does his duty as he sees fit."

"Those rules were set for officers of the law, Inspector. Not for lawyers. Or judges. They were drawn up for men like you. To ensure the proper treatment of prisoners. Among other things, they require that before being questioned, those in custody must be warned that anything they say can be used against them. When, after hours of questioning, you told my client that you were speaking on equal terms—that was your way of getting around those rules, wasn't it? Although she had been in your custody since early morning, you were attempting to create the fiction that you had just been having a friendly visit. You were covering yourself?"

Yarrow leaned forward. The threatening pose, instead of intimidating the bothersome woman as it was intended to do, triggered another smile of amusement. He looked down at his tie to see if perchance he'd worn the one with the spot on it. "Those rules have been revised, Mrs. Croft."

"Ah yes, the New Rules. A prisoner is not a prisoner until you decide she is. A person is not in custody until the moment a charge is laid. Unfortunately, we don't have a Miranda ruling to protect people like my client. We do not have the right to be cautioned. But we do have the right to a lawyer. Or is that outdated, too?"

"She called a lawyer."

"And you felt that was an indication of guilt?"

"I did. I do. A person with nothing to hide doesn't start off asking for a lawyer. That's not what happens."

That was exactly how it had happened with that nurse in Toronto who was accused of killing babies. She refused to speak until she saw a lawyer. The refusal was construed as guilt, she was charged, the investigation was halted, the charges were dropped for lack of evidence, the real killer—if such existed— was never found.

"You arrested Miss Taylor shortly after the finding of the body. Surely one of the shortest investigations on record?"

"We don't believe in wasting time." He had hoped she'd mention how quickly they zeroed in. A speedy solution made the department look good.

"And time is crucial, isn't it? Every day that goes by makes it more difficult to follow a trail? Easier for the guilty party to cover his tracks?"

"That's true."

"Naturally, once you had Miss Taylor in custody, you didn't bother to look further?"

"Naturally."

Harriet gave him one last, amused glance, turned away, then said abruptly, "No further questions."

Yarrow stepped down. He was pleased with himself. Even mildly pleased with the attorney for the defense. The slashing attack he expected hadn't materialized. The woman had actually been rather pleasant. At least she knew enough not to push her luck. To back off when she met her match.

Over lunch, Clarence accused her of "letting that bastard off too easy." Unperturbed, she finished her small steak and ordered pumpkin pie for dessert. "You're not listening," he complained. "What's the matter with you? You never used to eat like that."

"I'm hungry. It must be all this fresh air."

"Fresh air? That's sulphur, not fresh air. There's more pollution here than in the city."

"Maybe sulphur is good for you. Sulphur and brimstone."

"Speaking of brimstone—you had Yarrow on the hot seat. You could have fried him."

"The man with the one-track mind. He said what I wanted him to say. Forget about Yarrow. Think about Moore. He's next on tap."

"Speak of the devil. He just walked in. Moore and Yarrow, Frost and Charles. Are you ready to leave?"

"Donna hasn't finished her coffee." Donna drained the cup in a gulp. "You still have some Coke." Clarence drained the can and crushed it. "I thought I'd have another piece of pie."

Clarence picked up the tab and said, "Do as you like. Donna and I are leaving."

"That's one way to get you to pay, Clare." Harriet followed them out into the bright, crisp autumn day. She shouldn't have teased him. He was worried about Charles, concerned about her. Actually he was edgier than she'd ever seen him. "Clare," she said impulsively, "it's good to have you back. We missed you. And don't worry about Charles. With all these reporters, all this publicity, he'll behave like a perfect gentleman."

"And when it's over? When the trial is over and the reporters are gone, what happens then?"

"We'll worry about that when the time comes."

Donna had some shopping to do. Clarence decided to go with her. Harriet, wanting to review her notes on Doug Moore, returned to the courthouse. She leafed through the report Clarence had prepared, trying to concentrate. Instead, she kept seeing Leslie's face. The high cheekbones. The skin, fine-drawn. The dark eyes, frequently clouded, infrequently warm with laughter.

The hard part was over—that graphic detailing of what had been done to Marcie. Yes, the hard part was over, but the worst part was still to come. Marcie had been exposed physically on Spellman's autopsy table. Leslie would be exposed emotionally, spiritually, with equal precision, by Frost's psychologist. And it was she, Harriet, who had insisted on this public moment of truth. If she was wrong, if she had misjudged Leslie's inner resources, the case might be won, but her client would be destroyed in the process.

"I bought a blouse."

Startled by Donna's voice in her ear, Harriet realized that she had been staring into space for over half an hour. It was time for Leslie to be brought back in. Time for Nystrom to resume his role playing. Klyk made her appearance. Following behind her, Leslie in the heather tweed suit and crepe blouse with ruffled jabot. Simple. Elegant. A neat foil for the preppie Moore.

The machinery slid into motion. Moore was on the stand, solidly masculine in trim slacks and Harris Tweed jacket. Gone, the effete dandy with the chunky bracelet and heavy rings. Gone, the delicate mannerisms. Full-throated and resonant, he recapped much of what Yarrow had said and then shifted to the time spent alone with the accused. He spoke of her state of mind, her depression—a self-directed depression that contained no hint of remorse.

"The witness is yours," Frost said, and Harriet glanced at Leslie and walked toward Moore, saying a silent prayer against what she was about to do. The prosecutor's opening reference to an unnatural relationship had been fleeting. Almost buried. But there was the letter. Any why else the psychologist? With luck, she could contain him. With luck she might enable Leslie to continue her masquerade. With luck. . . .

She looked into Moore's eyes—confident, knowing eyes—and said, "That night, in the cell, the two of you alone, you knew, Sergeant Moore, that Miss Taylor was a lesbian?"

Stunned silence. Then a ripple through the spectators, a straining forward of the reporters, consternation on the Bench, stunned attention from the jury. The mocking confidence in Moore's eyes faded. They were hard now. Hard and round as worn pebbles. "Answer the question, Sergeant. You knew that Miss Taylor was a lesbian?"

"Yes." A lifetime of venom in a single word.

"How did you know? Did she tell you she was?"

"It wasn't necessary." The venom spilled over into his features, twisting the handsome mouth and planing his flesh.

"Was it something in her appearance? Her dress? Her conversation?"

"It was her general attitude."

"I see. What you are telling this court is that you can identify a homosexual by some sixth sense you happen to have." A nervous shifting in the jury box. Murmurs in the audience. A call to order from Nystrom. Harriet allowed herself a quick glance at the Taylors. Immobile, the couple stared straight ahead. Leslie, too, was in control, her face mirroring more interest than apprehension. So far, so good. "Would you say, Sergeant, that I am a lesbian?"

The question triggered another seismic wave.

Moore sensed the trap. If he said no, she was capable of saying she was. If he said yes, she could have him for slander. If he said nothing, he would lose credibility. Where was Frost? Why didn't he object?

"Answer the question, Mr. Moore. Am I a lesbian? Yes or no."

"I'm sure you're in a better position to answer that than I am, Counselor." There. Are you satisfied, Mrs. Croft? When in doubt, turn the table.

"Fair enough. What about him? Would you say he's gay?" Her finger pointed at Yarrow. "Or him?" A swoop toward Frost. "Or Mr. Crossley, my assistant?"

"Objection, Your Honor. This is ludicrous."

"I withdraw the question. You are aware, Sergeant, that the incidence of homosexuality is comparatively high?"

"I am."

"At least one in ten. And if you take Kinsey's bell curve into consideration, much higher. You're familiar with the bell curve?"

"Yes." Short and dour and without explanation.

"That we all possess homosexual tendencies. In greater or lesser degree. That rather than being abnormal, such feelings are completely normal."

"That is open to debate."

Harriet was conscious of a faint flow of empathy from the jury box. At least one member of that panel was with her. The buttoned-up conservative next to the plump woman in the floral print. "Based on your knowledge of the subject, Sergeant, I would like you to indicate the thirty persons in this room who are exclusively homosexual."

A right-and-left turning of heads in the audience. Suspicious glances and pulling away from unfamiliar seatmates. A storm of protest from Frost. A furious warning from Nystrom that if she returned to this line of questioning again, she would be declared in contempt.

Having made her point, one she knew would stick in the minds of everyone present, Harriet returned to the issue of credibility. "Before coming to Spruce Falls you were with the Morality Squad in Toronto?"

Moore showed the first signs of nervousness. Yes, that was true.

He had infiltrated the bathhouses, taken part in the raids carried out with fire axes and crowbars, destroyed the premises, ruined reputations, only to have the bulk of the charges dismissed when finally they were brought to court? Was it not also true that much of his time with the morality squad had been spent spying through a peephole at men who were using the washroom facilities of a major department store? Did he enjoy watching men go to the bathroom? Was it not true that he also engaged in physical entrapment? Had there not been an incident of fondling in a theater, overt masturbation in a hotel washroom? Had not many of his victims been respected family men, men who, aside from these few private moments, led conventional lives? Had he not destroyed, not just these men, but entire families? And isn't it true, Sergeant Moore, that you were paid handsomely for this dubious contribution to society—in one year, over forty thousand dollars in court time alone? "I hope," she said, her voice ringing above the clamor of objections, gavel pounding, uproar from the floor, "I only hope the taxpayers of Spruce Falls can afford you."

It was, Clare said that evening, "vintage Croft. There was a guy on the jury who couldn't take his eyes off you."

"Nobody could take their eyes off her," Donna said. "I didn't know that stuff about everyone being, more or less. You even had me looking around."

"I have a feeling Mr. Moore won't be around much longer." Harriet's face shone with satisfaction. "His picture will be all over the papers. The next time he pulls his limp wrist routine, he's likely to get flattened."

Clarence agreed that Moore's days as gay bait were numbered, but exposing the immorality of enforcement wasn't what this trial was about. "You made him look bad with that stuff about the money, Harriet. But you turned a lot of people off, too."

"Only nine out of ten," Harriet said lightly. "I was so busy with him, I didn't have time to clue in to the reaction."

"If you mean how did Leslie take it, she was O.K. She was a lot better than Charles. And Yarrow. They were ready to go into orbit."

Aware, suddenly, that she was exhausted, Harriet announced she was going to bed. Switching on the lamp in the bedroom, she stood looking down at the block of lucite that held, encased inside, the body and outspread wings of her monarch. In a small town on the outskirts of the city, Clarence had found the one man capable of casting such fragile beauty without damage—encapsulating it as a vivid reminder of a delicate strength that could ride the wind.

Leslie, too, was exhausted. Too exhausted to fall asleep. She closed her eyes and saw Doug Moore on the stand and thought she must have been mad to have considered reaching out to him.

Harriet Fordham Croft. Thinking of her, Leslie felt an easing of tension. Where Marcie had been soft and smooth and yielding, Harriet was fire and ice. The flashing brilliance of a perfectly cut diamond. She was willing to fight for what she believed in. And one of the things she believes in is me, Leslie thought.

The narrow cot, the cell, the bars, receded. She knew that whatever lay ahead, she would survive.

Chapter Ten

Amanda Peak placed Leslie at the scene of the crime, at the time of the crime. Her identification was positive. So was her sense of time. The Blue Jays were playing the Giants. The game had just started. Harriet had no questions.

The handwriting expert positively identified the signature on the letter, still unread before the court, as that of the defendant. Harriet had no questions.

Mrs. Bergstrom spoke of the Marcie that was before "that woman" made her appearance, of the change that came over her daughter, of the sense of relief she shared with her husband when Marcie turned away from "that life" and settled into a normal relationship with Mr. Denton. Charged with emotion, her testimony alternated between fits of weeping and outbursts of naked rage. Harriet knew the pain was real. She only wished that Mrs. Bergstrom had cared enough about Marcie's pain to have given her shelter when she asked for it, rather than turning her away. There were questions she would have asked of Marcie's mother, questions she knew she should ask. But the woman was so distraught, so genuinely torn by grief, that again she said, "No questions."

The three witnesses had taken up the entire day. A day in which Harriet had sat by and done nothing. There is a time to speak and a time to listen, she reminded herself, but she knew that this day had been more difficult for Leslie, harder on her than the furious give-and-take of the day before.

And tomorrow? Two names remained on Frost's list—Charles and Dr. Dunstan, the psychologist. Where Mrs. Bergstrom had the impact of a sledgehammer, Dunstan and Charles would have the cutting edge of a scalpel.

She should spend some time with Leslie. She should drop in on the Taylors. She should go over, once again, the material from the Coalition for Gay Rights. She should do all of these things, but she knew she would do none of them. "Here." She handed Clarence her credit card. "I want you and Donna to have a night on the town." Turning to Leslie, she said, "I'm going to go home and get some sleep. I want you to get to bed early, too." As Mrs. Klyk approached, she leaned close and told her, "Wear the silk dress tomorrow." The soft shade of butterscotch would not emphasize her pallor if she paled under Charlie's malevolent gaze or Dunstan's clinical dissection of her psyche.

Joe drove Harriet home where she fed Duchess, made herself a sandwich, showered, and went to bed. When Donna and Clarence arrived, they found the house quiet, her door closed. Donna inched the door open and peeked inside. Harriet was on her side, sound asleep, with Duchess lying full length beside her.

"She's spoiled that dog to pieces. When Leslie gets home, she'll have a fit."

"*If* she gets home." Clarence eased the door shut. "That's what she does when she's worried. She goes off by herself and sleeps."

"How do you know what she does when she's alone?"

"I know how she thinks, that's how." Clarence was touchy. Peevish. "She's got Charlie the Hun tomorrow and she's worried." There was no need to add that he shared her concern. He'd been worried from the beginning, before the beginning. From that morning when he'd cornered her on the steps of the courthouse in Toronto and warned her against getting mixed up in this case. He'd had a bad feeling about Charlie Denton then, but it was peanuts compared to the feeling he had now.

As a witness, Charles Denton was everything the prosecution could have hoped for, and more. Bereaved husband. Caring father. Victim of a senseless tragedy. Unknowing pawn caught in a sinister web. A web spun by a creature who fed on the helpless, "a creature who destroyed what she could not have."

"Objection." Harriet's voice was mild, almost indifferent. Why waste energy? Every objection she raised was promptly overruled. Not that she had raised that many. Fascinated by the range of emotion emanating from a man she had always considered incapable of anything but the most basic of feelings, she had been caught up in what was truly an incredible performance. Had she not seen Charles in his off-moments she, like the jury, would have been moved to pity. Pity for him. Anger toward the woman who had visited upon him this grief too great to bear.

"No," he said, in answer to a direct question from Frost, "I did not know that my wife had a sexual relationship with the defendant."

"That's a lie." Leslie's voice, outraged, rose one decible above a whisper. Harriet pretended she hadn't heard.

"The first I knew of it was that morning . . . ." His voice broke. Nystrom, solicitous, asked if he needed time to compose himself. Charles took a deep breath, gained control, said he was ready to continue. "I did not know," he said, "until we found the. . .the letter."

Frost had it at his fingertips. "Is this the letter you're referring to, Mr. Denton? The one you found in the pocket of your wife's suitcase the morning you were notified of her murder?" On the word *murder*, he whirled round and glared at Leslie.

Charles took it between thumb and forefinger, held it as though it would sear his skin. They rehearsed this, Harriet thought. He and Frost have rehearsed this in front of a mirror until they got it right. She felt a grudging admiration. The distaste on Charles's face, the long pause Frost allowed during which anticipation, curiosity, could build—a neat piece of showmanship.

She felt three pairs of eyes burning into her, willing her to stand up, to work a miracle: Leslie's, imploring; Donna's bewildered; Clare's, urgent and demanding. Caught up in the drama on the stand, knowing what was coming next, she kept her eyes on Charles as a rabbit keeps its eyes on the snake it knows is about to strike.

"Would you read it, please?"

"I'm sorry. . .I. . .I'd rather not." A beseeching glance at Nystrom, at the jury, followed by a long, penetrating stare at Leslie. He waited, willing every eye in the court to follow his.

"Keep your head up," Harriet whispered. "Look at him." Slowly, as though steeled by Harriet's will, Leslie's head came up and the dark eyes locked with his.

She knew what was in the letter. Until now, she would have died rather than have it read in public. But the letter itself no longer bothered her, the content was immaterial. It was the use being made of that letter that she found intolerable. To twist that admission of love into a reason to maim and mutilate and murder—was that what love meant to these people? To Charles and Frost and Yarrow?

"Perhaps, Mr. Frost, you will read it." Nystrom, being helpful.

Charles cleared his throat, said, "I'm sorry, Your Honor. I can go on." Harriet knew that wild horses couldn't stop him. "Marcie, darling." His voice carried to the last row. Probably into the corridor beyond. "Marcie, darling," he repeated, glancing at the reporters who were scribbling frantically. "I've missed you terribly. It's been such a long time. Last night I went to bed and thought of you here beside me. Your hair spread across the pillow. Tangling with mine. Your body, that wonderful, warm, magic body reaching up." Charles paused. Held his hand over his eyes. Shuddered. The reporters stopped scribbling and looked up expectantly. "Yes, I got the ring. It's beautiful and I'll wear it forever." His voice broke. The reporters scribbled. Stopped. "I'm so bad about birthdays, and you're so good. You never forget. Must go. I have tons of things to do before you arrive. I'm so glad—so awfully glad—that you've decided to come back." A strangled sob. A request for a glass of water. "This time, darling, it will be forever. You know I love you. I wonder if you know how much. Your Leslie."

The members of the press sat back, delighted. Even those who didn't take shorthand had managed to get the letter verbatim.

"And subsequent to your discovery of the letter you found, in your wife's jewelry box, the receipt for the ring?"

Charles nodded. Emotions well in hand for the remainder of his testimony, he accounted for every moment of his time on the fateful Saturday: an hour at breakfast, a walk with the children through the park where they met and talked with a woman with a small boy with a yellow balloon, an emergency business meeting in the afternoon; the friends with whom he had dinner, the play they attended, the after-theater supper club they visited.

The hour-by-hour account ended. Frost stepped back and said, "Your witness." Harriet responded, "No questions at this time, Your Honor. I reserve the right to recall this witness at a later date," and another day in court was over.

With the exception of the morning recess and an abbreviated lunch period, Charles had been on the stand a full day. He had spoken, spoken effectively and well, for over six hours.

"They believed him," Leslie said. "They believed every word. You should have told them he was lying."

For the first time since gaining her trust, Harriet saw doubt in Leslie's eyes. "Our day is coming," she said, hoping to reassure her. But she knew Leslie didn't believe her. She was no longer sure that she believed herself.

He was the last of Frost's witnesses, and Harriet hoped she was ready for him. Dr. Clement Dunstan—ex-professor of psychiatry, ex-clinical psychologist—at present in private practice and the public eye through his numerous court appearances, was imported from Toronto for the express purpose of profiling the defendant whom he had not interviewed but had "observed" on a total of three occasions. A seventy-year old who looked no more than fifty-plus, Dr. Dunstan was a fitness buff: he ate no meat, drank no coffee, preached monogamy, and jogged ten miles a day regardless of climate or geographic displacement.

The defendant, he said, is the victim of a serious personality disorder with areas of vulnerability that would, in layman's terms, make it difficult for her to think straight at times of emotional stress. Disappointed by the lack of response (usually in cases such as this the play on words drew a good-natured chuckle), he explained that she would tend to react to a distorted belief system rather than to the real world.

Persons such as Leslie Taylor, he elaborated, exist in one world but live, emotionally, in another. Maintaining this delicate balance inevitably leads to paranoia and psychosis. The fact that she has displayed no previous signs of violence is not germane. This contrast in behavior is typical of the passive-aggressive personality, a personality marred by antisocial features such as the hostility she feels toward men. He smiled at Yarrow. Had it not been for the private screening of the battered-wife documentary arranged by the Inspector, he would have had nothing on which to base this opinion.

Leslie, who saw men as people rather than a gender and

based her opinions accordingly, wondered how he could mouth such drivel, wondered if anyone listening could take him seriously, all the time knowing of course they would. He was an expert, had credentials, spoke with authority. Not too long ago, she might have accepted what he was saying as gospel, too.

There are those of us, he continued, who, at times of extreme frustration, resort to violence. With some it will take the form of verbal abuse. With others—a dramatic pause while he stared, steely-eyed, at the defendant—it erupts in mutilation and murder. In this instance, he said, an explosion was inevitable, given the combination of sociopathic psychosis, hostility, antagonism toward authority, and history of homosexual activity that indicated an inability to adjust to society. Because of the defendant's underdeveloped emotional condition, she would be unable to draw a line between fantasy and reality. In short, the sociopathic personality does not see the world as others see it.

In response to prompting from Frost, he said that homosexual murders are very often different from ordinary murders. There is an element of overkill. Mutilation. Very often genital mutilation. And strangulation. True, in the case in point there was no evidence of strangulation. This was understandable inasmuch as women did not tend to throttle their victims (as did men), nor was there evidence of battering. But the damage to the anorectal region, even though it occurred after death, was extensive. And, of course, the shaving of the hair spoke for itself.

There was a gleam of triumph in Frost's eye as he turned the witness over to Harriet. An answering gleam in hers, she smiled and said with a neat touch of deference, "You will have to bear with me. I am not as well-versed in this subject as you. You are a clinical psychologist?"

Yes, he had a background of clinical psychology. At present he had his own practice. No, he had not personally interviewed the defendant. For someone with his experience, that was not necessary. He had read the transcripts, listened to the tapes, seen the evidence. In addition, he had observed Miss Taylor both in custody and here in court. She was a classic example of the sociopathic personality.

"You've used that phrase a number of times, doctor. Precisely what is your definition of a sociopathic personality?"

He thought for a moment. "To put it simply, an individual born with a biologic defect, with something missing. Such a person may find it impossible to attain deep loyalty or genuine love. Sociopaths do not recognize and react to the same standards, the same goals and values, as the rest of us. The lack of satisfactions enjoyed by others, malformed aspirations, freedom from scruples and remorse—these factors leave such persons free to act without inhibition, to indulge any whim, to act out their rebellion without fear of consequence."

"But you would agree that a sociopath is not necessarily homosexual?"

"True. But, conversely, all homosexuals are sociopaths."

"You are aware that homosexuality has been reclassified by the American Psychiatric Association? Changed from *paraphilia* —I believe the phrase is—to *a sexual orientation disturbance*. How would you define paraphilia?"

"As a perverse liking leading to perverse behavior."

"So, if your own Association no longer considers homosexuality to be perverse, if it is now classified as a *disturbance*, we can assume it is a psychiatric problem only when it is disturbing to the person in question?" The benign smile was in sharp contrast to the cool green eyes. "Would it be fair, Doctor, to say that your experience with homosexuals has been limited to those who are disturbed? Those who have come to you as patients?"

Quite so, he admitted. But he had also read and studied extensively. Starting with the early work of Henrick Kaan, published in the mid-nineteenth century, almost without exception researchers had used such phrases as *congenital inversion, moral insanity, an error of nature, hereditary degeneration, sexual immaturity, a subdivision of neurosis, a disease entity*. Terms that reached well beyond the euphemistic *disturbance*.

Harriet looked pointedly at Leslie. Far from appearing immature, morally insane, or an error of nature, she seemed more centered and at ease than the drum-tight psychologist. "A belief system based on a faulty premise can hardly be accepted as fact, Dr. Dunstan. Saying the world is flat does not make it flat. Are you familiar with the work of Magnus Hirschfeld?" Hirschfeld was the German sexologist who, near the turn of the century, conducted a psychological survey of ten thousand men and women, a massive undertaking that remained a milestone in the field of human sexuality.

Dunstan reacted to the question with a tightening of lip and stiffening of frame. He was accustomed to delivering an opinion, not defending it. And in a boondock courtroom, of all places. A pox on the woman. Of course he knew of the study. Prodded further, he admitted that a universe of ten thousand was more than respectable, especially so in a time when mass communication was unheard of, and yes, the findings of that early research had indicated that homosexuality was congenital, that it existed independently of the individual wish or will.

Havelock Ellis? Yes, Ellis did view same-sex attraction as an inborn variation of the sexual impulse. Even in extreme cases, pathological only in the sense that color blindness or albinoism might be considered pathological? Again the answer was a reluctant yes.

And what of Freud, Harriet pressed. Was it not a fact that Freud felt all humans were born with a homosexual component? That bisexual feelings were normal? That true abnormality lay in the absence rather than presence of such feelings?

Fascinated by Harriet's grasp of a subject of which she had no firsthand experience, Leslie waited for the reply, remembering too late that Harriet had warned her not to smile.

It was also normal, Dunstan huffed, for those feelings to fade as one matured. One must also look at Adler. Particularly when speaking of the female homosexual.

Harriet felt the elation of a chess player watching an opponent move into a checkmate. He had saved her the trouble of bringing up Adler by doing it himself.

Mistaking her silence, Dunstan launched into Adler's "masculine protest theory." Women turn to other women in compensation for their lack of power. Lesbianism is based on an antimale bias, a mindset that sees every man as the enemy.

Harriet stepped back, smiling. "If what you say is true, Doctor, the women's rights movement is adrift on a sea of lesbianism."

Startled, he snapped, "I didn't say that." One of his daughters was an active feminist. Her daughter, his granddaughter, had insisted on retaining her own name when she married.

Smile broadening to a grin, Harriet said, "I'm finished with the witness, Your Honor."

"Finished with him?" Clarence protested as she slid into place beside him. "You didn't even start on him. I gave you a lot more information than you used."

"There are times when more is less."

It was time for the court to recess for lunch. They would resume with the opening for the Defense, preliminary remarks by Harriet, and her first witness, Dr. Max Kado.

Leslie was justifiably nervous. Frost had presented his case with little disruption and virtually no rebuttal from Harriet. Oh, she had managed to pick holes in the expertise of Yarrow's investigative team, but her quibbling had focused on technicalities, not on Leslie's guilt or innocence. Her few objections were disregarded; her questions on cross appeared to bolster the prosecution rather than weaken it.

Seated beside a silent Harriet, eyes fixed on the pen doing a maniacal dance between the attorney's slender fingers, she struggled with the panic pushing up into her chest. Trust me, Harriet had said. And trust her she had for reasons she still could not explain. Something about Harriet Croft had smashed through to the core of her. Instinct, intuition, whatever—she had responded by placing herself in a pair of hands as delicate as eggshell.

Conscious of her parents in the audience (for audience it was), of the Bergstroms, of Josie who attended every day as a sign of support—of Charles and Moore and Yarrow and Frost who made no secret of their contempt for women who slept with other women—she felt naked and vulnerable and frightened. The self-acceptance that had been building throughout the trial was still so new, so fragile, she did not know whether it would survive dissection by Harriet and onslaught by Frost. Once on the stand there would be nowhere to hide. Had she made a mistake? Had she miscalculated not only her own growing assurance but Harriet's ability as well? Were it not for this magnetic, compelling woman beside her, she would not be here. Would not be labeled. Would not be forced to sit day after day being studied, analyzed, taken apart by strangers.

She turned to say something to Harriet, caught the warning nod of Clarence's head, swallowed the question, and said nothing. Do not disturb her when she's thinking. There was no need for him to say it. He'd said it often enough in the past. "Let her be. She knows what she's doing." And yet often there was doubt in his eyes, too. She suspected he no longer knew what to expect, did not know the direction Harriet intended to take.

Nystrom swept into place, and she felt as she had when, as a child, she had first climbed aboard a roller coaster and realized with the initial loop that she didn't want to be there, but it was too late to stop, to get off, to do anything but cling tight until it came to a stop. And then Harriet was on her feet and you could hear a pin drop and she was standing before the jury box with her porcelain hands closed on the railing like a vise and that voice, that wonderful mesmeric voice, was flowing through the court.

"The jury system functions on the fundamental assumption that, once properly sworn, a juror will determine the guilt or innocence of the accused solely on the evidence. There must be no extraneous considerations. You must be free from prejudice either for or against the accused.

"It is not necessary that the defendant prove innocence. The burden is on the Crown to prove guilt. This must be done through evidence, either direct or circumstantial. Direct evidence ties the accused directly to the crime. Circumstantial evidence is based on conjecture."

Clarence nudged Leslie and shoved a scribbled message toward her. She scanned it quickly, not wanting to miss what Harriet was saying. *She's taking control of the court,* the note said. *Beating Nystrom to the punch. She's giving them the judge's charge.* He was beaming with the delight of confidence restored. It was a true fact, Leslie thought. Harriet had moved to center stage and was in command. But was that good or bad?

"Circumstantial evidence is based on conjecture." Repeated for emphasis, the line rang through the air. "And this case, ladies and gentlemen, is purely circumstantial. Oh, there is direct evidence. Evidence not placed before you by the Crown. Evidence that points, directly, to the murderer of Marcie Denton. I propose to show you who killed Mrs. Denton, and why, and your verdict will rest on that disclosure."

Ignoring the excited buzzing of the journalists, angry whispers among the prosecution team, she continued smoothly. "You will, during the next few days, learn that Marcie Denton's marriage was not a happy one. That she, like the women in my client's documentary, was subject to wife abuse. That when she turned to her parents for help and support, they convinced her that her place was by the side of her husband.

"You will also learn that Leslie Taylor was not the first female in Mrs. Denton's life. That it was she, Marcie, rather than the defendant, who initiated the relationship with Miss Taylor. And you will learn that the person who was in Unit Three, the person responsible for Marcie Denton's death, could not possibly have been the person who stands accused. We will prove that the letter upon which the Prosecution has based their case is totally irrelevant and has no place in this court of law.

"I now call on Dr. Max Kado, a family psychologist who specializes in marriage counseling, parental guidance, and group therapy."

Dr. Kado was youngish, bookish, and broadly experienced. He stated that he did not subscribe to the views espoused by Dr. Dunstan. Nor, for that matter, did most of his contemporaries. One of the problems faced by senior members of the profession, he said firmly, was their lack of contact with gays who were happy and adjusted to society's maladjustment. Until recently, the majority of homosexuals were in the closet. With the gay liberation movement, homosexuals had surfaced in greater numbers than ever before and as more and more of these once-hidden gays emerged, it became apparent that homosexuals were a microcosm of their heterosexual counterparts: happy, unhappy; mentally sound, mentally unsound; promiscuous, nonpromiscuous; ambitious, indolent.

He treated both homosexuals and heterosexuals and had found that their problems were virtually identical. Human problems, for the most part. Difficulties on the job. The breakup of a relationship. Economic worries. The problems that did relate to homosexuality were occasioned more by the attitude of society than the fact of being gay.

One of the greatest fears, he explained, is being disowned by one's parents. (He was addressing the court, but Leslie felt he was speaking directly to her. Rejection by her parents had always lain at the root of her concern. But now they knew and loved her still, and this major hurdle in her life was behind her.) A fear, Kado was saying, often attributable to a strict, highly religious family structure. This in spite of the fact that Christ made no reference to homosexuality. As a matter of fact, he understood from friends who had read the Bible in the original Aramaic, that homosexuality per se was not mentioned anywhere. And, of course—with a pause and smile for the jury—there are many laws set forth in the Bible that are broken every day. The mixing of yarns and fabric in a single garment, the trimming of beards, the rounding off of hair when it is cut, the sowing of a field with more than one type of grain. It had always seemed odd, he commented, that we should ignore specifics while adhering to fanciful interpretation.

Harriet moved to the matter at hand by directing Kado's attention to Leslie. "Like Dr. Dunstan, you have had an opportunity to observe Miss Taylor. Do you feel that she is maladjusted? Sociopathic?"

The bright eyes fixed on the slim figure next to Clarence. "I see no sign, none whatever, of psychosis. Miss Taylor appears to me to be as well-balanced as anyone in like position might be expected to be. Based on your conversations with the defendant which you have recounted to me, on my knowledge of this case, and what I have seen and heard in this courtroom, I would say that she is a normal, well-adjusted young woman. Also," he added, "a very attractive young woman."

The gratuitous compliment had no effect on Leslie but it registered with, and pleased, Harriet. Nodding agreement, she crossed to the defense table and picked up a printed flyer. "Would you read out the underlined passages, Dr. Kado?"

Kado took the paper, glanced at it, and read, "*Queers do not produce: they Seduce.*" Eyebrows arched in surprise, he continued, "*Queers exist to seduce and pervert our children. Queers are sexually depraved vampires. Queers include many left-wing liberals. The Human Rights Commission, who consider it a violation of a queer's civil rights if it wasn't allowed to seduce your child. All communists, rabble and misfits. It is time they all be put back in their closets and have them nailed shut. Do you want your children to be the blood of sexually depraved vampires?*"

"That's enough, Dr. Kado. I think this court can imagine what the remainder of that flyer is like. How would you describe that piece of writing?"

"This is clearly a piece of hate literature. Highly inflammatory."

"Hate literature—which is against the law." Harriet retrieved the flyer and held it up in view of the jurors. "And how would you describe the mind behind it?"

"Psychotic. With overtones of extreme paranoia. '*Everyone who doesn't agree with me is queer. Queers eat babies.*' I would say that the person responsible for this has a violent and unreasonable hatred—not just of gays, but of society as a whole. I would further consider him extremely dangerous. A time bomb."

"Would it surprise you, Dr. Kado, to learn that this piece of hate propaganda was distributed by the Spruce Falls Police Department? That it was written by the head of Homicide Division, Inspector Floyd Yarrow?"

Frost screamed an objection. Yarrow turned ashen. Kado silently marveled that anyone, much less a slip of a girl, would come out of the closet in a community that tolerated such blatant homophobia from those sworn to uphold the law.

Harriet entered the flyer into evidence and released the witness.

"What is the etiology of homosexuality, Doctor?" Frost zeroed in with jut-jawed pugnacity.

"I'm sorry, I can't answer that. No more than I can give you the etiology of heterosexuality."

"Listening to you, Doctor, it is obvious that you condone homosexuality." The prosecutor's voice dripped sarcasm.

"I neither condone it nor condemn it, Counselor. It is part of the human condition."

Frost turned with a gesture of contempt and walked stiff-legged back to his seat, brushing past Yarrow without a word, without a glance.

Harriet's final witness of the day was a retired medical examiner from Vancouver, now resident in a small community on the outskirts of Toronto. He had read Dr. Spellman's findings and felt the fixing of death based on rigor mortis alone was highly questionable.

Even more questionable, Harriet asked, if you had a powerful air conditioner, directly in line with the body, in a restricted space?

Frost roared an objection, adding, "There has been no prior testimony regarding an air conditioner. This is conjecture on Counsel's part."

"This entire case is based on conjecture, Your Honor." Abandoning the air conditioner, Harriet asked, "Based on the condition of the body, could you fix a precise time of death?"

"Not having seen the body, it's difficult to say. But from the cursory manner in which the autopsy appears to have been conducted, I would think not."

"What would you consider a reasonable time frame for the onset of rigor?"

"Again, that's hard to say. It can commence within three to six hours, or be delayed for as much as twelve hours. Fading can occur after twenty hours. I have known it to take up to forty-eight. There are a number of factors which must be taken into account. Without the necessary cross checks, it would be impossible to pinpoint the exact time of death."

More than satisfied, Harriet said lightly, "One more question, Doctor. Are you, by any chance, equally knowledgeable on the subject of watches?"

"Other than wearing one, I'm afraid not."

Under a slashing cross-examination, the retired M.E. held to his conviction that the degree of rigor mortis was a poor barometer. No, he did not know whether the air conditioner was functioning at the time. He did know that if it had been, it would have made a substantial difference in fading. When he finally stepped down, it was with confidence intact and the issue of time of death in doubt.

That afternoon, with the case for the defense firmly on the rails, Harriet decided it was time for a conference with her client. She had avoided Leslie intentionally. Given carte blanche to handle matters as she saw fit, she had not wanted to muddle her mind with post mortems of what had gone before, justification of what was yet to come. It was important to keep her thinking clear, to forge ahead on the course she had set without allowing fear and doubt to creep in. Such were the reasons she had given herself; reasons that, deep down, she knew were little more than excuses. In reality, it was increasingly difficult to be with Leslie, to sit beside her day after day in the courtroom and remain objective. Harriet knew that maintaining a proper client/attorney relationship was crucial. She was not about to make it impossible.

"I brought you some fried chicken."

The room off the matron's office in the old jail brought back memories of their first meetings, that time when Leslie was locked inside herself, silent and stubborn. Now even though changed back into the shabby cotton shift, there was no resemblance to that earlier Leslie.

"I don't even know if you like chicken." It came as a shock to Harriet to realize how little she actually knew about this young woman whose life lay in her hands. The important things, yes. Those she had sensed immediately—strength, integrity, character. The invisible inner workings were as clear to her as though they were her own. But what did she eat? What sort of books did she read? Did she sleep on her back or her side, or curled up in a ball? In pyjamas or in the flesh? The intimate musing triggered a warm flush and unaccustomed awkwardness. "Here." She thrust the box forward abruptly.

"I love chicken." Leslie flipped open the carton and offered it to Harriet. "Where have you been? I was beginning to think I'd never see you again."

"We see each other every day." A stiff stating of the obvious.

"That doesn't count." She bit into a chicken leg and said, "This is terrific. I hope you brought lots of napkins. Are you pleased with the way things are going? I'm getting nervous. That Dunstan character said some pretty mean stuff. Do you think I'm sociopathic? A diseased entity? Is that why you haven't come around, scared I'll go off in a fit?" Her black eyes danced with amusement.

Thank God, Harriet thought. If she'd bought all that psychiatric drivel, we'd be finished. She ripped open one of the wet towel packets. The chicken leg Leslie was devouring had left a smudge of grease on her chin. She leaned over to wipe it off, pulled back in embarrassment, and handed it across the table. "Here. If I'd known you were going to make such a mess, I'd have brought a bib." Then, "Have you talked to your parents?"

"Last night. They were pretty upset. I didn't think they'd be able to sit through anything like that. It's lucky they knew about me before, Harriet. At least they were sort of prepared. Your Dr. Kado helped."

"I arranged for them to spend some time together. He's with them now. Would you believe your mother invited him for dinner? They'll probably end up knowing more about homosexuality than you do. At least he'll get rid of all the myths." *Gays are unhappy, gays corrupt kids, gays are losers, gays can decide not to be gay, gays are gay because their parents did something wrong.*

"Gays have horns." Grinning, Leslie teased, "It sounds as though you've learned a lot too."

"I'm a quick study." A lot, Harriet thought, is putting it mildly. And not only me, but the good people of Spruce Falls as well.

"Why didn't you bring some of that stuff up when you were cross-examining?"

"Because it's better coming from someone with credentials. You can say the same things, but it makes a hell of a difference if you've got the right letters after your name. And we have to keep the emphasis where it belongs. Homosexuality isn't on trial. *You* are. I just didn't want to pass up the opportunity to shed a bit of light on the subject. The newspapers will pick it up. They swarmed around Kado. All you had to do was look at the two of them. Dunstan and Kado: the Dark Ages and the Enlightenment. It came across. And that flyer of Yarrow's—did you see the way the jury looked at him?"

"I saw the way Poulis looked at *you*. I hate him sitting there every day, Harriet. Hasn't he got anything else to do?"

"Nothing he considers more important, I guess. I think he was waiting for me to pick up on that moral insanity angle. 'There. See. She's not guilty because. . . .' "

"Because she's morally cuckoo." Laughing, Leslie dropped the last chicken bone into the carton. "I had a visit from Josie. She's got a job. Nights. As soon as the trial is over, she's going to try to get on shiftwork in one of the mines. That will pay enough so she can keep the kids with her."

"I'm glad. You're fond of her, aren't you?"

"She was good to me. If it hadn't been for her I don't know how I'd have come through those first few days. She's crazy about you, Harriet. Said she's going to get you something special to show her gratitude."

"Oh no. Not. . . ."

"Probably," Leslie said, straight-faced. Then seeing that Harriet was genuinely concerned, she added, "Don't worry. She promised whatever she got would be bought and paid for. Her boosting days are over. Aside from boosting you to anyone who'll listen." Her eyes grew sober and thoughtful. "Tell me the truth, Harriet. Are we winning or losing?"

"Can't you tell?" It was an effort to sound light-hearted. Who could tell what a jury would do? Until the votes were in, who could tell whether the strategy chosen was right or wrong? She didn't want to discuss the case. Didn't want Leslie to know she planned to pull a rabbit out of a hat: the hat she had, the rabbit she wasn't sure of. "I'd better go." Her manner was brisk. Businesslike. "I just wanted to drop off the chicken." She knocked for Mrs. Klyk, then said quietly, but with an implacable authority, "You know I plan to call you to the stand. I'll see you the night before to go over what you're going to say."

Mrs. Klyk materialized, allowing no time for remonstrance. No time for anything but a glimpse of Leslie's face, frozen with shock, as she was led away. It was not incumbent upon an accused to take the stand, and she had not expected to be called. Theoretically, failure to testify could not be construed as indicating either guilt or innocence, but Harriet was aware that refusal to speak under oath was almost always taken as a sign of guilt.

She knew it would be dangerous to deliver Leslie into the hands of Jeremy Frost. But she also knew it would be far more dangerous not to.

Leslie, her feelings in turmoil, accompanied Mrs. Klyk back to her cell. She did not want to take the stand. It would take so little, one thoughtless gesture—one unguarded moment—and what Harriet had gained she could destroy.

She did not want to go to prison. Enough of her life had been spent in a prison of her own making. But she wanted, even less, to see Harriet Croft go down in defeat before someone like Jeremy Frost. Leslie wanted Harriet to win as much for her, Harriet's sake, as for her own.

Chapter Eleven

*T*rials were all the same. High points, moments of stark drama, dull, dragging testimony in between, and often it was the latter that decided the outcome. Nuggets of gold could lie, near buried, in the nitty gritty of trivia and repetition. Such a week was the one just past. Carefully, as though building a house of cards or matches, Harriet had planted bits of information that in itself meant nothing, but were all part of a larger mosaic.

Walking Duchess along the creek—it was Saturday, Clarence and Donna were in Toronto, and she was alone—she reviewed the week that was. Days of seemingly insignificant detail enlivened by rants and raves from Frost, scoldings from Nystrom, and a scornful reference by the prosecution to Perry Mason histrionics which followed on the heels of her towel bar demonstration and was duly picked up and expanded upon by the press.

188

The towel bar. The one time in Harriet's career she had done what she had sworn she would never do—descended to the level of gut theatrics. But it had worked. God, how it had worked. Charmed into cooperating, a decision abetted by a craftsman's pride in a job well done, Amanda Peak's husband had taken the remaining towel bar from his bulk purchase and mounted it on a sheet of heavy planking. Not quite as solid as the wall-mounted bars, he warned, but close enough. It had been Harriet's intention to have one of the women on the jury attempt to dislodge the bar. That, however, was too much for Nystrom. So she had played stand-in, attempting unsuccessfully to tear the fixture loose. Accused of not applying her full weight to the task, she seconded one of the female spectators and finally, to the morbid delight of everyone present save the Crown and Homicide, she invited Leslie to make the effort. Not one of them had succeeded in jarring the bar by as much as a hair's breadth.

How effective was show and tell in the tension-packed atmosphere of a courtroom? Harriet didn't know. Nor did she care. Her goal had been to have the planking entered in evidence. Have it placed in the jury room. Once there, she knew that every member of the panel would do a hands-on test of their own.

Then there was the Dalton cleaning woman. The one who discovered Marcie's body and found herself a new job shortly thereafter. The first thing she noticed when she opened the door, even before she set foot in the room, was the chill that lay across the threshold like a barrier of ice. "It was like a refrig. I knew right off something was wrong." More hindsight than foresight, Harriet thought, but no matter. The woman left no doubt in anyone's mind that the room was cold. Frigid. The air conditioner was not merely on: it was working at top capacity.

The four post-slaying occupants of Unit Three also chalked up marks for the defense. There was a slim accountant with triple A feet, who described himself as a true crime buff; a portly middle-aged widow in sensible oxfords; a youngish woman in high-heeled strap sandals; a young man in jeans, sweater and sneakers. All, at Harriet's request, appeared on the stand in dress identical to that worn during their stay at the Dalton. None came anywhere near matching the prints ringing the bed.

And then there had been the friends and acquaintances of the deceased. Watching Duchess duck for stones in the shallow water, Harriet said, "I hurt her. If I'd stuck a knife into her I couldn't have hurt her more." The dog ignored her. "I'm talking about Leslie," she said sharply. "Don't you care?"

At the sound of a name both familiar and cherished, Duchess's head came up—attentive, dripping water. Sensing Harriet's mood, she trotted out of the creek and nuzzled up, warm body pressed close. Harriet hugged her and sighed and thought abut the girls, those willing to come forward, who had gone to school with Marcie. She had always had crushes on other girls, they said. There had even been a washroom incident when she was caught in the act. Embracing, kissing another girl. It was harmless enough, but gossip had spread like a brush fire. For days after Leslie visited the school, she had talked of nothing else. Marcie Bergstrom could be very persistent. They had not been surprised when she got to know the commentator.

The effect of their testimony on both the Bergstroms and Leslie had been devastating. Frost, with much of his case resting on *Leslie's* pursuit and eventual seduction of the victim, fought to have the witnesses excluded. Harriet countered by reminding the court that it was the prosecution itself that opened the way for this line of questioning. Nystrom, sword of a mistrial poised overhead, reluctantly agreed.

The school friends, now young matrons with families of their own, had been followed by Elsie Mak. "Thank God we didn't go for that change of venue," Harriet whispered in the dog's ear. "If we'd been on home ground, on her turf, she'd have up and disappeared." But Elsie hadn't disappeared. She had shown up ready and on time.

At first hesitant—this was, after all, the first time she'd been set under a microscope before a room full of strangers—she had gained assurance as the morning wore on. The Cameo Club was a place where gay women could come together and have fun. She had seen Marcie there with Leslie. She had also seen Marcie there on her own. It was after her marriage to him, pointing at Charles, that she, Elsie, had got to know her. Marcie had talked to her about her marriage, her fear of her husband. She had told Elsie about taking the children home to her family and being pressured to return, had said that some day she would get away. Just before she left that last time, Marcie told her she was going for good. Nothing would bring her back.

It was Elsie who opened the first cracks in Charlie's facade, cracks that widened with each revelation until Frost, alarmed by the surfacing rage that threatened to turn grieving husband from a Jekyll to a Hyde, thundered that the decedent and her family were not on trial and counsel for the defense would be well advised to stop beating the bushes and get down to the facts at issue.

Harriet cheerfully obliged by abandoning the relationship between the Dentons and moving calmly to the subject of the ring. Was it not true that she had been given a piece of jewelry by Marcie? Yes, Elsie said, and she had handed the ring to Harriet, who had then shown it to the jury, pacing the length of the box slowly, holding it up for each juror to study in passing. She had returned it then, without reference to the letter, leaving behind only the impression that this ring was significant and was part of a larger design of which they would eventually be apprised.

After Elsie came a young man of such sartorial aplomb that both Doug Moore and Charles Denton looked like the ghosts of fashion past. His name was Clifford Whyte Smythe. He was the president of the Stone Shirt House. They catered to an exclusive clientele, an international clientele, he might add. It was not in the least unusual to receive an order for an annual supply of shirts which would then be custom-tailored to the client's specs, which were kept on file. Yes, Mr. Charles Denton was one of his regular customers.

At this point, not knowing why Mr. Whyte Smythe had been summoned but beside himself by this invasion of his private life, Charles had to be restrained by the flanking Yarrow and Moore. Harriet had allowed time for the scuffle to subside before asking, "Your clients are very exacting?"

"Very."

"They spend a great deal of time over details that to many of us might appear minor?"

"To a man who takes pride in his appearance, Mrs. Croft, nothing is minor."

"Including the buttons used."

"Particularly the buttons. We carry the largest stock of buttons on the continent. Bone. Mother-of-pearl. Nothing synthetic, of course."

Presented with the button found behind the Dalton drapes, Mr. Smythe said it was similar to those favored by Mr. Denton although he could not say it was from one of Mr. Denton's shirts. The courtroom erupted into full-scale pandemonium and, unable to restore order, Nystrom wisely called adjournment for the remainder of the day. Charles was led away in a state of near apoplexy. Was it fury, or something more? As the court cleared, Frost had accosted her with accusations of character assassination and a threat of disbarment.

The following day had been equally hectic. The pace was set by Nystrom who refused to allow the button in evidence and ordered that all mention of same be stricken from the records. Harriet accepted the ruling with marked good nature. She well knew you could strike testimony from the transcript but not from the minds of those who heard it.

And then—was it only yesterday?—they had heard from the jeweler. This time, try though he did, Frost was unable to silence the witness. Harriet countered his objection with, "My learned friend in his opening remarks stated that the letter written by Miss Taylor to the deceased was, to use his words, 'the Crown's pivotal piece of evidence'. He opened the gate, Your Honor, and once open it cannot be closed."

Allowed to proceed, the jeweler had examined the receipt, looked at the date, and after examining the ring worn by Leslie, said no, he had never seen this ring before, it was certainly not the one sold by him and covered by his bill of sale.

Holding the ring up triumphantly, Harriet said, "This is the ring that Marcie gave the defendant years ago. Not when Leslie Taylor was living in Spruce Falls and Marcie *Denton* was settled in Toronto, but years before, when Marcie *Bergstrom* was back in Spruce Falls with her parents, planning to return to Toronto to resume her life with Miss Taylor.

"When you retire to the jury room you will examine this letter and you will see clearly that it is a copy and you will wonder why it is not dated. And you will further wonder if the date on the original was removed with liquid eraser and if the original was then destroyed and this doctored copy substituted in its place." And because she had expected the rising tide of protest from the Crown, the attempt to drown her out, she had adjusted her voice accordingly and it had soared above the bedlam and made her point.

But the letter and the ring were not all she brought up. There was also the watch. The watch that, according to Spellman, had helped frame the time of death, still keeping accurate time when the body was discovered. Slipping her own watch off her wrist, she had handed it to the witness. One of her prize possessions, the eighteen-karat, seventeen-jewel Cartier with cabochon sapphire set in the Cartier crown had belonged to her mother. A family keepsake that Harriet wore only on special occasions. Handing it to the man on the stand, she had asked how long such a watch would continue to run between windings.

Holding the timepiece with infinite care, his expression one of awe, he said, "This watch is very valuable, Mrs. Croft. One of the very first wrist models. An antique. This is the famous

Tank watch made by Cartier immediately after the WWI and so named because of the square, tanklike design. I would suggest you keep it in your safety deposit box."

How long would it run she had asked again, and he had replied a day, perhaps a few hours beyond a day. Certainly not much longer. A stemwind, any watch with standard movement, required regular winding.

And this, she had asked, handing him Marcie's Rolex Oyster. This, too, was expensive. A gift from Charles in the early days of their marriage. How long would it tell time with accuracy?

"You realize," he said carefully, "we are speaking of two different mechanisms. This model is self-winding. Responsive to movement. Depending on the wearer, the degree of activity of the wearer, it could run for forty-eight hours. Fully wound, worn by someone extremely active, such a watch has been known to function for as long as four days."

On that note, with another tiny building block in place, they had come to the end of the day and the week.

"Monday," she said, cheek flat on the top of Duchess's head, "Monday it's Leslie's turn. What she says and how she says it will make half the difference."

And the other half? The rabbit she hoped was there? That would take luck and timing and a pressing of exactly the right button at precisely the right moment in time.

Chapter Twelve

They knew that this was the day Leslie Taylor would take the stand. Harriet had so informed the reporters on Friday when they crowded round her as she left the courthouse. Yes, Miss Taylor will appear on her own behalf. No, Miss Taylor has nothing to hide. Yes, it was Miss Taylor's decision, born of her desire to set the record straight.

Now, as the cab rounded the corner at the end of the block, Joe slowed to a crawl, and Clarence whistled in alarm. "The whole city's here. We'll never get past that mob." Clare leaned forward and tapped Joe on the shoulder. "Maybe you should drive around the block and drop us at the back."

"We'll get through." Harriet was in no mood to sneak in the rear entrance. At any rate, she had hoped for a big crowd and was pleased that it had materialized. Let them see Leslie's team: relaxed, confident, and assured of success. Image was everything. Just pray they couldn't see through that image to the nest of doubt concealed underneath.

Clarence and Donna tried to shield her as they stepped out of the cab and the reporters closed in. The woman with the shoulder-pack pressed forward. "Is your client really going to take the stand? Did you plant that button? Do you think you have grounds for an appeal?"

The case hadn't even gone to the jury and she was asking about an appeal? The woman was either hung over from a mind-blotting night on the town, or she was hoping to provoke a damaging outburst. Controlling her anger, Harriet said pleasantly, "It's a bit early to worry about appealing. As for grounds, there is no ground for conviction. Naturally we expect an acquittal." Liar, she thought. If I really believed that, I'd be dancing in the street.

"What does your client think of the way things have gone?"

"You'll have to ask her. She'll be available for a statement later in the week."

Clarence had heard enough. Gripping her arm, he tugged her through the pack of bodies, stiff-arming a path toward the steps. Safely inside, he dropped her arm and said, "You're going to be the death of all of us, Harriet. You've been jumping all over the map with these witnesses. If you don't stop dragging your feet, I'm out of here."

Clarence was astute enough to know that a lot of the questions she had asked were meaningless, that she was playing for time. He also knew that there was no percentage in playing for time in a capital case with all the evidence in. What he did not know was that there was method in her madness and motive in her shilly-shallying.

There was no need to worry about Clarence. She was confident he would stay until she no longer needed him. She was worried about the Taylors, though, and about Leslie. The briefing last night had gone well, but not as well as she had hoped it would. Leslie's moments of assurance were punctuated by fits of indecision and acute self-consciousness. Finally, instead of coaching her on what to do with her hands, how to move and sit and react to difficult questions—all the trivia that went into being a model witness—Harriet had simply told her to listen to each question carefully, to take time to think, and then to answer honestly and without holding back. Now, looking down the aisle to the Bench, she thought of other things she could have said, and her heart pounded as she knew Leslie's must be pounding at the thought of this day that lay ahead.

The Taylors were seated at the end of a row near the front. Pausing beside Emily, she said quietly, "Try not to be upset by anything you hear. Just keep in your mind that whatever happens, it won't be nearly as bad as having her locked away."

Emily nodded, face set with determination. Adam's too, showed a surprising strength. Reassured, Harriet continued down the aisle. Past Haberdash, who threw her a glance of sly satisfaction that said she was about to get her comeuppance and if she'd gone for an insanity plea as he would have done, she wouldn't be in this fix. Past Charles, who stared at her with marble eyes and glacial composure.

This day would be taken up by Leslie. Frost, she knew, would keep her on the stand as long as possible. Not wanting to run over into a second day, to have Leslie go back to her cell with the specter of another session of questioning ahead of her, she planned to terminate her examination before the morning recess.

A hush of anticipation. The narrow door, opening. Mrs. Klyk. Beside her, the defendant. Clarence, whispering, "She looks O.K."

Outwardly, yes. But it seemed to Harriet that she was too still, too wrapped inside. Almost sleepwalking. If she didn't know better, she'd think she was on drugs. Cosmetically, she was well in hand: perfectly groomed, hair brushed and shining. Her eyes were shining too, but Harriet was unnerved by their glassy brilliance. The taut body slid into place beside her. Fearing the answer, Harriet asked, "Are you all right?"

"I'm scared."

Harriet reached for her hand and held it. As their fingers interlaced, she was conscious of the flow of warmth between them, of the knowing stares from Frost and Yarrow.

"I don't think I can do this, Harriet."

"If you can't do it for yourself, do it for me." The green eyes were hypnotic, compelling. And then Nystrom was on the Bench, and she was on her feet, and Leslie was in the witness box, and that first and hardest question was voiced. "You and Marcie Bergstrom were lovers?"

"Yes." Clear and sharp and unequivocal.

"How did that come about?"

Leslie sketched their early relationship quickly and economically. Admitted, but only when prodded, that the overtures came from Marcie. But, she added, tempering Marcie's culpability, it was not a matter of who did what first. She had always known she was different. Not like her friends: they talked about boys, she thought about girls.

"You knew, perhaps without applying the word to yourself, that you were a lesbian?"

Yes, she did. As for the ring, Marcie had given it to her the first year they were together.

It was she who had urged Marcie to return to her parents. She who had later relented and agreed to resume their relationship in Toronto. The letter in evidence had been written during that interval. Years before Marcie and Charles Denton met each other.

Marcie, she revealed, had come to her twice after her marriage. The last time, after a severe beating, Leslie had urged her to return to Charles but to seek the advice of a divorce lawyer. "She came to me. She went to her parents." She paused, stared at the Bergstroms, regained control. "She came to us for help, and we turned her away." Anger flared in the dark eyes, anger aimed as much at herself as at Marcie's mother and father.

"Was Charles Denton aware of your relationship?"

"He knew from the beginning. I think it was one of the reasons he asked her to marry him."

The answer lay there. A grenade. Let Frost pull the pin if he dared. Expressionless, Harriet turned to the Crown. "Your witness."

She had closed exactly on schedule. Nystrom would call a recess. Frost would consult with Charles. They would have to pick up where she had left off. With the male ego at stake, far better the explanation should be elicited by a male prosecutor than a female defender.

As expected, Frost was champing at the bit by the time the court was recalled. Voice dripping with scorn, he picked up the thread Harriet had left dangling. "You expect this court to believe that a man, *any* man, would knowingly ask a...a confirmed...lesbian...to marry him?"

"Objection. Miss Taylor did not say what she expected the court to believe." Frivolous nit-picking to Nystrom; to Harriet, a brief delay to heighten anticipation.

"Overruled. Answer the question."

"Many men knowingly marry lesbians, Mr. Frost. They do it because...."

"Just answer the question yes or no."

"Miss Taylor is attempting to answer the question, Your Honor. Counsel is harassing her."

"Overruled. Yes or no, Miss Taylor."

"Yes."

Harriet made a mental note to catch it on rebuttal. If doing so meant ruffling a few male feathers, so be it.

"Do you consider the feelings you had for Mrs. Denton to be normal?"

"They were normal for me."

Yes or no, he badgered. "Yes."

He continued to hammer at her. You were upset when she left you. Upset that she left you for a man. Another woman would have been easier to take. You had nothing but the victim's word that she was being beaten. You were obsessed by the subject of battered women. You were enthralled by Marcie's hair. You knew she considered it her best feature. You were ashamed of your relationship. You hid it from your family. You have never sought psychiatric help. Never attempted to find a cure for this sickness.

And finally, you knew Marcie Denton was in that motel room. Knew she was waiting there for you. Knew it was your last chance to get her back. Knew that if she rejected you again she would never leave that room alive.

And then it was over, and Leslie, shaken but holding together, was filling in under Harriet's guidance what she had not been allowed to say under Frost's rapid-fire cross: there were numerous incidents of men—and women, too—marrying known homosexuals; gays were considered a challenge by many heterosexuals; lesbianism struck at the very heart of masculinity.

As far as the beatings were concerned, she had seen Marcie's bruises. And psychiatric help? There had been no need. Had she married, as Marcie had, she would have required a psychiatrist. As it was—this said with a radiant smile toward Harriet—she felt completely at ease with herself.

Was she positive Charles had known about the two of them ahead of time? Absolutely. Marcie had told him while they were still together in an effort to discourage him. It was after that that he became more persistent—waiting outside their apartment building, calling in the middle of the night and insisting she speak with him, once even telephoning Leslie at work and warning her that if she didn't get out of Marcie's life, he would speak to her employer and have her fired. There was not the slightest doubt that he had known in advance that both she and Marcie were involved in a homosexual relationship.

Charles sat, rigidly composed, as she painted a picture of a frenzied suitor determined to go to any length to achieve his ends. Could the jury equate the two, imagine this upright citizen indulging in bouts of bizarre behavior? Harriet was doubtful. Had it not been for that unguarded moment in her office, she would not have believed it herself. Why, then, would strangers?

Still, Leslie had done as well—even better—than she'd expected. "You were wonderful," she said in the few moments between adjournment and Mrs. Klyk. "It's over. You won't have to go through that again."

"I couldn't." Leslie was tired, drained to the point of exhaustion. The front she had managed to hold intact through those grueling hours on the stand was still in place, but only barely. Watching as she was led away, Harriet saw her shoulders sag and wished that she could walk with her behind that closed door. Be there to hold and comfort her through the lonely hours ahead.

Settled in the cab, Clarence said bluntly, "It's her word against his. And anybody who doesn't know him isn't going to believe half of that stuff. I thought sure he'd come apart at the seams, having all that dirty linen washed in public. Instead, he sat there like butter wouldn't melt in his mouth."

"She was splendid, wasn't she?"

"Harriet, you haven't heard a word I've said." Clarence cleared his throat. "I think I'll go home and take poison."

"She didn't think she could do it. Frankly, I didn't think so, either."

"Cyanide. We'll all take cyanide."

"That's fine." Still staring off into space, Harriet said, "You and Donna go on ahead. I'll be there later. Joe, will you drop me at the Taylors'?"

Emily, she knew, would be expecting her. On top of which, she was anxious to assess the damage, see what sort of shape they were in. Leslie's testimony would have been as hard on them as it was on their daughter. Harder, perhaps, for they would have to live with it reflected in the faces of their friends and neighbors.

Unable to pull into the driveway—it was crowded with cars and more were pulling up at the curb—Joe dropped her in the middle of the street in front of the house. Emily answered the door, hair awry and expression distraught. "Harriet. I was hoping you'd come by."

"I thought you might need someone to talk to. I see I was wrong."

Emily laughed, actually laughed. "What I really need is a secretary. The phone's been ringing ever since we got in. Adam's on long distance now."

Harriet caught a glimpse of Dr. Kado in a corner of the crowded living room. "It looks as though you're holding a town meeting. What are all these people doing here?"

"Offering moral support, would you believe? And we've been getting calls from all over. A group called Parents of Gays. A few cranks. A woman who thinks her daughter is iffy—how should she handle it. And you won't believe this, Harriet, but one of our neighbors said she's been wondering about her son and asked if I'd talk to him. It's crazy. We even had a gay newspaper call from the coast and ask for an interview. I had no idea."

Drawing Emily into a quiet spot in the kitchen, Harriet said, "Don't talk to anyone publicly until you've thought it over. You're going to have to live with this for a long time. Make sure you know what you're getting into." Harriet glanced at her watch. There was no need to stay. The Taylors had company enough. On impulse she said, "How would you feel about a welcome home party?"

"Oh, Harriet, I don't even want to think about it. What if . . . suppose she doesn't come home?" The bright eyes clouded, shades of the despair lingering below the surface.

"She's coming home." A remark born more of stubbornness than conviction. "She's done her part. The rest is up to us."

She nabbed a cab being vacated by a grim-faced couple clutching a pale young girl in jeans. (The Taylors, she feared, had become instant authorities on the handling of gay offspring.) The trio started up the drive, the cab started off along the street, and she started an imaginary list of the people she'd invite to a victory celebration. Josie. Dr. Kado, if he was still in town. Haberdash Poulis? Why not. And just for the fun of it, Yarrow and Moore and yes, even Frost. They wouldn't come, of course, but the rubbing of salt would do them good.

She would plan it herself and tell no one ahead of time, and if worse came to worst, nothing would be lost. Nothing, she reminded herself as a chill crept through her bones, but Leslie herself. And if that happened, what would it matter? What would anything matter if Leslie Taylor was destroyed and she, Harriet Croft, had unwittingly engineered that destruction.

"The defense calls Charles Denton."

With those words, the die was cast. No one had expected him to be called back. Charles himself had not expected to be recalled. It was customary for the defendant to appear last. Customary but not mandatory. Seated in the box, Charles Denton watched Harriet approach him with the easy glide of a panther stalking its prey.

Simultaneously, Leslie stared at the man on the witness stand. For one brief moment their eyes met and held: in his, venomous hatred; in hers, searing aminosity. That Marcie could have gone to him—that she, Leslie Taylor, could have allowed her to go to him—filled her with a vast, helpless rage. Her gaze tracked from Charles to Harriet. This was the last day, the last witness. Why had he been called back? What more could he add? Tensed, she waited for Harriet's opening question.

"You told this court under direct, Mr. Denton, that you were not aware of your wife's previous relationship with Miss Taylor."

"That is correct."

"You suspected nothing until you found Miss Taylor's letter in your wife's suitcase?"

"That is true."

"Did you find the receipt for the ring at the same time?"

"The same morning, yes."

"In the same place?"

"No. The receipt was in her jewelry box."

"And you assumed that the ring referred to in the letter was the same ring covered by the receipt. Did you not notice that the date on the letter did not match the date on the invoice?"

"There was no date on the letter."

"Ah yes. The original letter was destroyed. All we have is a copy. So you naturally assumed that the letter, instead of being written years ago, was actually written after the purchase of this second ring. The ring given to Elsie Mak."

"I'm having trouble following you, Counselor."

"Did you or did you not know that letter was written years ago?"

"I did not."

He knew that she knew he was lying. They both knew there was no way she could prove it. "Would you mind repeating your schedule for Saturday, July 13th?"

"Objection. That information is on record."

"Then perhaps we can have it read back."

Nystrom glanced at the court reporter, wavered, and said, "Witness may answer the question."

In the same words, the same monotone, Charles logged the events of that Saturday.

"You have a wonderful memory, Mr. Denton." Harriet allowed time for the compliment to sink in. Then, innocently, "What did you do *last* Saturday?"

"I returned to Toronto. Spent some time at the office. Had dinner with friends."

"Come, come. Surely you can be more specific. What did you have for breakfast? What did you do after breakfast? What time did you leave for the office? Where were you at three o'clock in the afternoon? At eight o'clock that evening?"

"Counsel is harassing the witness. May I remind my learned friend that Mr. Denton is not on trial here."

"That is true, Mr. Frost. But his memory is. And it's a highly selective memory, isn't it Mr. Denton? You can remember every minute of a day, weeks ago, that at the time was a perfectly ordinary day, but you can't remember what went on over this past weekend."

"Objection sustained."

"You have heard testimony that your wife died at the hands

of a dangerous sociopath. A psychopathic personality triggered by rejection into an overwhelming rage. Would you agree with that?"

"I would think any normal person would agree with that, Mrs. Croft."

"We have a meeting of the mind, Mr. Denton." Harriet's friendly manner housed a lethal intent. "I understand that you are known among your colleagues as a man of impeccable taste. Did you have trouble matching the button from your shirt?"

"Objection."

Charles ignored the interruption and answered the question. "I am not missing any buttons, Mrs. Croft." He smiled, but his eyes were icy. "Nor marbles, I might add." The remark eased some of the tension.

He's playing with her, Clarence thought. Actually enjoying himself. He knows that wherever Harriet is heading, she won't be allowed to get there. Frost will object and Nystrom will agree and . . . the gavel descended as though the thought were father to the deed.

"Objection sustained." A ruling after the fact.

"What size shoe do you wear?" The question coiled through the air with the snap of a whiplash.

"Irrelevant."

"According to your secretary. . . ."

"Irrelevant."

"Who runs most of your personal errands. . . ."

"Irrelevant, Your Honor. I insist. . . ."

"You wear a size eleven." Snatching up a toeprint tracing, she waved it in front of him. "Would you care to step down, Mr. Denton, and match your print to this?"

It had happened so quickly that Nystrom was still back at the button stage. Frost, beside himself, demanded to approach the Bench. Summoned to join him, Harriet countered his harangue with a cool, "It is my intention, Your Lordship, to show presence in that room of someone other than my client. This is a capital case. She is entitled to as full and fair a hearing as possible."

Unsure of his ground, Nystrom looked to Frost for help. The prosecutor responded with, "Every case must be tried on the evidence, Your Honor. Not on supposition and slander."

The pot calling the kettle black. Harriet vowed to quote him in her summation, if they got that far.

Nystrom breathed a sigh of relief. "Quite right." He smiled at Frost, glowered at Harriet. "You have walked a fine line from the beginning of these proceedings, Mrs. Croft. I am coming to the end of my patience."

Rather than risk further censure, Harriet abandoned the shirt button, the shoes, and returned to the events surrounding the weekend that Marcie left home. "When was the last time you saw your wife?"

"Friday morning, July 12th. We had breakfast together."

"When did you realize that she had deserted you?"

"She did not desert me, Mrs. Croft."

"When did you realize that she was gone and would not be back? At what point did you begin to worry?"

"I did not worry. She had been away from home before. She was free to come and go as she pleased."

"Free to return to a lesbian lover?"

The thin lips twitched. A tiny knot of muscle formed in his cheek. "That was never a possibility." There was a slight roughness in the cool voice, the first real sign of slippage.

"It was more than a possibility, Mr. Denton. Surely, when you found the letter. . . ."

"I found the letter on Sunday, Mrs. Croft. After the fact, not before."

"Ah yes. But surely you suspected something. You heard Elsie Mak say that your wife was a frequent visitor to the Cameo Club, that she'd had a number of one-night stands."

"That's a vicious lie."

"How did it make you feel, knowing that your wife would rather sleep with other women than with you?"

Charles frothed. Mrs. Bergstrom screamed. Frost thundered. Nystrom beat a tattoo. Harriet's voice soared above the din. "You knew the only person your wife ever loved was Leslie Taylor. You knew it, and you hated her for it. You hated both of them. And it was you in that room. Not on Saturday, but on Friday night. You knew and you were waiting for her in Spruce Falls and you trailed her to the Dalton and when you couldn't talk her into returning with you, you killed her."

Charles was screaming now, his voice cutting through the air in a high-pitched whine of fury. "She's the one I should have killed." Crazed, he bounded out of the witness box and headed towards Leslie—gasping, grasping with hands formed into claws.

Clarence slithered across the table, his body a shield in front of Leslie. Harriet moved to intercept him. Guards rushed forward. Halted by a wall of blue, laid hold of, he continued to struggle and scream obscenities.

It was over. Harriet leaned on the defense table. A pillar of strength a moment before, she needed the support of something solid to hold her upright. They had come so close. Charles had held together for so long. A few more seconds and Nystrom would have cleared the court, and the moment would have been lost.

As her shaking subsided, she picked up the envelope Clarence offered her and crossed to Frost. "You'll need these." She handed him the packet of gas receipts—the receipts Clarence had retrieved from a service station mid-way between Spruce Falls and Toronto. One was dated Friday, July 12; the other bore the date Clare had followed him on his return for the trial. Both were made out to Charles Denton.

Shocked into silence, Frost stared at her helplessly. "You have more than enough to put him away," Harriet said. Back in control, her voice was calm, but she felt as though her body was floating, rising off the ground in soaring, heady euphoria. "What was it your psychologist said? A sociopath. Victim of a serious personality disorder with areas of vulnerability? He was pretty close to the mark. He just had the wrong mark." There was more she wanted to say. Much more. But there was a matter of greater importance to attend to. Crisply professional, she asked, "How quickly can you arrange my client's release?"

Stunned by the turn of events, Frost stared at her blankly. "I don't know. I don't know how long it will take. We'll have to talk to him. Corroborate your. . .your allegations. We may still have to go to the jury."

"I want her out tomorrow, Jeremy. Tormorrow at the latest. I could insist that you do it now. What we have here is a case of wrongful arrest. Based on nothing more than bigotry. If it weren't for Miss Taylor's sexual orientation, she would never have been charged in the first place. We have enough grounds to bring suit against the city. And you. And your Homicide Division."

In the background she heard Nystrom vainly calling for order, heard him finally and in desperation declare the court dismissed. None too soon. It had effectively dismissed itself on the heels of Charles's outburst. The spectators were milling in the aisles, all but a few die-hard reporters had rushed off to file their stories. Those who remained, shoulder-pack lady included, were heading for Leslie and a hot-off-the-press exclusive. Harriet got to her first, and said, "Tell them you're glad it's over. You'll have a full statement tomorrow."

She stepped back to make way for the newshounds and felt herself engulfed in a bear hug from the rear. Adam Taylor lifted her up, swung her around, planted a kiss on her forehead. "You did it," he roared. "You actually did it." And then he was pushing through the reporters, scooping Leslie up in his arms, laughing and crying and telling her how happy he was. How proud of her.

Bedlam, Harriet thought. Wonderful, glorious bedlam. The Taylors were jubilant. Donna was crying. Clarence, looking as though he was about to do cartwheels, caught her eye, grinned, then said, "I didn't think he'd break."

"To tell you the truth, I was beginning to doubt it myself."

she confessed. "We never would have got those receipts in if he hadn't blown. They'd have done the trick eventually, but it could have taken months." She nodded toward Moore and the Inspector. "Look at Yarrow. He's positively green."

"If I had my way he'd be black and blue," Clarence glared. "Ah, to hell with it," he added, "I'd say you're just about ready for a double brandy."

"Truer words were never spoke." She'd rather spend a few moments with Leslie, but that was impossible. Her client—ex-client, she reminded herself, and felt a quick sense of loss—her soon to be exclient was barely visible through the press of family, friends, reporters, and Johnny-come-lately well wishers. Everyone looked pleased, even Mrs. Klyk, who for once was in no hurry to perform her duty and whisk her charge away.

Waving to Leslie over the heads separating them she called, "Just one more night. I'll see you tomorrow."

Joe knew, even before they climbed into the cab, that things had gone well. He did not know how well until Harriet told him he was invited to a party for Leslie. Tomorrow night. She hoped he could come. She hoped he would bring his wife. She hoped he would have the time of his life because that's what she intended to do.

Only later, when some of the euphoria wore off, did the niggling sense of loss sneak back and take hold. Leslie's welcome home party would be her, Harriet's, good-bye party. Soon, within days, Leslie Taylor would no longer be part of her life. There would be other cases to prepare, other charges to defend, more long, lonely weekends in retreat.

Joe dropped them at Leslie's, and as they started up the walk, Clarence, sensitive as always, said, "You're going off into one of your moods."

"Post-trial letdown." She opened the door and saw Duchess waiting, tail wagging welcome, and felt regret knowing this was the last time she would enter this house as occupant-in-residence. Tomorrow night Duchess would greet her as a visitor. She would be here as Leslie's guest. And the nights after that, she would not be here at all.

Suddenly, she no longer wanted the brandy. She wanted nothing at all.

Chapter Thirteen

Strange. The squat red building no longer seemed malevolent. Today it appeared almost benign. Harriet turned off the engine, leaned across the passenger seat, and opened the far door. Duchess stared at the figure on the landing at the top of the jailhouse steps. Memory stirred. She tensed. The powerful shoulders bunched as she sprang onto the sidewalk.

Leslie saw her coming. Knew this had to be Duchess, although it was a Duchess far removed from the timid droop-tail she remembered. Kneeling, she threw her arms around the dog and buried her face in the heavy ruff.

In her designer jeans and fisherman's sweater, hair tousled by the wind, Harriet walked toward them slowly. Duchess was wild with excitement. Leslie, hugging her, looked up, saw Harriet, smiled. Harriet's breath caught in her throat. Leslie's face was radiant with the sheer joy of being alive and free.

"Your father insisted I borrow his car." A dumb thing to say, Harriet. She can see you have her father's car. Would she think you took it without permission? "They would have come, but we weren't sure how long the red tape would take." No need to say that she hadn't tried to talk them into coming. At any rate, they had other things to do. Adam had taken the day off. Both he and Emily were at home preparing for the gala evening which Emily had decided would be held at home rather than in Leslie's tiny bungalow. "They're expecting you later. For dinner."

The party was a surprise. Her instructions were to keep the guest of honor away from the house until preparations were complete. Harriet had been delighted to oblige. This day, these few hours, would be her only time alone with this young woman who had dominated her life for so many nerve-racking weeks. "Is there anywhere you'd like to go? Anything special you want to do?"

"I want to go home." Finger hooked in the dog's collar, Leslie started down the steps. "You did a wonderful job with Duchess. She's better than when I left her. You should wear jeans more often. They suit you. I suppose you can't wait to get back to the city. I feel like a drink. Is there any gin at the house? Stop at the corner, and I'll pick up some tomato juice. I don't suppose you drink Bloody Mary's. Do you drink? Let me guess. White wine. Dry. Chablis."

Talking nonstop, she put Duchess in the middle and sat tight against the door on the passenger's side. "Would you believe—Poulis came up to me yesterday after you left and said he knew all along I wasn't guilty and he was glad things turned out the way they did. I felt like stepping on him. And Mrs. Klyk. She was as nice as could be. Where did you run off to? Why didn't you wait?" She gave a self-conscious laugh, then said, "I'm sorry, Harriet. I can't seem to stop talking. Here's the store. Do you mind stopping for a minute?"

Nose pressed against the window, Duchess whined until Leslie reappeared. "She doesn't want you out of her sight," Harriet said. And neither do I, she thought, and accelerated along the street. She screeched into the driveway and slammed the door hard as she got out.

"Did I say something to upset you?" Wearing a worried frown, Leslie waited while Harriet turned the key, opened the door, forged inside. "I know we haven't talked about what I owe you, Harriet. I'll write you a check now. It may have to be on the installment plan."

"I'm not worried about the money." Harriet poured herself a brandy. Single. Double. Triple. Forced a smile over the rim of the glass. "Your father said he'd take care of it."

"I pay my own way." Leslie mixed herself a drink and they moved to the living room. "It's good to be home. You don't realize how much you miss things till you think you'll never see them again."

"Ain't it the truth," Harriet said dourly.

Leslie prowled around the room, running her hands over the furniture, taking books down from the shelves and replacing them unopened. Suddenly she turned and faced Harriet. "I was very frightened. More frightened than I've ever been in my life. If you hadn't come along...."

"You'd have found someone else." Steadied by the brandy, Harriet said coolly, "Have you thought about what you're going to do?

"No. There wasn't much point in thinking about the future. Not until yesterday. How did you know it was Charles?"

"I didn't. All I knew was that it wasn't you. I was convinced it couldn't have been you. But I didn't see how it could be Charles, either. He had that damned alibi. It was airtight. Then we got to thinking that it was just too good. Who can tell you every damn thing they did on a particular day? It was pretty obvious he'd covered himself. If he didn't do it Saturday, it had to be Friday. You can thank Clare. He did the legwork. We knew that Charles is a creature of habit. We also knew, thanks to his secretary, that he cancelled an important meeting and took Friday afternoon off. That was the meeting he rescheduled for

Saturday afternoon. He drove to Spruce Falls—we assumed he would drive because at that point his intention was to bring Marcie back. By force if necessary."

"So you knew he'd have to stop for gas. Dad told me about the gas bills."

"We knew he'd have to stop. So Clare did to him what he did to Marcie. Followed him when he came up for the trial. Sure enough. He stopped at the same service station. The attendant remembered him, Head Office dug up the receipt. That clinched it. We had quite a party that night, although your parents didn't know what we were celebrating."

"How did you find that Mak woman?"

"Clarence. Did I tell you we interviewed her at the Cameo Club?"

"Harriet, you didn't. You must have caused a sensation." The dark eyes shone with an admiration approaching awe.

Voice cool against the rising tide of warmth flooding through her veins, Harriet said, "I don't think so. Some of those women were stunning." But none quite like Leslie. None with a brooding beauty that could light, instantly, with such dazzling radiance. "Someone did ask me to dance, though."

"You're lucky that's all that happened. No one made a pass? I'm surprised." Duchess at her heels, she disappeared into the kitchen and returned with a fresh drink. "I still don't understand how Charles knew where Marcie was staying. And how you found out about the plane ticket."

"The plane was the easy part. We knew when she booked in at the Dalton. We checked the incoming arrivals from Toronto, and it wasn't the bus or the train, so it had to be by plane. The rest was conjecture. Marcie had a habit of keeping things in her jewelry box, in the well under the ring tray. Probably the one place she thought he wouldn't look. We guessed he found it, drove up ahead of time, and was parked at the field when she arrived. One thing about these small airports: there are so few people coming in that it's easy to see who goes out. Who, and how, and where to."

"And she came straight to the Dalton, thinking it was the last place anyone would look for her."

"Right. And said Dalton just happens to have a boarded-up hamburger stand directly opposite. A perfect blind. I used it to check up on Yarrow after we told him about the footprints in the room. Knowing Charles, he'd be mortified if anyone, even a stranger, saw him going into a place like the Dalton. Which, as you said, is likely the reason Marcie picked it in the first place. My guess is that he left the car there, out of sight, and walked over. Mrs. Peak is a baseball nut. We checked with the television station. There was a game that night. Which meant she would be glued to the set. Which meant he would have no trouble getting in without being seen."

"Why didn't you tell me all this instead of letting me worry myself crazy? Why didn't you go to the police?"

It was Harriet's turn to refill her glass. "We did. With what we found in the room. If we hadn't made those tracings, taken photographs, we'd have wound up with nothing. Yarrow packs a lot of weight in these parts, and he believed you were guilty. That much I'll give him. He genuinely believed it. He was convinced it was you because you're gay and this is the kind of thing gays do."

"Like hell it is."

"You know that, and I know that. But that's what he believes, and he wasn't going to let anything interfere with that belief. He couldn't afford to because it would have meant reexamining his entire value system."

"That was my future you were playing with. Didn't you care?"

"Of course I cared." How could she ask? "We might have got you off on the strength of argument. I honestly don't know. But I didn't just want a jury to stand up and say you were innocent. I wanted the whole damn thing thrown out of court. Nystrom wasn't about to listen to fact. Look what happened to the button. We had enough built-in safety nets to take up the slack. Errors in law. Unadmitted evidence. I'd have got you out eventually, but that would have taken months. Appeals.

A new trial. And always that lingering doubt. I wanted it signed, sealed, and delivered, and that meant wearing Charles down. Working on that ego of his. I wanted him to come apart in front of everybody. Thank God he did."

The phone rang. Harriet reached for it automatically. Then, remembering this was Leslie's house and she was now nothing more than a guest, she handed it over.

Leslie listened, grinned, and said, "I'll think abut it," and hung up. "That was my boss. He wants to know when I'll be ready to come back to work."

Pleased for Leslie, trying to ignore her own spreading emptiness, she asked, "Do you want to go back? Do you think you'll stay here?"

"Yes. For a while. Would it be a mistake?"

"No. You'd be wise to stay. Long enough to prove to yourself that you don't have to leave." A pause. "It won't be easy for you. There'll still be gossip and whispers. But we've let some air in. Spruce Falls will never be quite the same."

Leslie's laughter was as joyous and carefree as a child's. "Nor will I. I couldn't have done it without you, Harriet. Never in a million years. Have the real Leslie Taylor stand up in front of all those people? Now it seems so simple. But when you first brought it up? You asked an awful lot."

"It's one of my shortcomings," Harriet said dryly. She had been told the same thing often enough by Clarence. Thinking of Clarence, she remembered. Harriet walked into the bedroom and picked up the lucite cube with its blaze of orange at the core. "I have a gift for you," she called out, and turned to find Leslie there facing her, so close they were almost touching. "It's a monarch. From your nesting tree."

Leslie held it on her palm, balancing it so that the color shimmered in the ray of sunlight falling between them. "It's beautiful." Her face sobered. "Living things shouldn't be turned into ornaments."

"It wasn't alive," Harriet said gently. "I found it like that. Lying on the grass. We thought it was a good omen, didn't we

Duchess?"

Duchess pushed against her, tail wagging happily. "They're incredible. So beautiful." Harriet knew she was beginning to babble but was unable to stop. "So fragile. Yet they travel thousands of miles. Go south in a flock. Through hurricanes. Tornadoes."

Leslie's breath was on her cheek. "Billions of them. Some have even traveled to England."

Leslie's breasts brushed against hers. "They cross miles of open water. Ride the wind."

Leslie's eyes, dark and compelling, pulled her forward. "They reach speeds of twenty miles an hour."

Leslie set the crystal-clear cube on the night table. "They go south in bands so high they block the sun."

Leslie picked up the photograph of Marcie and herself, studied it with a sad, searching intensity, and laid it face down beside the monarch. "The females come back alone. Flying low. Their wings faded so no one will notice."

Leslie removed the ring from her finger and placed it beside the photograph. "And they arrive back home, the cycle begins again, and you see them as they really are."

Leslie's arms were around her now, and her lips were on Harriet's. It was a touch as soft and light and sensuous as the brush of a butterfly wing in flight.

Harriet closed her eyes and wondered, briefly, at the rightness of this moment and the years it had taken to reach it. She knew that she, like Leslie, was at last set free.